I Wish You Would

I Wish You Would

EVA DES LAURIERS

Henry Holt and Company
New York

Henry Holt and Company, *Publishers since 1866*
Henry Holt® is a registered trademark of Macmillan Publishing Group, LLC
120 Broadway, New York, NY 10271 • fiercereads.com

Our books may be purchased in bulk for promotional, educational, or business use.
Please contact your local bookseller or the Macmillan Corporate and Premium Sales
Department at (800) 221-7945 ext. 5442 or by email at
MacmillanSpecialMarkets@macmillan.com.

Library of Congress Cataloging-in-Publication Data
Names: Des Lauriers, Eva, author.
Title: I wish you would / Eva Des Lauriers.
Description: First edition. | New York : Henry Holt Books and Company, 2024. |
Audience: Ages 14–18. | Audience: Grades 10–12. | Summary: At the Senior Sunrise
overnight, Natalia must work with ex–best friend Ethan to find seven of the class's
confessional letters before any secrets, including their own, are revealed.
Identifiers: LCCN 2023030214 | ISBN 9781250910554 (hardcover) Subjects:
CYAC: Best friends—Fiction. | Friendship—Fiction. | Love—Fiction. |
Letters—Fiction. | LCGFT: Romance fiction. | Novels.
Classification: LCC PZ7.1.D47726 Iaw 2024 | DDC [Fic]—dc23
LC record available at https://lccn.loc.gov/2023030214

First edition, 2024
Book design by Abby Granata
Printed in the United States of America

ISBN 978-1-250-91055-4
1   3   5   7   9   10   8   6   4   2

For Justin, who loves with a love that is more than love.

CHAPTER ONE

Natalia

Prom Night, 2:08 AM

I CAN THINK OF about nineteen reasons not to follow Ethan to his room right now.

One: track practice in the morning. Two: finals study group after that. Three: the whole "avoiding these feelings at all costs" thing.

But then the corner of his mouth lifts in that half smile of his, and in a voice that's gone gravelly from the late hour he asks, "Speaker duel?" and the reasons sputter out at three.

With everyone else crashed around us in a post-prom haze, *really*, the smart thing to do would be to go to sleep, too.

I grin and follow him up the stairs.

When I shut his door behind me, it's finally just the two of us. My favorite thing.

Or, well, it used to be.

I look around his room for changes I've missed in the months I've avoided coming over. Nothing drastic. As usual, it's orderly but lived in. The sky-blue walls are as familiar as my own. Stacks of books sit by the bed. Devices and cups litter his massive desk. I scan the framed photo

I gave him last year of us laughing on the beach, eyes squeezed shut, shoulders pressed together, our hair wild in the wind. His whole room is cozy and quiet and comforting. Just like Ethan.

"Here," he says, tossing me one of his sweatshirts.

I suppress a smile. I didn't even have to ask.

"This better be clean," I mutter.

He rolls his eyes and stretches out on his giant bed to choose some music. All limbs and length and lean muscle honed on the basketball court.

I pull the sweatshirt that smells like him over my head, dislodging a few hairpins from my updo in the process. I adjust the strands of hair that fell down and gather the too-long sleeves into my fists.

When I turn, Ethan's gaze is fixed on me, like he was watching me. He darts his eyes back to his phone.

I changed out of my cheap black prom dress earlier and cringed as I hung it next to Ethan's perfectly tailored suit. I'd accepted my dress would be nothing compared to the designer outfits the rest of the school wore tonight. I'm used to that. But I didn't expect to *feel* like nothing myself. That's new.

Different worlds.

The words echo in my mind. The warning I haven't told Ethan about. I haven't told my best friend a lot of things lately.

We settle onto his bed in our usual positions, lying side by side, arm's length apart, propped on our elbows, facing each other. Our bodies know the choreography of our friendship, even if I don't anymore.

I grab my phone to choose something for speaker duel, which is what we call it when we race to see which one will pair with his Bluetooth speaker first. It's silly, but it's classic Ethan-and-Natalia-best-friend vibes. Which is exactly what we need to ease the tension that's found a home between us lately.

"Let me guess, you're going Sad Girl Indie Album?" he asks.

My thumb pauses scrolling. That's exactly what I was going to choose. But I refuse to give him the satisfaction. "You'll have to wait until I win."

He dips his chin so we're at eye level. "You haven't been over in so long, the speaker probably won't even remember you."

He's teasing, but there's a slight . . . *something* in the way he says it. Hurt, maybe. Confusion, for sure. I sidestep it by rolling onto my stomach, crossing my ankles like a mermaid tail.

Ethan blinks at my feet once, then looks back at me. "Natalia," he says evenly, "are you wearing shoes on my bed?"

I look over my shoulder at my dangling feet. "No? Flip-flops don't count."

"Anything that brings sand in my bed counts," Ethan says, glaring at me.

"Don't be such a Virgo," I say, kicking my feet back and forth, messing with him.

"Says the control freak," he mutters, shaking his head. He pushes up on one arm. His large hands easily wrap around my bare ankles to stop my kicking. He slowly pulls off my sandals, and they land on the thick carpet with a soft thud. My stomach swoops as his fingertips drift down my legs a little before he lets go. "You're such a monster when no one is looking."

I flutter my lashes. "Part of my charm."

"I'm aware," he says affectionately.

As he settles back into position, I can't help but study the sharp lines of his jaw and cheekbones. The angles and curves I know by heart. For the hundredth time, my fingers itch to sketch him, and I squeeze my hands into fists to suppress the urge.

Even though he's beyond embarrassed, it's no wonder he was voted prom king tonight. As a freaking junior, no less. That inky mussed hair, those piercing eyes . . . He's a dark prince fantasy come to life.

"Why are you looking at me like that?" he asks, squinting with curiosity.

"I don't know. Like what? Shut up," I say in a rush.

"Oh . . . kay."

A soft *bloop* sounds from the speaker, indicating a phone is now paired. We wait. When a lo-fi beat comes on, I groan and Ethan gloats. Maybe he was right and his speaker doesn't remember me. That makes me sadder than it should.

"Did you know—" he starts, then stops. He clears his throat. "Never mind—it's stupid."

"I doubt it," I prompt.

Ethan never used to call himself stupid before the popular crowd started paying attention to him, and it sets my teeth on edge. I like his conversational left turns using facts and trivia and quotes. They're clues to what he's thinking about. I give him an expectant look.

"Fine . . . Did you know that *Virgo* means 'virgin' in Latin?"

"Yeah," I say, like, *duh*. Everyone has to take one year of Latin at Liberty Prep. I use my bitchy tone because it's hard enough to lock these feelings away when it isn't prom night and I'm not alone with him. But now he's looking devastating in the moonlight and talking about virginity? What's he going to bring up next? Our ridiculous pact from freshman year?

Ethan pulls on a loose thread of his T-shirt, wrapping it around his fingertip one way, then unwinding it and wrapping it the other.

"Historically it also was interchangeable with 'maiden,' which is messed up, since that implies it's a status only girls can have."

Wait.

I sit up, eyes wide. "Ethan Forrester, is this your way of telling me you had sex with someone?"

His eyes bug. "What—no!"

My relief is annoyingly palpable. I don't want to think about Ethan with anyone like that, but I'd be lying if I said I hadn't wondered. He's always been beautiful, but *everyone* noticed when Gawky Ethan grew into Hot Ethan. And it's not like I'm immune to noticing, either.

"So, you're still a *Virgo* Virgo?" I joke.

"I mean, it depends on your definition," he says, not looking at me. "But, yeah, technically."

Heat creeps up my neck. "Oh. That's . . . specific," I manage. "When exactly did we decide this is something we talk about?"

"You literally just asked!"

Girls like you make boys do bad things. Is this one of those things? I really need to change the subject.

"Besides"—Ethan cuts his eyes to me—"we talk about everything else."

Guilt needles my sternum. Not everything.

Ugh, what am I doing? I shouldn't be lying beside Ethan in the middle of the night talking about our sex lives. Or lack thereof in my case. But . . . I can't make myself move, either. I chew on my lip, every nerve in my body at attention.

"I mean, I hope you know you can tell me if you ever . . . have something to share," he says.

The silence between us is short but charged. Like when the tide pulls back just before a thunderous wave.

"Who says I don't?" It's definitely just my competitive streak putting that edge in my voice.

He sits up fast, dark curls falling over his forehead that he pushes back. His usually pale skin is flushed in the dim light, and we're close enough that I can see his pulse pick up in his neck. "Do you? Was it Tanner?"

"No," I admit. "He wanted to, but . . . no."

It's why I ended up flying solo at the prom I organized. Tanner Brown dumped me at the last minute for being, and I quote: "not worth it." Not sure if he meant his time, the prom ticket, or the fact that I didn't want to get a hotel room with him after. But we had only been together three weeks. I wasn't about to lose my virginity with someone who hadn't even outlasted my most recent tank of gas. No matter how curious I am about the whole thing.

Ethan flops back on the pillow beside me, obviously relieved. "Good. I can't believe you ever went out with that guy."

Honestly, I can't, either. But no one else asked me to prom, and it would be pathetic if the president-elect showed up alone. Which it was. So, you know, beggars and choosers and all that.

"We don't all have them busting down our doors the way you do," I say.

Ethan rolls his eyes as if he isn't constantly fielding texts. He got asked to prom by *three* different girls. He said he turned them down because he could tell they only asked him because of his dad. It's possible, but it's equally as possible they like him. Everyone does now.

"That doesn't mean you should go for just anyone. Tanner's such a dick. You deserve so much better."

"Like who?"

Ethan nudges me with his shoulder. "I would've taken you."

"Pity date? No thanks," I say. Shoving the *feelings* away, away, away.

He frowns a little. "You were down freshman year."

I push the sleeves of the sweatshirt above my elbows because I'm warming up now. "What're you talking about?"

"Don't you remember? Our pact," he says, finally meeting my eyes.

He really went there. The canvas in my mind flushes in pinks. Blooming and vibrant and rosy.

"I remember," I say carefully.

As if I could forget. At the time, we pinkie swore to be each other's firsts if we were still virgins by senior year because I didn't want to lose my virginity to a jerk, and Ethan was so terrified of girls he figured he'd die a virgin otherwise.

"But I was also the only member of your Waluigi Appreciation Club. I wasn't exactly making great choices." I keep making jokes to quell the tingly feeling in my stomach.

He stares off into the middle distance, his expression pensive. "If you can't love me at my Waluigi, you don't deserve me at my prom king."

I laugh and tuck a strand of hair behind my ear. His gaze follows the motion.

"I still can't believe it. I don't think a junior has ever won before," I say.

He returns his attention to the ceiling, his thick eyebrows coming together. "It was probably rigged."

"Rude. I counted those votes personally." In a tone like I'm breaking bad news, I say, "You're going to have to accept that you cornered the ironic emo vote."

He laughs, but I can tell the whole thing makes him uncomfortable. The only bright lights Ethan likes are the glow of his gaming PC and his reading light. He's shy and doesn't get why anyone would pay attention to him other than the fact that his jerk dad is just a *wee bit* famous. He has no idea how cool he is in his own right.

A sharp breeze brings the briny scent of the ocean through the window, and I close my eyes and inhale deeply. Warm fingertips start tracing a lazy path up and down my forearm. I'm not sure if Ethan knows that he does this when he's thinking, but I've always loved it. His touch leaves a trail of goose bumps in its wake. On a sigh, I settle deeper into the bed.

We lie like that awhile in contemplative silence. The plush blue bedspread is so cozy, fatigue pulls on me. Ethan tracing my arm, my eyes getting heavier.

I'm almost asleep when he says, "I think you're my favorite person, Natalia."

My eyes flutter open, and our gazes lock.

I *hate* how badly I want to kiss him.

I can't believe what I'm saying, but the words fly out of my mouth anyway. "What if we did it? Our pact."

Ethan's hand freezes. "What?"

"I mean. Why not? We're almost seniors, we're both single, we care about each other. You're not—you know, *horrible* to look at."

"Thanks?"

"I'll never feel comfortable with some random guy the way I do with you."

Whenever guys start to get to know me, they all say versions of the same thing: I'm too intense; I stress them out; I need to relax. They think they're getting the girl I pretend to be. Nice. Confident. Happy. No one wants the real me—the wreck I am inside.

Hello, dumped before prom night.

But here is my best friend who's . . . prismatic. Light shines through him, and he creates color for me. It's the way he's exactly himself. The way he lets me be exactly who *I* am. No armor, no fake smiles. And I'm his favorite person. And he's mine.

His expression is unreadable. "You're messing with me."

I sit up, the idea gaining momentum in my mind. "I'm not. I know it's . . . kinda awkward . . ."

"Uh, yeah, *kinda*," he says, a flush dusting his cheeks. "We're just friends."

I ignore the unexpected twist in my gut. "I know—I'm not, like, proposing marriage. It would just be to try. The whole point of the pact was to learn what it's like with someone . . . familiar, right?"

I tell myself if we do it this way, our friendship will survive it. We'll get whatever *this* is out of our systems and be friends like before. No more feelings. Everything will be okay again. *We'll* be okay again.

"I mean, you brought it up. And it *is* prom night," I say.

"Wait, you mean *tonight*? Like right now?" His voice gets higher.

I shrug, my heart racing. "No? Maybe? What do you think?"

"Um. This is a, um, very surprising turn of events."

The more nervous Ethan gets, the more formal he becomes. It makes me pause. In that pause I hear everything I just said from his perspective and I kind of want to die.

"Totally. Never mind. This is clearly my worst idea yet."

He fights a smile. "No, that title still goes to Lobster Day."

I bury my face in my hands. "Oh god. Don't remind me."

"Hey, if it wasn't for you, I'd never know just *how* allergic I am to shellfish."

When I peek at him over my hands, we both crack up. I assume that's the end of this weird conversation where I was obviously possessed by a sex-crazed Demon Natalia who was ready to get naked with the same guy she shot up with an EpiPen last summer after challenging him to a lobster-roll-eating contest.

But as I lie back against his pillows, Ethan starts tracing again. My arm. Then my collarbone, which is new territory. Our eyes meet. And then everything shifts when he curls his hand around my waist and brings me closer to him. He's propped on his elbow, looking down at me, searching my face. The music's stopped. The only sound is our breath, picking up faster and faster.

"Would you . . . really want to do this?" he asks.

Never one to follow, I pull both the sweatshirt and my shirt over my head with trembling hands. His eyes widen as he takes in my bare torso. I'm still wearing a bra, but I can't help but blush under his look.

I force my voice to sound calm when I say, "C'mon. We've seen each other in less at the beach."

"This is different," he says.

I swallow. "I know." I can tell by the way his gaze is lighting my skin on fire that it is. "It's okay if you don't want to."

"No, I—" His voice breaks, and he clears his throat. "I do."

Then in one smooth motion, he pulls off his shirt and drops it in a heap on the floor. I thought I could handle it, seeing him like this. But when the guy you feel safest with in the world is beautiful and his bare skin brushes against yours, apparently it unlocks . . . everything.

"Do you have condoms?" I ask.

His throat bobs with a swallow, and he nods.

Girls like you . . .

But the warning falls away when he nudges close. Resting his forehead against my shoulder, his breath hot on my neck, he murmurs, "I can't believe this is happening."

"I can't believe you're talking," I say dryly.

His chest shakes with laughter, and I smile into his hair. Hesitantly, I reach up and slowly twine my fingers through it. I can feel him tremble. He pulls back to look at me, his hazel eyes holding mine.

"God, Natalia," he whispers.

Then my best friend leans in and kisses me.

CHAPTER TWO

Natalia

Senior Sunrise,
Two and a Half Months Later, 7:07 AM

THE SKY IS FULL of secrets today. I hate secrets.

Fingers of coastal fog weave through the cedar trees that line my street. Way too spooky of a vibe for a late August morning. If I believed in signs, it'd almost feel like the whole freaking atmosphere is trying to tell me something about today. So, it's a good thing I *don't* believe in them because Senior Sunrise has to be perfect. *Is* going to be perfect.

Even if I have to see Ethan.

The front door creaks open behind me, and Mom's slippered feet pad down the porch steps, almost catching on the edge of the giant poster board I have propped against my legs. I move it out of the way as she finishes a phone call to one of my aunts in rapid Spanish. When she's done, she settles beside me, wrapping a pink sweater tightly around herself with one hand and cradling a steaming cup of coffee with the other. Her expressive brown eyes are tired, and her black stick-straight hair that looks nothing like my wavy tangled mane is gathered high in a sleek ponytail.

"Still not here?" she asks.

"Obviously," I mutter.

I check my watch. I've been waiting for Ethan under this moody morning gloom in front of our—well, I guess now *Dad's*—house for seven minutes. Because no matter what, no matter where, it seems like I'm always waiting for Ethan. If I could afford to get my car fixed, I wouldn't have to rely on rides from my best friend in the first place.

If we even are best friends anymore.

I still can't believe we haven't talked all summer. Okay, sure, we talk on the group chat with Rainn and Sienna, but we're both super careful to never actually respond to what the other says so it doesn't count beyond knowing the other is still alive.

Mom sighs, heavy and foreboding. "I really wish you hadn't planned this overnight trip. Tonight, of all nights."

I somehow manage to control my eye roll. "It's not some conspiracy against you. It's Senior Sunrise."

Senior Sunrise is a sacred tradition at Liberty Prep. The senior class gathers at sunrise the weekend before school starts to set goals and intentions and kick off our last year together by writing the infamous Lion Letters. I shudder at the thought of actually writing down anything I've been going through.

"When your dad went to Liberty, it wasn't overnight."

She's right. It's usually only a few hours, but I suggested we turn Senior Sunrise into a one-night camping trip to make it extra special. It's my job as student body president to get everyone hyped for the year, even if I'm not feeling it myself.

When I don't respond, Mom sighs. "Mija, I know this summer hasn't been the easiest, but your father and I think . . ."

I look back at the dark sky, tuning out the rest of what she's saying as I drop into my head and begin mentally painting.

I imagine the way the sky will crowd with light tomorrow morning. The splash of color it'll cast across my senior class. Golds, pinks, purples if we're lucky. The new beginnings the sunrise promises. I could really use one of those right about now.

"Are you listening?" Mom's tired voice cuts through my thoughts.

"Yeah," I lie.

She sighs again. "We'll figure this out. We will."

This. The word my parents collectively decided represents my world falling apart. *This* meaning the divorce. *This* meaning the impossible choice I have to make by the end of the weekend. Mom or Dad.

If I stay with my dad, I have zero chance of pursuing art, since it's "a damaging, insecure lifestyle." If I move with my mom, I lose Liberty and my whole life here. The beach, my presidency. Ethan.

Finally, low headlights stream through the fog before a car comes to an abrupt and apologetic halt in front of my house.

He's here.

But this isn't right. Ethan's car is a nondescript clunker with an I NEED SPACE NASA bumper sticker on one side and a faded Golden State Warriors sticker on the other. But this thing—this sleek, fancy, electric car that only the richest, douchiest kids at school drive—is the exact opposite of Ethan.

"Looks like Roger finally got him to cave," Mom says.

My stomach sinks. Ethan's dad loves throwing his money around like it's the only thing in the world that matters. Ethan always resisted. Or, at least, he used to.

The driver's side door drifts open like a freaking bat wing, and everything slows down as Ethan climbs out.

Two and a half months apart did nothing to make this part easier.

His mop of curls is slightly tamed with product, and the gray day makes his hazel eyes brighter, his dark eyebrows more striking. He's wearing rust-colored jeans—cuffed at the ankles to reveal black high-top Chucks—and a plain black hoodie that's snug around his lean frame.

Ethan is here, beautiful and tangible and *late*.

He jogs to me through the dense fog, and his searching look makes my fragile heart squeeze.

I'm hit with the urge to throw my arms around him and breathe in the long weeks of him that I've missed. But I can't do that. And we don't have time besides.

I pick up my tent and shove it into Ethan's arms, cutting off his chance to say anything. He grunts at the impact, and I pile the sleeping bag on top of it, blocking his flawless face for good measure.

"Oh . . . kay," he says from behind the pile. His voice is still scratchy and rough with sleep.

I'm glad he can't see my smile.

I give my mom a quick hug and grab the poster board from the porch steps before I run down the driveway to the car. Only, I can't get the thing open because there isn't a freaking handle. I stare at it a moment. There's a shiny silver strip where a handle should be but no latch. Does it want my fingerprints? A hair sample? I'm a smart girl who is more than capable of opening a door. And yet.

When I look up, Ethan's watching me, his eyes bright with amusement. It's such a familiar expression, I soften a little.

"Hi," I say. It just tumbles out, this tiny word that yearns to pull him back to me. And it's like he knows.

"Hi," he returns, the corner of his mouth lifting.

Something beeps, and the passenger door drifts open like his did. "Finally—"

But I stop because Claire Wilson is sitting in the passenger seat. *My* seat.

"Hey, Natalia," she says with a small smile.

My hackles engage. If I were a cat, I'd be puffy as hell. But I plaster on my best presidential smile to cover it. I have a lot of practice in pretending I'm okay. Apparently today will be no different.

"Hey!"

But seriously, since when do we give Claire Wilson—with her dewy freckled skin and glossy blue-streaked hair—a ride anywhere? Let alone to the kickoff event of our senior year that I've been planning all summer? After Ethan and I haven't seen each other in basically a decade?

"Ethan offered me a ride," Claire says. As if that's a perfectly normal thing to have happened.

They've lived across the street from each other ever since Ethan moved to Cliffport Heights last year. The neighborhood is known for its massive houses and amazing views of the ocean. But Claire has never been on his radar. Until now, I guess. The pinch in my ribs must be from the cold.

"Great! The more the merrier!" I say brightly. "Guess this explains why you were late."

"Nah, my fault," a grumbly voice from the back seat proclaims. "My alarm didn't go off."

Rainn is splayed across the entire back seat, his long legs bent awkwardly, his hair a wild mess of sunshine blond. He's wearing a T-shirt with a screen-printed image of a wolf howling at the moon, and tie-dyed sweatpants.

I walk around the car and climb into the back seat behind Ethan, wrestling my giant poster board inside. I'm instantly hit with Ethan's familiar scent, piney and heady and comforting, and I have to slam my eyes shut as memories of prom night flood my system. His strong grip on my waist, his hot breath on my neck—

Rainn slings his legs across my lap, and I'm back to the present. I would normally shove them off, but I'm grateful for the distraction and extra warmth.

He points to the poster board. "Oh man, are those pictures from freshman year?"

I nod. "To show how far we've come."

It took me three nights to cut out every senior's photo from three years ago and decorate it. I even hunted down photos of the few students who came to Liberty after freshman year. Rainn points to our cluster of old photos and laughs. Me and my frizzy hair and braces. Rainn with his shoulder-length surfer hair and skinny neck. Sienna with her broad grin and goggle glasses before she found sleeker ones. And then Ethan and that unfortunate buzz cut because he had no idea what to do with his glorious hair. That was right before his dad's show came out.

Even though a lot changed after that—Ethan's house got bigger, his stuff more expensive—*he* never did. I still want to believe that the only thing that's really different is that he knows *exactly* what to do with his hair now.

But if we're in a spaceship car giving Claire Wilson rides, that's obviously not true.

I press my hands to the heater vents and wriggle my fingers back to life. I eye Rainn's ridiculous shirt again and his surfer-tan arms that are covered in goose bumps. "Aren't you freezing?"

Without opening his eyes, he says, "Cold is a state of mind, Natalia."

"It's also a factual state of temperature, but okay."

I pull out the extra sweatshirt from my bag and toss it to him. It lands on his chest, and he cracks one eye open.

With a grateful grin, he balls it up and puts it under his head like a pillow against the window, and slumps down farther. "Always thinking of me."

I shake my head and check my phone. I note with a vague panic Sienna hasn't responded to any of my wake-up texts. "If Sienna isn't awake yet, I swear I will *cut* her."

Ethan snorts.

"You're grumpy," Rainn mutters.

"More like hungry," Ethan says, eyeing me in the rearview mirror. His gaze is steady, like he was watching us talk. This is what he's leading with after ten weeks of ghosting me?

The growling in my stomach betrays me then, and he gives me an expectant look. I have to tear my gaze away, watching my neighborhood with its small houses and apartment buildings fade as we make our way toward the beach.

"I'm just waiting to eat, since Sienna is picking up doughnuts and coffee as we speak."

"I guarantee you she hasn't even left yet," Rainn says, eyes still closed.

"Don't say that. We're already thirteen minutes behind schedule. I swear if Prashant starts setting up without me—"

"You'll cut him?" Ethan suggests.

I glare at the back of his head. Which is kind of a bad idea because my fingertips remember that's where his hair is softest, curling just so against the nape of his neck.

"Prashant's like the smartest guy in the class, why can't he set up?" Claire chimes in.

I purse my lips. Is she really that clueless? Prashant may be smart. He may be the vice president of the class and on track for valedictorian, leaving me in the dust thanks to my freaking econ final last year. He's also clever and conniving and has been trying to usurp my position as class president the past three years.

As if I'd let that happen now that I'm the student body president and finally have some real power to make a difference. Especially for scholarship students. It's the only thing keeping me upright.

"Who invited her?" Rainn jokes so only I can hear him. I hide my laugh with a cough.

Though Ethan and I have always been closest, we've been a group with Rainn and Sienna since eighth grade. They mellow us out. Usually, Rainn is closer to Ethan like Sienna is closer to me. But this summer, Rainn and I hung out more in Ethan's absence.

I rub my hands together and blow on them for extra warmth. "Can you turn up the heat? Wait, Ethan, no, don't take Main Street—all the stoplights—*ugh!*"

He turns onto Main Street, and we are now going to be stuck at an endless string of red lights when Maple Avenue would have gotten us there in half the time. I scowl at his reflection in the rearview.

"You're so stressed. I had to."

I smack the back of his seat. "You did that on purpose? What is wrong with you?"

"Lots of things."

"It's not funny, Ethan."

"I'm not laughing."

But he's smiling. One of those dagger grins that makes me feel warm all over. "Why do you insist on torturing me?"

"It's my favorite pastime."

"I hate you."

"You love me."

The air in the car goes taut, and Claire shoots us an odd look. It's the look that every girl who has a crush on Ethan gives us eventually. It holds all the questions:

Are they flirting?

Do they like each other?

How big of a threat is Natalia Diaz-Price, anyway?

Answers:

Sometimes.

It's complicated.

None at all. Prom night proved that.

"Especially because I brought treats," Ethan announces.

I perk up at that. We come to the next torturous stop, and he reaches across Claire to open the glove box. He reveals a handful of dry, slightly crumpled granola bars. The sad-tuba-sound equivalent of a treat.

I give him a long look. "I almost die of hypothermia waiting for you, and now this?"

Ethan scoffs and mutters, "Hypothermia? It's fifty-four degrees out."

"Nice try. I'm holding out for doughnuts."

Ethan shakes his head. "You know, I'm not hearing a lot of gratitude for driving your carless ass to a school function we're not required to attend *and* bringing food."

I roll my eyes. "Counterpoints?" I hold up my fingers, tapping each one as I go down the list. "As student body president, I *am* required to organize, attend, and set up Senior Sunrise. I'm only carless because mine is in the shop getting fixed, and *that* does not qualify as food." I shoot a look of disdain at the heap of wrapped bars.

Ethan frowns. "What happened to your car?"

I shift uncomfortably. "Fender bender last week. No big deal."

"Seriously? You okay?"

I hate the way his voice softens. I pull my hair over one shoulder and begin playing with the ends. "The hypothermia was worse."

Ethan rolls his eyes, but I can see he's holding back a smile.

"You two are so cute," Claire interjects, full of confidence.

"Aren't they just?" Rainn teases, jabbing my leg with his shoe. The car lurches to yet another stop.

Claire spins around to smile at me. "Ethan told me you were close."

I force my smile wider. She's acting like she doesn't know Ethan and I have been best friends since middle school. Liberty Prep isn't that big, everybody knows everything.

Then again, Claire is one of those popular theater kids convinced she's going to be a star. She doesn't look outside her own bubble. Which is why her being in the spaceship car with us makes no sense.

Even less sense? That Ethan has obviously been talking to her this summer, instead of to me.

All our phones ping at the same time, pulling me out of my spiral.

"Yeah, Sienna just woke up," Rainn announces.

Ethan bursts out laughing. It's been so long since I've heard his laugh, loud and rolling like that. Everything about him is so . . . overwhelming. Different. Sienna on the other hand is exactly the same. For someone who can do complex equations in her head, she is the most scatterbrained class treasurer ever.

"Uuuughhhh," I groan.

Ethan's arm appears over his seat, bent at the elbow and dangling a granola bar behind him like a taunt. I grab for it. When our hands touch, my freezing fingers against his warm ones, he squeezes them—whisper soft, but there. A signal of some kind. Ethan language I can never quite decipher despite spending years trying to become fluent in him. He could be saying *hi*. Or *calm down*.

Or *I can't stop thinking about that night, either.*

We lurch at the next stoplight, and Rainn's legs fall off my lap. He stretches, his neck audibly popping, then slings his long, outstretched arm around me, pulling me close in that flirty way he has all summer. "This is going to be such a good year. I can feel it."

I snuggle closer to Rainn's heat and optimism and return his smile. I hope that's true for everyone, even though I know it's not for me. No matter what decision I make about where I end up living. But I can't say that because nobody knows.

Ethan's gaze snaps to mine in the mirror again.

Yeah. Secrets suck.

CHAPTER THREE

Ethan

Senior Sunrise, 7:19 AM

COOL. SUPER COOL. LIKE, ice-cold cool. I hate camping and setting up tents and sleeping on the ground. I only agreed to come to Senior Sunrise to try to fix this thing with Natalia, and now I guess she and Rainn are . . . what? Into each other? Together?

After what he told me at prom, I guess it's possible.

I mean, they've never been the kind of friends that *touch*, and I'm not hallucinating that his arm is *still* around her, and she is *still* smiling up at him. I grip the steering wheel until my knuckles turn white.

This is a disaster.

When I saw her standing on the porch, I swear her blue eyes lit up the way I felt inside. But I obviously imagined it, since she's barely even looked at me since.

The quote "Sometimes not getting what you want is a wonderful stroke of luck" pops into my head. I think the Dalai Lama said it. But even that doesn't help. I rip open a granola bar with my teeth and shove the thing in my mouth, the stale flavor just this side of offensive. She's right as usual. These suck.

I have to double back when I miss the turn toward the beach campsite, and I barely register Natalia's groan of annoyance from the back seat. Why didn't anyone fucking tell me about her and Rainn? Why didn't *Natalia* tell me?

Oh, right, because she ghosted me all summer.

I'd hoped that the summer would have chilled us both out, that she'd be ready to talk about what happened, but that was wishful thinking. It's Natalia. World's Best Grudge Holder. People think she's nice, but she's really not. I mean, yes, she's kind, she's thoughtful, she's generous, but *nice*? Nope. That's the armor she wears. Inside, she's petty and sharp and angry. God, she's one of the most twisted people I know.

She's the best.

I shouldn't be surprised she disappeared on me. She started drifting away long before prom. She does that, retreats into her head or her art or her to-do lists so she doesn't have to actually talk. But on prom night, she was present. It was like she swallowed the moon; she was glowing from the inside out. I finally had her to myself after months of her pulling away, and then . . . I don't know, my asshole brain drudged up that pact.

One minute we were talking on my bed, and the next, her shirt was on the floor, my fingers exploring her skin. When our lips touched, a dam broke inside me. I could hardly process what was happening except that I liked it too much, never wanted it to stop. This was *Natalia*. It should have felt weird or funny or wrong. Nothing had ever felt so right.

That's the problem.

I barely got a taste of her before she made it very clear she didn't feel the same way.

"This is better," she'd said almost to herself after we'd kissed like the world was ending, after I drew out that shaky, fragile sound from her when my lips found that dip between her collarbones. "If we do it this way it won't change anything."

And I froze. It was clear. She didn't want me for real. She never would've touched me if it hadn't been for the pact.

"Talia . . ." Her nickname scraped across my throat. "I—I don't think I—this is stupid. I don't—with *you*—not like this."

It all fell apart then.

She wrenched herself away from me, stumbled off the bed, groping for her shirt. "Totally. You're right. I'm sorry—ugh, *move*."

"Wait, whoa, Talia, hold on," I said. I reached for her, grasped only air.

"It's fine, Ethan."

"You're pissed."

She was a frenzy of hairpins as she yanked them out, her dark hair falling in lush waves down her back. I wanted to push my fingers through them again, bury myself in them. But it was too late.

"I'm fine. I'm—I'm just going to go home," she said.

I followed her down the stairs as she cycloned through my house, grabbing her stuff, never looking back at me. Not *once*.

"Wait—don't leave," I said from the front porch as she climbed in her car.

The last thing she said to me before she disappeared all summer was: "Please forget about this."

I watched her drive off into the dark, taking the possibility of us with her.

I flick my gaze back to her now. She has a hold on Rainn's shirt, tugging it between two fingers while she teases him for how awful it is. He laughs, and she bites back her own smile.

This is all my fault. What if I've really lost her because I was too scared to tell her the truth that night?

"Thanks again for the ride," Claire says, cutting through my thoughts.

I'd forgotten she was here. "Oh. Yeah."

"It makes sense, us carpooling. We should do it more." She gives me a sweet smile.

"Sure," I say.

Claire's cute, but she literally never looked in my direction until recently. Things started changing after the Showdown basketball game last season, and then the weird prom king thing after that, but it still doesn't make sense to me.

When I got back from my summer in Seattle last week, she'd showed up at my house with a book she'd borrowed during the school year that I'd completely forgotten about. We got to talking, and then, out of nowhere, she kissed me. And, I mean, I didn't hate it, but I haven't really thought about it again. Natalia and everything going on at home has taken up every square inch of my brain lately.

God, I miss Natalia. No matter what happened that night, I should've texted her. This summer sucked for me in a way I could only tell her about. The messages I found on my dad's phone, Adam's struggle with recovery.

I'd hoped visiting my older brother for the summer would help get my mind off everything—Natalia, Dad, school, the team, *Natalia*—but instead it just made it clear how much I couldn't say. Like every time I wanted to tell Adam about our parents, what it's really like at home now that both he and Dad are gone, *why* Dad is gone, the words got stuck. I can't stress him out with what I know. I won't risk his recovery.

He asked about Natalia until I caved and told him everything. All he said was "Dude, don't get in your own way. You've wanted her for*ever*."

"No, I haven't," I answered automatically.

He just rolled his eyes, then he snatched the basketball out of my hands and spun around me to make a fadeaway jump shot.

Riiiiing!

The entire car erupts as my phone rings. A picture of my dad's face appears on the mission control–esque screen that I still can't get used to. This fucking car. One of the many things I'll never be able to forgive my dad for.

I hit DECLINE. No thanks. A few seconds later, *riiiiiiing!* I hit DECLINE again.

When it rings a third time, I have to count my breaths. What part of *Leave me the fuck alone* does he not understand?

"You're not going to answer it?" Claire asks.

My jaw hurts with how hard I'm clenching it. "Nope."

"Seems like it might be important," Rainn says.

"It's not."

Even if it is, I don't care. I notice Natalia and Rainn exchange a look, and the way it slices through me is a new kind of pain. They have a shorthand now. Like we do. Did.

I scrub a hand across my jaw, the slight stubble scratchy against my palm.

"Isn't he on location right now?" Claire asks, her voice filled with excitement. "I read the new season takes place in New York."

I shift uncomfortably. "Um—"

"Ugh, it's so overcast! It better not be like this tomorrow," Natalia exclaims, cutting me off.

I look at her in the rearview, and she won't meet my eyes. But I know she did that on purpose, and I try to telepathically thank her. She knows I hate talking about my dad and his job.

I was friends with Rainn, Sienna, and Natalia long before his show, *The Beltway*, premiered. They were by my side as Dad started being . . . everywhere. The only thing any of them outwardly said about the shift was from Sienna after my gaming PC died.

"Tell Daddy Warbucks to get you Alienware. He can afford it now."

Honestly? It ruled. Them not giving one shit about the celebrity thing.

But not everyone is like that.

"Do you think we'll even be able to see the sunrise tomorrow?" Claire asks, looking out the window.

"Yes," Natalia says, a note of finality in her tone. She says it like she has total control over the weather. Adorable.

"Even if we don't, it's still a fresh start. Every day is if you think about it," Rainn says.

Natalia bumps him with her shoulder. "That was profound, Rainn."

He grins. "Don't sound so surprised."

She laughs, and the soft tripping sound of it makes my chest hurt.

"Did you know astronauts on the International Space Station see sixteen orbital sunrises a day?" I blurt. When no one says anything, I blaze on. "The first art ever created in space was a drawing of an orbital sunrise. You can look it up, it's really cool."

"You're so smart," Claire says, rubbing my arm.

For a second, I'm sure she's making fun of me. But there's no sarcastic glint in her eye. Only a wide, cute smile as she scrunches her nose. So I return it with a self-conscious one of my own.

"We don't have sixteen chances, Ethan," Natalia says, her tone turning icy again. "We have one."

I get the feeling we aren't talking about sunrises at all anymore.

CHAPTER FOUR

Natalia

OF COURSE HE KNOWS about the first art ever created in space. Because he's so freaking cool. Ugh, I miss him. I almost say it out loud until Claire shoots him a smile. The kind Ethan would usually be suspicious of, like he was of all the girls who asked him to prom. But my heart sinks as I watch Ethan smile back. One of his sweet, shy ones.

First a ride and now this? Is there actually something going on between them?

My phone chimes with a taunting text from Prashant just as we pull up to the group campsite at Ventoso Beach.

Miss Perfect is late??? Not a great start to the year . . .

I grit my teeth and see through the window that, except for Sienna, every other senior officer from student council is already here including Leti Mitchell, the class secretary and Sienna's sole obsession for the past year.

Thankfully it looks like they've barely made any progress. Nothing I can't undo.

We unload the car quickly, and as we walk toward the group, Rainn wraps an arm around me again. I don't mind, because it's freezing and windy, but it's definitely not our usual style. He's been flirty like this lately, and I have to admit that sometimes it's nice to feel like I'm a girl someone could want.

"What's up with you and Forrester?" Rainn asks. He pushes his free hand through his shaggy hair, catching it in a fist against the wind.

"Nothing. What do you mean?" I ask, sounding panicked even to my own ears.

Rainn shrugs. "Awkward vibes."

"Weird not seeing each other all summer, I guess."

"Oh, I thought maybe . . . because of him and Claire."

Him and Claire. I suck in a painful breath. I guess Rainn knows something I don't. I go to the canvas in my mind, and it quickly becomes a deep, melancholy blue. I want to lie on top of it until the paint seeps into my skin. Until I'm hidden inside it.

But not now. I have to be President Natalia now.

I plaster on a smile and use my best camp-counselor voice. "Okay, everyone, we need to hustle before the rest of the class gets here! Can you all"—I vaguely gesture toward Ethan and Rainn—"set up the bonfire benches? Mason, you're buff, why don't you help Ethan."

Ethan shoots me a mutinous look, and I barely keep my expression innocent. We do our damn best to avoid Mason Hartman because the guy is like a walking energy drink. He's Liberty's notoriously competitive quarterback, with smooth white skin, light brown hair that is vaguely pushing mullet territory, and huge muscles. The guy never stops talking.

He slaps a big congenial hand on Ethan's shoulder, making him wince.

"Whoa, you been lifting this summer, Prom King?" Mason asks, squeezing his shoulder. But Mason doesn't wait for Ethan to answer before he launches into a long, meandering story about his favorite protein powder. I can feel Ethan's soul leaving his body the longer the story goes on.

The chatter fades to the background as I get to work. Historically, Senior Sunrise is held on the football field at school, but that never made sense to me. We're a town of beach bums, and our school is ten minutes from this beautiful beach campsite that's a short walk to the water. You can hear the waves crashing as you sleep.

Now, as I try for the third time to unroll a plastic tablecloth that keeps catching in the wind, I get why we've never done it here. It's effing windy and cold and entirely possible I've made a huge mistake for the class—all in an attempt to avoid my mom packing up the house. The tablecloth flies into my face, and Leti runs over to help me.

They're wearing a boxy sweatshirt that shows off a sliver of their bronze tummy, and baggy jeans that swallow their feet. Their jet-black hair is cropped short in the back and sides and styled messily on top.

"Thanks—this wind is wild," I say.

"Why they named this beach Ventoso, right?" Leti exclaims, laughing.

When I look at them blankly, they say, "Right—I forgot you take French. It means 'windy' in Spanish."

My cheeks heat up. "Oh. Gotcha. Yeah, I probably should've taken Spanish . . . but I have this dream of going to the Louvre in France someday, so . . ." I trail off.

Since they're the only other Latine person in my class, I expect Leti to judge me for not speaking Spanish. I mean, *I* a little bit judge me. I know the basics, and random words like "guapo" because my abuela uses it all the time to tease me about how cute Ethan got. But that's it.

I already struggle to feel like a Diaz sometimes since the Price DNA really decided to take over with my light-skin-blue-eyes combo. Being mixed and white-passing is confusing. It feels like I don't really *count* in either space.

But the only judgment in Leti's expression seems to be about my choice of art museums.

"I went to the Louvre last summer and it's dope, but hella crowded. You should go to the more underground places—I went to this studio called Douleur Peinte and it was so inspiring. My art has not been the same since."

I smile. Leti is the kind of unbridled artist I wish I could be. Brash and bold. Not stuck in their head or their roles or everyone else's expectations. Free.

"You gonna keep our deal?" they ask. "About art school?"

I showed Leti some of my work last year, and we made a low-key pact that we'd both apply this year. But I don't know why I did that. It can never happen. As a scholarship student, I have to keep my focus on my academics and not on my "little hobby," as my dad calls it.

I think of the last time he found me painting. How he pulled up my school schedule to see why I had so much free time. My smile falls.

"My parents would never go for it."

Leti frowns. "You'd get in. You're good."

I'm stunned still for a second. I try not to think of my paintings as good or bad. They're my insides; pent-up, explosive emotion. Color and feeling and all the words I can never say. Silent screaming.

"Thanks."

We lay out the notebooks for the Lion Letters next, and my palms go slick in anticipation. The letters are the heart of Senior Sunrise. The foundation the entire event rests on. Everyone writes an anonymous note to themselves about our final year at Liberty; what we want and what we would do if we were braver, like the lion, our school mascot. I heard from my senior friends on student council last year that some people *actually cried* writing them.

But what can I possibly write that would make a difference? I already know I can't have anything I want.

Leti's attention snaps over my shoulder, and I notice they're watching Sienna, who has *finally* arrived, haul a tent from her trunk.

"Do you think she needs help?" Leti asks so hopefully, it almost makes *me* blush. Leti doesn't even wait for me to answer before jogging over there, causing Sienna's entire being to light up when they do.

Ethan passes by and notices. He shoots me a knowing look about Sienna—because oh my god, she's tomato red—and then it's like we realize at the same time how strange it is that *we* aren't talking. I want so desperately to walk over to him.

He walks to me first. "Hey," he says.

It hurts to look at him this closely. All I see when I do is the way he pulled away from me that night. The way he's changed—we've changed— since then.

He pushes a hand through his hair. "I just wanted to—I mean, thanks. For before. When my dad called," he says haltingly.

Ugh. His dad. I try to control my face because Ethan doesn't know that disgust rages through me whenever his dad comes up. But no matter the strain between us, I will always have his back.

"Of course," I say.

Still, I have about a thousand questions as to why Ethan didn't want to answer the calls. I may not like his dad anymore, but the two of them have always gotten along fine. It might just have been because Claire was there, but what if it was because . . . I was there? That I'm even wondering that forms a new knot inside me.

"So . . . we're good?" he asks.

On the surface it's an easy question, but inside those words, it's impossible to answer. I'd tell the truth if I had any idea what it was. So I reach for my default instead.

"We're great," I say, and I shoot him my presidential smile quickly, not lingering on his hazel eyes or wind-tousled hair a millisecond longer than I have to. But I do catch his frown.

"So, are you and Claire . . . ?" I trail off. It comes out accusatory and way harsher than I mean it to. *Deep breaths, Natalia.*

He rubs the back of his neck, his voice getting all high like it does when he's uncomfortable. "Oh, um, yeah, it appears to be . . . going that way?"

My lungs actually feel like they stop working for a second. Even though I could tell by the possessive tone in her voice, those little glances and smiles they shared in the front seat. He's waiting for me to say something. I don't. I can't. Maybe all I *can* do is outrun this. All of this will go away permanently if I choose Mom.

I'm a riotous swirl of gray inside.

At least Sienna being late has its uses. She walks over with a stack of pink bakery boxes in her arms, saving me from having to respond with my heart in my throat.

"I know, I know! I'm hella late. I'm sorry! It's Ethan's fault," Sienna exclaims.

Ethan blinks. "What? How?"

She throws him a leveling gaze. "I was up all freaking night playing *Dwarf Fortress*."

He bursts out laughing. "You seriously need to give up on that game."

"Never! It's utterly chaotic, but so am I," she says, setting down the boxes. She pushes her long auburn hair back and adjusts the strap of her faded black overalls, then sidles up next to me.

"How goes the reunion?" she asks, dipping her voice low so only I can hear.

I flick a look to Ethan. "Bad."

"Hmmm. Awkward bad or you've-already-planned-a-painting bad?"

My cheeks warm. "Both."

"Yikes."

Rainn runs over, too. He grabs me around the waist and moves me so he can snag a bear claw out of one of the boxes. His hand lingers on my lower back a long moment before he drops it, and then he says, "Did you guys hear that Jackson Ford got fired from Liberty this summer?"

Sienna rolls her eyes. "He was always super sus, even when he went to school with us."

"Truth," I mutter.

Jackson Ford was a senior when we were freshmen. Everyone in the theater department was so excited when he was hired to direct the musical at Liberty last year, but I never got it. He's the kind of guy I'd never want to be alone with.

"Everyone's talking about it like it's so shocking. Please, I should've bet on it when he posted those pictures," Sienna says.

"You have a gambling problem," Ethan says.

"It's a probability problem," Sienna corrects, picking up a sugar doughnut.

Rainn points a finger at Sienna. "Speaking of, you owe me ten bucks."

She glowers at him and throws her hands in the air, exasperated. "Okay, fine, *technically* I overslept. But to be fair, when I made that bet, my calculations didn't account for *Dwarf Fortress*!"

Rainn drapes an arm around my shoulders from behind, pulling my back to his chest. I blink at the sudden closeness. I can feel his deep voice between my shoulder blades when he asks Sienna, "And whose fault is that?"

"Apparently mine," Ethan states. His gaze fixes on Rainn's arm around me, then slowly lifts until our eyes meet. "Like everything else these days."

We stare at each other as my heart slams against my rib cage.

Sienna looks between us a few times before she says, "I was just kidding—"

"I have to go help Prashant," I say quickly, slipping out of Rainn's grasp.

I march over to a table across the campsite and rip open a bag of jumbo marshmallows. The bag seems to disintegrate in my hands, and the marshmallows scatter all over the dirt. Of course.

"Great, she's Hulking out already," Prashant mutters. "What did the bad marshmallows do to you, Natalia? Go on, you can tell me."

I shoot him a glaring side-eye as I scramble to pick them up. "I'm hungry," I say, and shove three clean ones in my mouth. And it's not like I was going to stand there eating a doughnut while Ethan made comments under his breath about how much I suck.

"Well, get it together. Everyone's here and, according to the agenda—" Prashant begins, but I cut him off.

"I'm aware of the agenda, Prashant, I wrote it."

He folds his arms across his chest. "Don't take your Ethan drama out on me. I have enough to deal with today."

"Ethan drama? There's no Ethan drama."

Things are just *going that way* with him and Claire Wilson. He's entirely forgotten about prom and the kiss I've been obsessing over for two months. It's fine. I'm fine.

"I have eyes," Prashant says dryly.

"Do they see that there's no drama? Ethan and I— Oh my god, it's none of your business."

He adjusts his black rectangle glasses primly. "Whatever. The more of a mess you are here, the sooner I'll be able to take over as president, anyway."

I throw a box of graham crackers at him that he, unfortunately, catches just as Ms. Mercer and Mr. Beckett appear to check in.

"It's time to begin," Ms. Mercer intones. Ms. Mercer is the psychology teacher and student council faculty adviser. She has glowing olive skin, a pixie haircut. The scent of sage wafts off all her clothes, and she constantly talks about *energy*, but I like that she doesn't treat us like little kids.

"Right on," Mr. Beckett agrees. He's our AP History teacher and a total hippie, with a full black beard and goofy grin. He tells us, like, all the time, that schools have way too many rules, so he's lenient and distractible.

They're the perfect chaperone combo.

Ms. Mercer scans the campsite as if reading its aura. I mean, maybe she is. "We'll start with the Lion Letters first."

Panic leaps through me. I'm feeling too many things to be able to write any sort of coherent letter yet. I haven't had time to figure out what I'm allowed to want.

"But"—I grab the clipboard from Prashant's hand and show her the agenda I painstakingly typed up, color-coded, and printed for everyone—"the letters aren't supposed to be until tonight—not until the bonfire."

We have to warm up to it. *I* have to warm up to it.

Ms. Mercer's beatific smile broadens. "Oh, but you must feel it."

Prashant and I exchange glances.

"Feel what?" I ask.

She sucks in a lungful of air, her eyes rolling back in a kind of ecstasy as she lets out a super awkward moaning sound. "The *energy*."

I look around and notice nothing but the fact that everyone seems bored already. Not great. Ms. Mercer watches me expectantly.

"I don't *not* feel it," I hedge.

Prashant rolls his eyes and says, "It'll throw the entire day off."

"Then let's throw the entire day off!" Ms. Mercer exclaims. "Isn't Senior Sunrise all about living braver and bolder?"

"But we still need a schedule—"

"Nonsense. You're not *trains*." She says this with so much disdain, like someone actually suggested we were.

Prashant and I exchange another look, trying not to laugh.

"But—"

Ms. Mercer cups my shoulder. "Be brave, little lion. This ritual is begging to be done. It's time." The wind picks up just as she says it, and goose bumps ripple down my arms. I don't believe in signs but . . . maybe Ms. Mercer knows what she's talking about. I study the agenda one more time, fighting the anxiety thrumming under my skin.

I guess if we do this now, I won't have to worry about it all day. We can just get it over with.

"Fine," I say. "Let's do it."

CHAPTER FIVE

Ethan

Senior Sunrise, 7:45 AM

MY CHEST IS ON fire watching Natalia walk away. Again. Is she ever going to slow down long enough to actually talk to me?

Claire cuts off my thoughts when she loops her arm with mine. "It's going to start soon. Want to sit together?" she asks.

When she looks at me with big hopeful eyes, I can't turn her down. "Um, yeah, sure."

We start toward the semicircle of benches Mason and I set up, passing an older couple walking in the opposite direction past our campsite. The woman smiles at me politely. But then it gets weird. Because she does a double take and stops.

Oh god.

She stares at me and stares at me, and it's probably only three seconds in real time, but when a stranger stops the trajectory of their walk to stare at you, three seconds feels like approximately nine hours.

I'm entirely unsurprised when she says, "My goodness, has anyone told you that you are the spitting image of a young Roger Forrester?"

Yes. Yes, they have. When Dad got his role on *The Beltway*, the fast-talking political drama that won him a SAG Award and launched his career into ludicrous speed a few years ago, he was lauded the next Jon Hamm. And that's when strangers started coming up to me way too often to tell me I looked like him. Dad. Not Jon Hamm. We would both only be so lucky.

I always pretended I had no idea who Roger Forrester was because it was funny to me, and I never really saw it myself. But now that I'm taller and less gangly, even I have to admit I'm like a clone of him when he was my age. Same dark hair, same jawline and smile, same color eyes. My mom jokes if it wasn't for the fact that she was, you know, *there*, she'd question my maternity.

"Doesn't he, Dale?" the woman prods.

I smile as politely as I can muster and try to turn away, but Claire hooks a hand around my arm to keep me in place.

The man beside the woman, Dale presumably, looks at me. "Yeah, I see it."

"Ha, thanks," I say awkwardly and try to walk again, but Claire pulls on my arm with a surprising amount of strength.

"That's because he's his son," Claire says triumphantly. Smugly.

The sharp pain in my jaw is a sign of how hard I'm clenching my teeth.

The couple share an impressed, delighted look.

But I mean, c'mon. What's so impressive about being born? I didn't choose my dad's career. And it's not like I grew up in the industry, so I have no idea how to handle this kind of thing. Since Mom's job as a surgeon keeps her at the research hospital here, and Dad can film anywhere, they decided to stay here in the Bay Area when he booked *The Beltway*.

"Well, we're *big* fans of his," the lady says. "Aren't we, Dale?"

Dale shrugs.

"Who wouldn't be? He's *so* talented," Claire gushes, squeezing my arm. She leans closer to the lady as if sharing a secret. "And he's so nice, too. When I was the lead in our school's production of *Mamma Mia!* last year, he made a point to tell me how well I did. My director totally agreed when Roger told me I have a future in the business. Like, *so* nice."

I squeeze my eyes shut so I don't roll them. He only went to *Mamma Mia!* because the drama teacher asked him to introduce it as a way to get donations for the theater program. But guess who never comes to my basketball games? Yeah.

"Doesn't surprise me at all; he's such a family man," the lady says.

His publicist deserves a raise.

"Please let him know I just love him in *The Beltway*," the lady says to me.

"'Fame is proof that the people are gullible,'" I say. When the three of them look at me like I've spontaneously sprouted a fungus, I follow it up with a quiet "Ralph Waldo Emerson said that." I try to smile, but it feels ill-fitting and full of acid. I tug my arm out of Claire's grip so she can't keep me here any longer.

They walk on, and so do I.

"*Ethan*," Claire hisses, running up behind me. "That was *so* rude."

"Okay."

I don't care. It's not going to make one fucking difference in my dad's career if Dale and Lady Dale think his son is an asshole. But it's not the fans I'm mad at. Not really. It's Dad. And that *brand*. Roger Forrester: family man? *Bullshit*. Though if I'm really honest, it burns worse that it used to be true.

Rainn motions for us to sit with him and Sienna. I haven't really talked to him since we got here. He hasn't exactly been available, what with him spending all his free time feeling up Natalia.

I clench my jaw and shrug at him in response. Confusion passes over his face when I let Claire pull me to sit with her group, including Tanner Brown. He looks rough. His eyes are red, and I can smell the booze coming out of his pores.

"Ew, Tanner, shower much?" Janelle Johnson asks, plunking down next to him.

He groans. "Fuck off."

"What, did you go to another Jackson Ford party?" she asks.

"Stop talking," he says, massaging his temples.

A Jackson Ford party? Is that why Ford got fired? Even if he's not that much older than us, who would willingly want to hang out with a teacher? Especially one like him.

When Tanner notices me his lip curls. "'Sup, Prom King?"

I grimace. I haven't really thought about the whole prom king thing because it makes my skin feel too tight when I do. It's obvious that everyone at Liberty is either in on some elaborate, long-con prank, or they only voted for me because of my dad. I kept looking up for the bucket of blood to fall on me like in *Carrie*, standing on the stage with the same people who used to throw trash at my head.

The same people I'm sitting with now.

I wouldn't even care about it, but if Claire Wilson is kissing me and Mason Hartman is joking with me like I'm some jock in his orbit, it's as if there's this pressure now to be, like, *that* guy. Prom King Guy. I never asked to be that guy. I don't want to be that guy. Fame changed my dad into a person I fucking hate. Rotted him from the inside out. Popularity can't be much better.

I don't want to be the kind of person who has to live up to everyone else's opinions of me. Who even are you, then, if you're constantly giving pieces of yourself away?

God, if Adam could hear me complaining about all this . . .

Oh, poor Ethan. Must be so hard to be you. These aren't real problems, buddy. Grow up. He'd ruffle my hair in that gruff way that actually really hurts, and I'd throw something at him. But deep down I'd know he was right. Ignoring the shit going on with my parents, I don't have real problems. Not like him or anyone else. What am I even upset about?

Claire shakes me out of my head by holding up her phone for a picture. She leans in close and snaps it.

"Look at *us*," she says, grinning at the photo and getting it ready to post.

"Hey, that's going on a private account, right?"

None of my profiles are public. Not that I think I'm on anyone's radar, not really, but the media will use any sliver of content they can if it's a dry news day. Worse if some big story about Dad breaks.

I've learned it's best to keep everything on lock.

Claire looks up from her phone and grabs my arm. "Of course," she says seriously.

"Cool. Thanks."

We share a smile, and her cheeks go pink.

I feel eyes on me, and, sure enough, Natalia is watching us. Does she even care that I told her Claire and I were a thing? *Why* did I do that when it isn't even true? I guess I didn't want her to think I couldn't move on from what happened between us as easily as she did.

God, I'm pathetic.

Before my thoughts can spiral further, the teachers start welcoming everyone, then going over the long list of rules for today. Natalia is sitting up front with them and Prashant.

I try not to stare at her, but it's an effort. The moody sky brings out the dark blue of her eyes, and the wind keeps lifting the tumble of her long hair away from her face. I realize with a significant gut drop that I could look at her forever and never get bored.

I can tell Natalia isn't paying attention, either. She's deep in thought, churning on something. What I wouldn't give to know what is going on in her head right now.

I think back through what she posted on her profiles this summer for any clues I might've missed. But she didn't share anything personal. Not like usual. Nothing about her fender bender last week, or her annual camping trip with her parents in July. Obviously, nothing about Rainn, or I would've been prepared for all the goddamn *touching*.

How serious are they?

I comb through the conversation with Rainn from prom. When he told me he liked Natalia.

When I carelessly told him to go for it.

"Since when are you into Natalia?" I asked, genuinely surprised. Rainn usually goes for the kind of girls who are as relaxed as him. Natalia is a lot of things, but relaxed is not one of them.

"I dunno, tonight, I guess. Look at her," he said.

So I did. And she looked . . . perfect. She wore that long black dress and had her dark hair swept up, showing off her neck. The red lipstick was cruel. I hadn't stopped staring at her mouth all night.

But it wasn't just that. I saw her adjusting a vase of flowers on the refreshment table instead of dancing with everyone else. I saw her holding Sienna's purse while Sienna and her date took their prom photo.

She should've been the one getting a crown on the stage, but she kept to the sides, managing and straightening and shrinking as if trying to blend into the walls around us. As if she ever could.

"Have you two ever . . . ?" Rainn trailed off.

"No," I answered truthfully, and probably too quickly. Not because I didn't think of her like that. But because I knew she didn't think of *me* like that.

Doesn't think of me like that.

The best friendship is sacred ground, and I wasn't going to go messing that up just because I'd started to notice how I looked for her in every room, rushed through homework every night so I could talk to her before bed, woke up smiling every morning because she texted me, stressed about her to-do list that day.

So when Rainn was looking at me all expectant, I played it off. "I mean, c'mon, we're friends."

"Then it's cool if I go for it?" he asked.

"I don't know why you're even asking me."

"I dunno, you've got like a protective-brother vibe going."

I shuddered at that. God, not even close. "Whatever, dude, she's so gonna turn you down," I said jokingly, but I meant it. Or, at least, I'd hoped.

He laughed. I honestly thought that would be the end of it.

I didn't have a fucking clue.

"Natalia?" Ms. Mercer prompts, and Natalia and I both blink.

"I'm sorry, what—" Natalia starts.

Prashant stands up and opens his arms out wide. "Welcome to Senior Sunrise, a sleepover extravaganza!"

Everyone starts clapping, and Natalia scrambles to stand. She slaps him a little too hard on the back and gives him her nicest smile. "Thanks, Prashant, I got this."

She turns to the group. It's subtle, but I notice her shoulders slowly roll back and her spine straighten as if she's assuming a role onstage. President Natalia at our service.

"Hey, everyone! Thanks for coming. We've all heard stories about Senior Sunrise since we started at Liberty—how special it is. How important it can be. It's like Liberty's own version of New Year's Eve."

Suddenly, her eyes cut to me. In that second an expression passes over her face that drops my stomach like a stone. Like she's trying to tell me something. Or maybe she's trying *not* to tell me something. But . . . she's kept so much of herself from me for so long, I have no idea what she's trying to say. She continues with a short speech about how hard student council worked on this event and goes over the agenda for the day. But I'm distracted by the stress just beneath her features. There's an edge to her today that seems to be about more than what happened with us after prom. I've missed something going on with her. Something crucial. I *hate* it.

When she's done, she and Prashant start handing out the little notebooks with yellow lined paper inside while Ms. Mercer explains the purpose of the Lion Letters. When she uses her yoga voice, I almost always fall asleep in class. But today, it's hypnotic.

"This ritual can be very powerful, so keep an open mind. Take this moment of reflection in this beautiful setting to think about your time at Liberty." She folds her hands delicately at her chest, like she's holding a secret.

"Think, *really think*. What do you wish to cultivate in your last year? What would you do if you were free from fear? What sits heavy on us, holds us back. Confess it so you may release it. Remember, these are entirely private. You can get real with yourself. Wishes can become reality if we're brave enough.

"If it helps, start your letter with the words 'If I were braver . . .' and see what comes out. Once you're done, tear out your letter, fold it up, and slip it into this glass bottle."

She holds up a large jar that looks like a retro milk jug, with a white resealable lid and metal mechanism to close it.

"As we do every year, we'll cast our letters into the fire at dawn."

Everyone is quiet. Reverent. Ready.

Ms. Mercer smiles. "You have an hour. Get writing."

I grab my notebook and walk over to a bench that's overlooking the water. The wind has pushed the fog away, and I can see forever into the distance. It's quiet over here save the rhythmic crashing of waves.

Get real with yourself.

To start, I guess I know what I *don't* want my senior year to be like. I don't want to be someone I'm not. I don't want to leave Liberty knowing I was some sort of asshat that I'll cringe to think about when I look back.

I don't want to look for escapes the way my brother did. I don't want to look outside of myself for some sort of fix for what's broken inside of me and our family.

I don't want to keep letting bad things happen to people I care about by not speaking up.

I don't want to lose Natalia.

How exactly did we get to this place where it's unbearable to look at each other?

Confess it so you may release it.

Maybe we really can fix it today. We can clear the air and start our friendship on a clean slate if we're brave enough. I miss her too much not to try. I will force myself to be brave enough. To write just to her.

My heart hammers in my chest as I put pen to paper:

I wish you would talk to me again. Everything is changing so fast. I have a lot of regrets lately. About school and my family. And I don't know what to do about most of it . . . but I know that if I were braver, I would have <u>begged</u> you to stay that night. Because you have no idea how much I wanted you. Never in my wildest dreams did I ever think you'd be topless in my bed.

But when you said it wouldn't change anything, I just . . . I knew I couldn't be with you if that was true. I couldn't finally have you in my arms to only lose you again in the next breath. Because I know now what I was only piecing together then.

It would change everything for me.

It already has.

But I didn't say any of this because I was afraid you would freak out. I don't know how you feel. Sometimes I'm convinced there's no way you'd even look at me like that for real. And other times, I don't know, I guess I wonder if you feel the same way. Because after that night, I only barely know what it's like to have you in my arms . . . to lie next to you like that and think you might want me, too. It's knowledge that's seriously incomplete.

I was sure that if I ever told you all this, I would lose you.

But I'd rather <u>know than wonder</u> forever. So, if I were braver, I would ask you. And I would tell you everything inside me. Because you are worth fighting for.

My hands shake a little as I fold the paper. This is . . . too honest. But I remind myself it's going in a bottle where no one will ever read it. You can't fix it if you pretend it isn't broken.

I walk up to the glass jar and, with a deep breath, drop it in.

CHAPTER SIX

Natalia

Senior Sunrise, 8:53 AM

AROUND ME, I HEAR sniffles and see honest-to-god tears. People are really taking the letters seriously. Everyone is either bent over their notebooks or staring out at the horizon, thinking and wistful. *Emotional.*

Now, if only I can get there myself. Ugh. I stare at the blank sheet, willing the words to come. It's already been forty minutes, and I feel like I'm the only person who's frozen. Too scared and weak to face what my mind is throwing at me.

Why did I have to compare Senior Sunrise to New Year's Eve?

Flashes of that night start surging through my head like headache-inducing strobe lights.

The way Mr. Forrester talked to me. The way he *looked* at me. It makes me shudder. I slam my eyes shut trying to run from it the way I have all year. I pull in a breath thinking of Ethan's strong, comforting arms around me. The safety I've always found there. Would that safety still be there if I told him?

I wish I could paint this jumble of fear and yearning that forces my words into corners I can't reach. But if I have any hope of figuring out what I want this year, of figuring out a way through this, I should do my best to reach for the right ones . . .

> If I were braver, I would tell Ethan everything.
> I would tell him what happened on New Year's
> Eve and why things have been so weird between
> us. Why I've been so off since then. I haven't
> known how to tell him because I didn't want
> everything to change between us. I know it
> has to and that once I tell him it will but . . . I
> swear I didn't want any of this to happen.

My chest tightens. I cross out the line about New Year's Eve but keep going:

> If I were braver, I would tell Ethan why I
> ran off that night. What I really wanted. How
> scared I was that I ruined everything. I just
> feel so out of control when I'm with him—

Nope. I draw a line through that whole paragraph and try to say it a different way.

> If I were braver, I'd accept that nothing
> can ever come from these feelings, no matter
> how big they are, or right they feel. His dad
> was right—we're in different worlds. I get it

> now, what everyone else seems to understand:
> I'm not good enough for him. I never have been.
> I'm not rich enough. I'm not pretty enough. I'm
> not smart enough. I keep waiting for a cure for
> this feeling, and I'm terrified...

I rip the page out of the notebook, *this* close to eating it to ensure it can never be read by another soul.

It's too much. It's all too specific and personal.

But it's clear to me now that there is nothing else I could do to change my life or my time at Liberty. The task of the Lion Letter is to write about the thing that we need to be bravest about as we start senior year. Even if I don't finish high school here, even if I end up moving with Mom, there is nothing that will impact my senior year more or requires more bravery than facing this thing with Ethan.

I inhale, uncrumple the paper to reread my letter. I can still read through the crossed-out lines, and suddenly, it's clear what it boils down to. I add a final point to the long page of scribbled-out thoughts. One simple sentence:

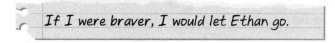

> *If I were braver, I would let Ethan go.*

I'm the last one to slip my letter into the bottle.

CHAPTER SEVEN

Natalia

LAST New Year's Eve, 9:06 PM

I'M SIX MINUTES LATE to Ethan's New Year's Eve party. His parents throw one every year, and our group always has our own version in the downstairs living room to stay out of their way.

I don't bother knocking and walk right through Ethan's front door like I do every time I come over. Though, now that he's moved to this giant house in Cliffport Heights, it feels like I'm breaking in or something. I can hear my friends gathered in Ethan's living room, particularly Sienna, speaking animatedly. My sparkly purple dress flares around my knees as I wince-walk, feet throbbing, to the entryway bench to rip off these heels.

I should never have worn them to Abuela's house to batch-cook the tamales, but I didn't think it would take so long, either. Besides, the dozens of reviews I read said these were comfortable and could be worn for hours without incident. *Hours*. Liars. One freaking star.

I peel off the heels, sighing. The relief is instant. I drop them under the bench, where they land next to Ethan's high-top Chucks he wears everywhere. His thunderous laugh echoes, and it makes me smile. With him in Tahoe and me so busy, we haven't seen each other all winter break. I can't believe how much I've missed him. I touch my hair self-consciously, wondering what he'll think of the cut. Then I roll my eyes at myself. He probably won't even notice.

When I stand up, my eyes snag on a new framed painting hanging on the wall by the stairs. It's abstract, bearing slashes of deep black against cobalt blues, an off-center maroon blob in the middle, like a weeping gash. I drift across the foyer as if pulled by a tractor beam to examine it more closely. The cold marble is heavenly under my throbbing feet.

I study the brushstrokes, looking at it from the side to take in the textures. Suddenly my eyes are burning like I want to cry.

"Isn't it absorbing?" a deep voice asks.

I turn around, and Ethan's dad is walking across the foyer, his eyes on the painting, too. He's wearing a pristine black suit and holding a crystal glass of brown liquor in his hand, his perfectly coiffed hair falling over his forehead just so. He's older than my dad, but he looks about ten years younger. It's that celebrity thing. That money thing. All the products and procedures that make them look like gods, as opposed to the years of work and stress that are worn deeply into the grooves of my own father's face.

I smile politely. "Hi, Mr. Forrester."

He puts a hand on his chest, like I wounded him. The ice in his glass clinks, some of the amber liquid sloshing onto his wrist. "You've been friends with Ethan since you were kids and still you call me *missur*?" The last word slurs a bit.

"Sorry," I say. Though, I'm not really. I could never call him *Roger*. It would be like calling a teacher by their first name—weird and *way* too familiar.

His gaze returns to the painting, so mine does, too. "I saw it at this small gallery in SoHo and even though it cost a fortune, I just had to have it," he says.

"It's really cool," I say, squeezing my eyes shut in embarrassment. *Cool?* It's so much more than cool. It's magnificent. Strange. At once it makes me feel like despair is bottomless but worth crawling away from with every ounce of fight left inside me.

"It's . . . special," I try again, a little breathless.

"I'm glad you think so, Natalia." He takes a step toward me. "How's your painting going?"

My eyebrows spring up, surprised. I don't know if I've ever talked about my art with him.

He leans forward even more as if sharing a secret. "Ethan always talks about how talented you are."

The flush heats up my cheeks in spite of myself, thinking of Ethan talking about me and my art. "He's exaggerating."

"I doubt that; he's got quite a discerning eye. Like his dad," he says proudly.

People compare Ethan and his dad a lot, but I don't really get it. Yeah, there's a resemblance, but nothing drastic. Ethan's eyes are kinder, his smile wider. And there's an edge to Mr. Forrester that thankfully Ethan doesn't have. Maybe it's just the fame on him that he's not able to shake.

He's watching me, I guess expecting an answer about my art.

"I don't really have a lot of time to paint anymore."

Mr. Forrester frowns at that and takes another step toward me. I have to lean away to look at him clearly. My shoulders hit the wall. Since when was I standing so close to it?

"Take it from me," he says, his red eyes shining, "if you don't prioritize your art, no one will."

"I've, um, never thought of it like that."

I try to step around him, and he brings his arm up, resting his hand against the wall. He probably doesn't realize he's caging me in, but my heart picks up anyway. I'm cornered and can't get by him without blatantly pushing him back.

"I'd love to see your work sometime. I know a lot of people in the art world I could connect you to."

"Really?" I say, unable to keep the interest out of my voice.

He grins, shining this megawatt red-carpet smile on me. "I'd be happy to."

I haven't spent a ton of time with Mr. Forrester, especially in the past few years, since he's always out of town shooting for his show or some new movie. But usually when he's around, he tells funny stories about Ethan and Adam as kids, never fails to order tons of food when we all come over, and has gotten tickets for all of us to basketball games and concerts as a surprise. He donates a ton to Liberty, especially in support of the Lion Scholarships, which is really cool, since I wouldn't be able to afford school without one.

But right now, his intent gaze is unnerving. "I almost didn't recognize you before. You look radiant."

My stomach twists, and I press my shoulders harder against the wall in an effort to create some space. Does he realize how close he's leaning? "Oh. Um. Thanks."

"My costar Sofía always complains about her curves, but men love them, you know." He says this as if it's sage wisdom I should be honored to hear instead of fetishizing and objectifying.

I glance around him, toward the living room, trying to telepathically beckon someone to interrupt our conversation. Whether he's aware of what he's doing or not, I do *not* want to be alone with him anymore.

Then my eyes fall on the pictures that line the walls with all the family portraits from vacations and holidays. I'm probably overreacting. This is Ethan's *dad*. Yeah, he's a celebrity, but he's also the same guy who's taken us out for pizza and sings off-key in the car and makes corny dad jokes—like my dad. He's probably just drunk. I've noticed that some guys can get *weird* when they drink. I try to push the uneasy feeling away.

"I had a girlfriend like you when I was younger," he says.

I fix my eyes on the painting. "A . . . painter?" I ask, trying to follow the sudden topic change. His gaze slides down my body in a way that feels . . . wrong.

"A siren. The kind of girl who makes boys do bad things."

Every muscle tenses with warning.

In my mind I'm sinking my fingertips into all the murky colors—browns and grays and blacks—and spreading them from the middle of the canvas, dragging them toward the edges. The smears resemble a rib cage with a tornado inside it.

He inches close enough that I can smell the booze on his breath. "If he hasn't yet, Ethan's going to notice soon, too."

He's eyeing me the way he eyed the painting. *Just had to have it.* I hold back a shudder, and I fold my arms around myself, trying to hide my chest. Trying to get smaller so he stops looking at me like *that*. Trying to remember the few self-defense moves I learned in PE if it comes to that.

He leans even closer. "But we both know you're not the right kind of girl for him."

I squeeze my hands into fists so he can't see how hard they're trembling. "What?"

He keeps his glassy eyes on mine, a pitying, condescending smile curling his lips. "Different worlds," he says, spreading his arms wide around the foyer that half my house would fit inside.

My mouth falls open in shock.

"His brother is a lost cause now that he's gotten himself injured, but I have big plans for Ethan. Best if you . . . keep your distance. You get it, right?"

He's waiting for me to say something. All I want to do is burst into tears, but instead I nod once. Because I do get it. He's telling me what I've always known; I'm not good enough for Ethan. I never have been. Even his asshole dad knows that.

Suddenly, a peal of laughter echoes from the other room, and it snaps his attention for a second. I take the opportunity. "I should—"

He steps aside immediately. "Of course. Didn't mean to keep you. Happy New Year, Natalia."

Mr. Forrester raises his glass toward me in a toast, pushes himself off the wall, and stumbles a bit on his way back to the adult party.

My skin is crawling, and I spin on my heel to leave. I have to get out of here. Just then Ethan's voice echoes into the room, "Talia! You're here!"

He bounds over to me, pulling me into a warm hug. Safety. Comfort. Even though he put on way too much cologne, I want to curl against him, hidden from everything and everyone else. But I pull away quickly, imagining his dad hovering on the staircase watching us.

Ethan's hair is slightly messy in a purposeful way. He's wearing a navy button-down shirt, sleeves pushed to the elbows, and dark, expensive jeans cuffed at the ankles. I smooth a self-conscious hand down the dress I got at Target.

Different worlds.

"What took so long?" he asks.

"I—your dad," I say, my voice still shaking. I don't know what to say, though. Was that real? Did Mr. Forrester really mean what I think he meant? What did I do?

I must've done something to make him think it was okay to talk to me like that, right? He called me a siren. Like I purposely beckoned his attention with . . . what? The fact that I wore a dress to a fancy party?

If I can figure it out, I can be sure to never do it again. I need to never feel like *this* again.

Ethan grins, unaware of my inner collapse. "Was he showing off that awesome new painting? He did the same thing to Rainn when he got here."

Even though he looks exasperated, there's a swell of affection in his tone. And that's when I realize the tragedy of the situation.

It's his *dad*.

How could I ever tell Ethan what just happened? Especially when I can't even explain it. Even if Ethan did believe me, what would he think? Would he wonder if I flirted back? Disgust roils my insides.

No, I can't ever tell him. His dad didn't actually *do* anything, anyway.

I force out a laugh. "Yeah, the painting's really cool. Sad . . . but hopeful."

"I thought so, too," Ethan says warmly. He grabs my hand and pulls me toward the group, smiling. "Your haircut is really cute, by the way."

Ten minutes ago, a comment like that from Ethan would've sent my blood fizzing. But now, I don't want anyone to ever look at me like that again. Not even Ethan. Maybe especially not Ethan.

CHAPTER EIGHT

Ethan

Senior Sunrise, 9:00 AM

AFTER AN HOUR OF silent writing, Natalia is the last one to drop a letter in. I watch her as she squeezes the top on the bottle to close it and rests it back in the center of the table, her face a mask of unease. The bottle is full to the neck with folded-up slips of yellow notebook paper.

Our eyes catch, and I want so badly to know what she wrote.

"Well done, Lions! You opened your hearts, and I thank you for that." Ms. Mercer presses her palms together in a prayer pose and bows toward us. "We have one more announcement before we begin the fun and games. The only way you're going to find true presence today is if you're focused on yourselves and your fellow seniors. Not busy scrolling your attention away. When you pick up your senior T-shirt, you will turn in your phone."

Everyone groans.

"But! In exchange, you will also be picking up one of these." She pulls out a Polaroid camera and shoots me a knowing look. "Thanks to

Ethan's dad, Mr. Forrester, you each get one and plenty of film for the day to keep your memories!"

There are some excited murmurings, but bile rises in my throat. There goes Dad throwing his money around again. Trying to buy me back, as if it worked like that. Sure, Dad, I'll forgive you for cheating on Mom with your costar. All it took was a camera! That makes complete sense.

I slump down as far as I can, but when I look to Claire to commiserate, she's wide-eyed and leans close. So close her warm lips brush right against my ear. "Your dad is the coolest."

He's *really* not.

Despite the free cameras, people are still talking and complaining about their phones. I can hear some people threatening to leave.

Rainn stands up. "Seriously? You all can't be away from your phone for one day? C'mon," he says in that easy surfer way of his, "we'll be asleep for part of it. Let's do this!"

Somehow that turns the tide, and the complaints die down.

Natalia mouths *thank you* to Rainn, and he winks at her.

Don't mind me, the miserable jerk who just stuffed his heart in a jar completely ignoring the fact that Natalia basically has a boyfriend.

I eye the bottle, sitting on the middle of the table. Dread ripples through me at everything I put in that letter.

"Okay, line up and let the cord-cutting begin!" announces Mr. Beckett.

We get in line. Next to me, Claire and Janelle won't stop complaining about having to turn in their phones.

"If I had known we couldn't have them I never would've come to this. It's like, illegal, I think? We use them for literally everything. What if I need the calculator?" Janelle asks.

"That's such a good point," Claire says.

This goes on for a while, and I'm contemplating how much it would hurt to hurl myself off this bluff and straight into the ocean. Probably not more than this conversation.

Just then, Natalia cries out. I step around the line to see Rainn standing in front of her, his arms outstretched to block the wind while she cleans up the box of shirts that fell over.

"My hero," she laughs.

My hands ball into tight, straining fists at my sides. I don't release them until Rainn jogs down to the beach for the volleyball games.

The group in front of us moves, and we're finally at the front of the line. Natalia looks at us, and her eyes go flinty. I'm sure my expression matches hers.

Claire has her arms crossed, this deep V between her eyebrows. "What do you think, Ethan?"

"Huh?"

"About the *phones*."

Natalia's eyebrows drift up as she catches on. "Yeah, Ethan. What do you think about the phones?"

In truth, I'm usually glued to my phone. Scrolling and deep-diving on every single curiosity of mine relaxes me. Besides, reading through Wikipedia is the best way to avoid awkward conversations. I should be more upset.

But at this moment, they can burn the thing for all I care. Mine has been buzzing with calls and texts from my dad for the past hour. Varying levels of *Call me when you get this. IMPORTANT.* That implies I care. Or want to talk to him. I don't.

The pit in my stomach is growing, knowing that unless I ice him out forever, I'll have to talk to him about it at some point.

But not yet.

To be free from my dad in a real way, for even one day, sounds liberating as hell. Claire is staring me down, waiting for me to take her side.

Yep, here comes another awkward conversation.

I keep my eyes on Natalia when I say, "Um. Well, many studies have found excessive phone use linked with higher levels of depression, anxiety, and insomnia."

Janelle crosses her arms. "Oh, yeah, I forgot about your whole factoid thing."

I press my lips together. I'm surprised she doesn't remember considering that's the only way I used to converse in seventh grade. Especially for that whole day she and I went out. Which was a joke by the way. The bored, popular crowd *paid* Janelle to tell me she liked me, and she pretended to be my girlfriend for as long as she could stand it. An entire school day. Ah, fun, soul-crushing memories.

"He's so smart. He's like a walking Wikipedia," Claire agrees.

"Ethanpedia!" Janelle exclaims.

She and Claire giggle uncontrollably while my entire head gets hot. Am I actually friends with these people? See, this is where I would pull my phone out and look up "Stockholm syndrome," wondering if I have, in fact, crossed over to the dark side.

"Don't forget, excessive phone use is also linked to diminished academic performance," Natalia says. Her hard eyes cut to Janelle, who doesn't seem to realize that Natalia is insulting her.

I smother my smile with a hand, just as the corners of her mouth tug up.

Rolling their eyes, Claire and Janelle turn in their phones and each grab a camera. They walk away talking about how cute the senior shirts are without even acknowledging Natalia again, who I know spent hours designing them.

Before I turn in my phone, I shoot a quick text to Adam.

Won't have my phone today. Call mom if you need anything. Miss you dickhead.

I chew on the inside of my cheek. I hope he'll be okay without our usual call today. I don't know how much it helps him, but it helps *me* to hear his voice clear instead of slurring. To be reassured he's not using. To know that he's stronger than Dad could ever be. When I look, Natalia's holding up my T-shirt and watching me curiously.

But when I try to grab the shirt, she keeps a hold on it a beat. "Hey. Whatever's bothering you, it's not as bad as your spiraling ass thinks."

My heart lifts a little. "How do you know?"

Sweetness and pettiness are at war in her eyes. Her expression folds over on itself when petty wins. "Because I'm also *so* smart," she says in an imitation of Claire's voice.

She bats her eyelashes and flips her hair, then looks down at her clipboard. "By the way, do you prefer to be called Prom King or Ethanpedia? I need to update my files."

If she's trying to get under my skin, it's working.

"Cool new friends by the way," she says, replacing her frown with this radiant smile that kinda knocks me out for a second. For some reason that irritates me even more.

"Cool new boyfriend," I say, and snatch the shirt out of her hands, walking away with my face on fire.

I hate that I'm glass to her. That she sees right fucking through me. Except right now she's using that superpower to see only what she wants to see. My flaws. My mistakes.

Why is she giving me shit about Claire when *she's with Rainn*? And am I ever going to have a conversation with her, let alone fix this, when all we do is set each other off?

I swear, at this point it's going to take nothing short of divine intervention.

CHAPTER NINE

Natalia

Senior Sunrise, 9:15 AM

MY BOYFRIEND? WHAT IS Ethan even talking about? Was he making a joke, or does he actually think Rainn and I are together? They must not be talking, either, which is *really* unlike them. Ethan sounded angry and . . . jealous. Which shouldn't make me smile. Like, at all.

And yet.

But my face falls quickly thinking of Ethan and Claire again. The way she's absorbing him into her group. The way his voice gets a little deeper when he talks to her.

Now that everyone else has turned in their phones and headed down to the beach, it's my turn.

I'm honestly relieved about this no-phone rule. Mine has been going off all morning with texts from my parents. Like a screenshot of my fall class schedule with the text from Dad that says,

Studio art? Must be a mistake. Going to call to switch it back to statistics. One of my favorite classes senior year!

Like from my mom:

Which set of sheets should I take? The red flowers or black stars? Want all your favorites when you're with me!

Like they don't care they're ripping my life in half, leaving me only the tattered edges to work with.

I don't respond to either of them. I'm about to turn off my phone when I notice I missed a notification from earlier.

@ClaireBearWilson tagged you in a photo!

That's weird.

I tap it quickly, and my pulse spikes when I see a selfie of her and Ethan together captioned "no summertime sadness here." Her face is pressed into the crook of his neck that I know smells like shaving cream and *him*, and he's doing that easy Ethan prom king smirk that makes him feel so far away from me.

She *tagged me* to be sure I saw this. To send a message.

Ethan is particular and private about what he allows online. She posted it because he let her. Which means they're even more serious than I thought.

I take a shuddering breath as the back of my nose starts to burn. This is exactly why I need to let him go. Things are "going that way" with another girl.

In my mind I start on a giant canvas. As big as a house. It has rich, thick globs of violent reds and angry slashes of orange swirled together. The paint so thick you could climb it. A wall of fire.

I turn off my phone and shove it in the large plastic tub with the others under the table. I wish I could seal up my feelings in the same way.

As I rush toward the steps down to the beach to catch up with the class getting ready for beach games, a sharp glint of light catches my eye and I stop. Ms. Mercer left the glass jar of Lion Letters in the middle of the table like an offering.

I approach it, my head on a swivel looking for anyone who might be nearby. But no, it's just me.

Me and the jar of secrets.

Out here exposed where anyone could grab it and take it, read everything. *Know* everything.

Is she seriously planning to leave the letters here all day? There are several breaks scheduled. Plenty of opportunities for anyone motivated enough to steal them. I can't believe I trusted her to keep these safe.

I can't have my letter sitting out where someone as conniving as Claire could get her hands on it.

I grab the jar, but to do what, exactly? No matter where it ends up, the fact remains that my letter is in there, too personal, too alive, too *true*. I should never have written such private stuff in the first place. I wrote Ethan's name, how much I want him, mentioned his dad—New Year's Eve! No matter that it's crossed out, it's readable. All of it.

I really should've eaten it.

I was the last to put mine in, so I can still see it, right on top. The selfie with Claire flashes in my mind again. I need to let Ethan go, but on my terms. In private. Not in some public ritual. Not in a crowd of other people's wishes and secrets—people who have no idea what I'm going through. Who could never understand just how much it hurts to bear something so painful inside.

All I need to do is open the jar and pull mine out. No one will ever know. Leaving it here is too risky. If I'm going to do this, I have to do it now while everyone is down at the beach.

My pulse slams through me with guilt even though the letter is mine.

I pop the lid open with my thumb. Trying to get my fingers in the thin neck, I struggle. It's narrower than I expected. Even when I reach into it with one finger, it still isn't long enough to grab my letter. Maybe this is a sign.

I frown. No, I don't believe in signs. I press my lips together and turn the whole thing over, shaking it like a ketchup bottle.

Once. Twice. After three hard shakes, I get my letter close enough to the top that I'm able to catch the corner of it with a fingertip. Dragging it against the glass, with one final, triumphant swoop, I pull it out.

Big mistake.

I watch in horror as a cascade of letters comes tumbling out and is caught on a sudden strike of wind.

"No!" I cry as the next gust swirls and scatters them like yellow leaves.

Secrets, everyone's private thoughts and wishes and fears and regrets, are flying all over the campsite, catching against brush and eucalyptus trees and some, oh god, some tumbling toward the cliff's edge that overlooks the sea.

The blood drains from my face. *What did I just do?*

CHAPTER TEN

Natalia

Senior Sunrise, 9:23 AM

I SPRINT AFTER THE little yellow pages. Desperately lurching and stomping and catching the papers in the wind. I stuff them inside my shirt to keep them from flying away again. I dart around a tent and run smack into a warm wall, letters crumpling against my chest.

"What the—" the wall says.

I blink. *Ethan*, coming out of the bathroom in a change of clothes for the volleyball game.

My galloping heart leaps to my throat. I'm caught.

He clocks the letters spilling out of my shirt, in my hands, and his eyes fly wide with understanding. "You didn't."

"It was an accident!"

He shoves a hand in his hair. "Natalia . . ."

"Help me or move!"

Another slip of yellow paper catches my eye, and I sprint to snatch it before the effing wind steals it away. The letter blusters right up to where Ethan is standing, and he stomps on it, catching it under his shoe.

We share a look, and he picks it up.

"What do you need?" he asks.

Without any time to waste on the leap of joy my heart makes, I tell him to look everywhere and make sure there aren't any left. We both run.

I scan the campsite again, finding a few more under the greasy barbecue pit grate and another two behind the girls' bathroom. I do another frantic lap, running the perimeter of the entire area, from the tables to the cliffside. I circle back to the tents, my arms full of letters spilling out of my shirt, my eyes everywhere looking for any last scrap of yellow paper that I missed.

When I'm sure we got them all, Ethan grabs the jar, and we duck into my tent. I zip the door behind us, shaking my shirt out. Dozens of crumpled, dirty papers flutter onto my sleeping bag between us.

"Okay, there are sixty-seven seniors in the class, but only fifty-eight signed up for today," I say between panting breaths. "Based on the sign-in sheet, two didn't show."

In unison, Ethan and I say, "Jensen twins."

"Slackers," he mutters. "Okay, so there should be fifty-six here?"

I nod, swallowing down the rising panic.

We count furiously, then share a dismayed look when we only get to forty-nine. We count again. Same number.

Seven. Seven letters still missing. Seven potential bombs, grenades, personal land mines are out there in the wild that I *must* find before anyone else does.

The color drains from Ethan's face. "*Fuck,*" he says under his breath. "This is *bad*, Talia."

I think about all the people who were crying while writing their letters, and my breath stutters. "I know."

"I—" He stops and swallows. "Some of us wrote *really* personal stuff in those letters. In the wrong hands . . . you know how they are."

He doesn't have to say any more. These are the same people who poured trash on Ethan's head and threw him into lockers. Who just tagged me in a photo to stake their claim.

I know how they are. It's why I was trying to get my letter back.

But what do I do? It's an impossible task. They could be anywhere. *They call it Ventoso for a reason.* I almost laugh through the sob building in my throat.

I press fists to my eyes. No. Now is not the time to wallow. I just need to *think* so I can fix this. But I thought I was already doing that by touching the letters in the first place. If I had just left the jar alone . . . but nope, can't focus on that right now, either.

Our teachers always throw around the term "solution-focused mindset" when we get stuck on an issue. I just need to think about all possible solutions instead of fixating on the cause of the problem.

(Me. Me. Always *me*.)

"Okay. Tomorrow at sunrise, Ms. Mercer will pour all the letters into the bonfire on the beach, so it's not like anyone is going to count these. No one has to know their letter is missing. No point in upsetting anyone—especially when it's possible that some of the letters went over the cliff," I say.

This sounds extremely shady even to my own ears, but Ethan nods slowly, slipping the letters back in the jar one by one. "And we'll be outside all day, so we can keep our eyes peeled for them just in case. Like an Easter egg hunt. Helpful that they're yellow," he muses.

The ache builds stronger in my throat. "We?"

His hand stills on the top of the jar. Our eyes catch, and the tent gets smaller. He shrugs one shoulder up. "I always knew you'd get me to bury a body for you someday."

My almost laugh loosens the knot in my throat. "I miss you," I blurt.

About a thousand emotions flicker across his face. "I'm right here," he responds softly.

He is. My skin is singing with his nearness.

Then his face shifts with anxiety. "Wait." He studies the pile of letters scattered around us that we haven't put back yet. His eyes widen with alarm. "Did you read them?"

"*No*," I say immediately. "I would never. I accidentally knocked all of them loose and the *fucking* wind carried them. I—I was just trying to get mine back."

I realize with a stone-cold dread that I lost track of my letter in the madness. There isn't any way to check through these for mine without violating everyone's privacy even more than I already have.

Mine could be one of the missing seven letters. *Shit.*

He frowns, his dark brows meeting in the middle. "Why were you trying to get it back?"

But before I can respond, I hear footsteps and put a finger to my lips to shut him up.

Double shit.

We haven't gotten all of them back in the bottle yet. My lap is still covered in over half the letters. We couldn't look more guilty even if we were covered in blood at a crime scene. This is bad—it looks like we stole them on purpose. Like we *were* reading them.

"Natalia?" It's Prashant. "Being your keeper isn't in the vice president job description, so let it be known I resent this." He's right outside the tent.

My heart is working overtime. "Then what are you doing here?" I ask, somehow keeping my voice even.

"I was chosen as the messenger to ensure you weren't murdered or something. Our volleyball game can't start because of the uneven teams."

"I had to pee and now I'm changing," I say, the lies slipping easily off my tongue.

"I don't need your life story. I need you on the beach."

Even in my panic, I manage to flick a baleful glare at Prashant's silhouette. Ethan shifts, his entire back pressing against the side of the tent. I gesture at him to keep it together. He gestures like he's trying.

"By the way, have you seen Ethan?" Prashant asks, his voice going . . . weird.

Our eyes lock.

"No."

The silence gets louder the longer Prashant stands there *not* responding.

"Stop hovering, I'll be down in two minutes," I say, annoyed.

"Fine. But if you two are naked in there, it's going to take a lot longer than two minutes," he says before walking off.

Well. I shove the rest of the letters into the jar quickly, wishing I could bury my hot face in my hands. Ethan seals the jar closed, his eyes not meeting mine, either. I kick him out, and he returns the jar to the table while I change. It'll look way too conspicuous if we arrive at the beach at the same time anyway.

As I peel my sticky shirt over my head and pull on a dry one, I say a silent prayer that all seven missing letters are currently disintegrating at the bottom of the ocean where no one can find them. That I didn't just ruin anyone's life. That I didn't just ruin my own.

Being braver would ruin EVERYTHING. I'm so scared my dreams will never come true since I'm pretty sure I have no talent. Like, I've gotten compliments or whatever, but sometimes I feel like I don't deserve anything I've achieved. If anyone found out about me and Jackson, that's exactly what they would think, too. I mean, Jackson said that wasn't true. He swore that even if we never hooked up, he was going to give me the part ... But then he stopped saying stuff like that after we did. I don't know what to believe anymore. I wish he was going to be here this year. I wish he would text me back. I still can't believe he got fired.

Anyway .... I guess if I were braver, I would believe in myself more. But all I can do is try not to ruin my life more than I already have.

CHAPTER ELEVEN

Ethan

Senior Sunrise, 9:58 AM

I JOG TOWARD THE beach, scanning every plant, crevice, and pile of dried seaweed. No luck. When I mistake a discarded burger wrapper for a letter, there is a near altercation with a seagull. Terrifying. What the hell else is Natalia going to get me into today?

What was she thinking messing with the letters? What could she have possibly written that she wanted to take back that badly?

If anyone else had found her besides me . . .

I know her. I trust her. If she says she didn't read them, then she didn't. But this is so bad.

I survey the class, some already playing their volleyball games, while those on Natalia's and my teams are waiting for our game to start. Thankfully, everyone seems oblivious to what just happened. We have to keep it that way.

Things are hard enough right now, but if this gets out, our senior year is *fucked*. The entire class will *hate* us. I've been at their mercy enough to know they will make our lives a living hell, especially if their secrets are as personal as mine.

Oh *god*, what if mine is one of the letters out there?

I take a shaky breath in and tell myself it's probably one of the safe ones still tucked away in the bottle. I don't believe me.

I eye Prashant because I'm 99 percent sure he knew I was in the tent with her. Did he see anything else? I don't know him very well, but I do know he'd have no problem holding it over Natalia.

Prashant notices me looking at him and starts toward me, his expression inscrutable. *Fuck.*

Can he see the guilt on my face?

Guilt that I'm an accomplice. That his letter could be out there. That in the tent my hands weren't only shaking because of the letters but with the effort of not reaching for Natalia.

But no matter how confusing or painful or fucking infuriating things get with her, I can't stop myself from protecting her. I have to play it as cool as possible until we fix this. Prashant narrows his eyes when he gets to me.

"Look, it's not what you—" I start but am cut off by Prashant shoving a pole in my hands.

"Help me set up this net."

All I do is blink.

"Time is of the essence, Ethan, let's *go*."

There are several other volleyball games going on at the permanent nets, so I guess we need to set up an extra one for us to play at the same time. I grab the pole and study him carefully, looking for evidence this is the start of some double conversation. I don't see any. I exhale in a *whoosh*. "Um, I'm not really good at stuff like this—"

He stares at me blankly. "It's not something you can be good or bad at, it's an entirely neutral task. We're running behind, hurry up."

Once a few minutes go by, I'm sweating and Prashant is cursing under his breath.

"No, Ethan—just hold it up—"

"What? Like this?"

Prashant looks at me like I just kicked a puppy. Then he drops the net into the sand. "I don't admit this often, but I was wrong."

Sienna barks out a laugh.

"You could help, you know," I grumble to her.

"I'm busy," she says.

"Doing what? Staring at Leti?"

"*Ethan*," she hisses, turning bright red again.

She pulls agitated fingers through her hair and starts working on a complicated braid, while still very obviously staring at Leti Mitchell.

Then Natalia grabs both our attention as she scurries down the stairs to the beach, sweeping her hair into a ponytail while she runs. Her face is lined with worry.

Sienna frowns, watching her. "She's so stressed."

"She's not the only one," I mutter.

I do another scan of the beach for any yellow papers. Nothing.

Sienna gives me an odd look, her fingers flying through her hair. "She's having a hard time, Ethan. And you know how she is. The crappier she feels, the more she tries to control things. It's like making things perfect for everyone else helps her feel better."

My hands still. Sienna seems like she's in outer space half the time with the way her mind is always calculating probabilities, but then she'll make an observation like that, and it's clear she's paying closer attention than I think.

"You're right," I say, chastened. The need to protect Natalia, to fix what she did—what *we* did—surges through me anew. I have to force myself to ask the question I would already have the answer to if things were still okay between us. "Why is she having a hard time?"

But Sienna can't respond because Natalia comes over. Now she's wearing leggings and a black tank top, the peek of a pink bikini top tied around her neck. Her cheeks are flushed with exertion.

We exchange a look, holding yet another secret just between us. She subtly shakes her head, telling me she hasn't seen any letters, either.

Maybe they really did all fall into the ocean. Are we that lucky?

When Sienna eyes us curiously, I quickly return my attention to the net at my feet. It looks as mixed up as I feel.

"I will defeat you," I say to the tangled heap.

"I think it already won," Natalia says.

When our gazes meet, my heart skids to a stop. God, I've never realized how hard it is to look at her and talk to her at the same time. She's so close and so pretty, and I'm so confused. Not just about the letters but about everything. *Everything.*

She's the first to turn away. "Why does Prashant look like he's lost faith in humanity?"

Prashant's squatting in the sand, rereading the instructions for the fifth time, muttering to himself.

"I tried to help."

Natalia shakes her head slowly. "Why would you do that? You know how multistep instructions terrify you."

"I tried to warn him. But he said it wasn't that hard."

"It's not; you're just useless," she teases.

"Hey now—"

She starts tackling the net herself. "Hold this."

I do.

A minute later, the net is upright and staked and Natalia's tossing me a volleyball with an intensely smug look on her face. She steps back to admire her work, wiping her palms across the tops of her leggings. "Et voilà!"

I shake my head slowly, assessing her work. "Wow. Crushed it." I extend my fist out for her to bump. After a second of hesitating, she does.

Progress.

The morning sky is bright blue now, the wind having pushed the last of the fog away before downshifting into an easy coastal breeze. I peel off my hoodie down to my gray T-shirt, the cool temperature raising the hair on my arms. But it feels good.

After a beat, I shoot her a side-eye. "You're staring."

"No, I'm not," she says, looking away.

She really is, though. At my chest and arms mostly. I run a hand through my hair, my face on fire.

The thing is, when I couldn't follow a straightforward novel this summer because my head was such a mess, I figured I should listen to Coach, who is always on me about bulking up. Adam pounced on the project and put me through his spring training regimen. Working out became the only time we both relaxed; the only time it didn't feel like I was trying to breathe underwater. I didn't realize it was making *that* big of a difference.

"You're blushing," she says.

"No, I'm not," I say, imitating her.

She smiles. It's small, but it's real, and I can't believe how much I missed it. But it flickers out just as quickly when Claire bounds over to us and slings an arm through mine.

"I've been looking for you everywhere! What took you so long up there?" Claire asks me.

"Oh. Just . . . couldn't find my . . . sunscreen."

Natalia's expression tells me how bad of a liar I am. Perfect trait in the guy covering up a massive secret.

Claire watches us closely but doesn't say anything else about it. She turns toward the net. "Natalia, you're such a beast. You put that up in, like, two minutes!"

The corners of Natalia's mouth rise higher, her plastic smile now replacing the real one I finally got out of her.

"I'm used to these kinds of projects since I go camping every summer with my parents," Natalia says. But a flash of pain passes through her eyes when she says it.

"Ew, I hate camping. This is as rustic as I get," Claire says, squeezing my arm and laughing. I laugh, too, not because it's funny but because I'm so relieved Claire changed the subject from why we were late getting to the beach.

Natalia's smile gets tighter, faker, as she looks between me and Claire laughing. "Cool. Well, have fun today!" she responds, holding my eyes a second longer before walking over to Rainn.

"She's so nice," Claire says, watching her go.

I snort. That wasn't nice. That was Natalia's version of flipping me off. Dismissing me like she isn't going to see me the rest of the day.

What the hell? What about the letters?

So much for progress.

"Finally," Prashant says, assessing the net, then his clipboard. "Okay, Ethan, you're on my team, and Natalia, you're on Rainn's."

"Nice!" Rainn exclaims.

Of course.

"Look at you being all kinds of late today," Rainn teases her.

"Don't rub it in," she says, poking him in the ribs for emphasis.

He laughs and grabs her hand. "Careful, you know I'm hella ticklish."

"Are you?" she asks, eyes wide.

He studies her with suspicion because we both know she can't help herself. Once she knows the weakness, she must exploit it.

With a renewed vigor, she attacks his ribs with her fingers. He yelps, and in one swift motion, she's in the air, hanging over his shoulder, sand trailing off her bare feet. She yells at him to put her down.

"Told you to be careful!" he says, laughing.

She drums on his back. But then he starts spinning her, and a laughing shriek erupts out of her.

And I'm just watching. Fuming. I think about the Trojan War from Greek mythology. How an entire city was under siege for a *decade* because of a beautiful girl.

I get it.

It's not that Rainn's managed to pull laughs out of her all day when I've barely gotten a smile. Only. It's that when he puts her down, she pulls him into this . . . hug. And she looks undeniably happy.

The *ache* in me.

It's never been this bad before. Natalia's had boyfriends, and I've never wanted to pull their arms off. Then again, that was before the memory of her fingertips trailing down my bare stomach kept me up at night. Before the letter I just wrote about her could be *anywhere*.

Maybe I'm so pissed because I let this happen. If I had just been honest that night, with Rainn, with her, with *myself*, none of this would've happened. I push a hand through my hair.

Mr. Beckett blows the whistle to start the game.

If my letter *is* out there, I just hope I find it before she does.

CHAPTER TWELVE

Natalia

Senior Sunrise, 10:15 AM

ONE OF THE THINGS I've always loved about Rainn is that he's relaxed. Fun. When anxiety is taking hold of me, he somehow manages to make me laugh. Like he knows when I need it, even if he doesn't know why. Like when Claire is hanging all over Ethan.

Or when I violate the trust and privacy of our entire class.

When he finally puts me back down, I slide my arms around his waist to give him a quick squeeze. A silent thank-you for making me feel better for a second. When I pull away, he's flushed. There's a twinge of something in his look that makes me think that hug was maybe a step too far for "just friends."

But then he nods once and says, "Madam President."

I laugh again, rolling my eyes. He's the only one who calls me that. I don't need to worry about Rainn. He's as easygoing as the coastal breeze.

When I look up, Ethan's gaze quickly flicks away from me. I'm not doing anything wrong. I'm not doing anything he isn't doing with Claire. But guilt snakes through me anyway.

"See? Ethan drama," Prashant mutters.

I shoot him a murderous look while the teams get set up. It's Ethan, Prashant, Tanner, Janelle, and Claire on one team. Me, Mason, Leti, Sienna, and Rainn on the other. I scan around the beach, looking for any rogue yellow papers that could've blown this way. *Nothing.*

I squeeze my eyes shut and say a silent prayer for more time. To find them. To fix this without anyone getting hurt. Without anyone finding out what I did.

What was I thinking? On my first official day as student body president, I go and screw it up immediately.

Whose private worlds did I just let out? My own? My friends'? I can't take a deep enough breath.

I must've completely lost my mind. I got so focused on my own letter, I didn't even think about anyone else. It was impulsive and selfish and the opposite of a leader. I don't *do* things like that. I don't break rules or make mistakes or rope Ethan into being my accomplice.

That he still has my back is shaking me up. The way he immediately sprang into action. I don't deserve it. But I am so freaking thankful for it. If I had to figure this one out by myself, I don't know what I'd do. There is too much I'm holding, too many secrets piling up.

Secrets are like a wall. They protect you by keeping others out. Or they protect others but keep you locked in. Either way, they leave you in a prison of one with no way out but total destruction.

But . . . how am I ever supposed to let him go when he does things like this? My mind keeps drifting back to the tent, his eyes on mine. Alone for the first time in months and it felt like we were right back on his bed.

I need to focus on this game.

It's my turn to serve. I'm genuinely pleased when I get a decent underhand serve over the net on my first try. I'm less pleased when Ethan spikes it and gets his team their first point. He holds his arms out in a wide shrug, his eyes on mine in a *Sorry not sorry* gesture.

So that's how it's going to be.

After a few rounds, Ethan is scoring points off everyone. Sweat glistening on his forehead, cheeks flushed, eyes narrow and focused. He has the same instincts here that he does in basketball. It's this whole other side of him where he's confident and sure.

Claire hugs him whenever he scores. Janelle's on the volleyball team at school and stays poised at the net, dominating with her tall stature, blocking and spiking point after point.

When their team has a sizable lead, it's my turn to serve again.

Mason claps at me. "C'mon, Natalia! You got this! Just get your head outta your"—he makes eye contact with Mr. Beckett—"clouds."

I don't know what does it—maybe Ethan covering his laugh with the back of his hand or Tanner looking at me like I'm a waste of his time—but the competitor in me who has placed in hurdles the past two seasons takes over.

I serve into the opposite corner, and though Ethan dives for it, for the first time, he misses. Sand clings to his arms and chin when he stands. When he looks at me, I mirror his *Sorry not sorry* shrug back at him, and he pushes down a grin.

We slowly battle back to being tied.

It's really warming up now. I'm pouring sweat. Maybe too much. I vaguely note that I don't feel great, but I can't step out now. We're *so* close.

Thankfully, it's Leti's turn to serve, and they're killer. The ball sails just out of Tanner's reach. Though he dives, he misses, and we get the point. Now we only need one more to win.

I start to feel light-headed. I really should've had more than three marshmallows this morning. Especially because I was too nervous about today to eat much dinner last night. I pull my sweaty ponytail off my neck and squint my eyes to focus.

Mason slams an overhand serve that lands squarely at Prashant's feet. Prashant looks at it, shrugs as if he couldn't care less that he just lost, and walks to watch the other games. Rainn swoops me up in a victory hug, and when he releases me, my vision goes a little spotty.

I wobble toward the sidelines, but my foot catches on a piece of driftwood and I pitch over. I'm about to hit the sand face-first when a strong, familiar grip catches me around my waist. Ethan pulls me upright.

But he was on the other side of the net, how did he know? He calls out, asking if anyone has juice or soda with them.

"You're pale as a fucking ghost," he says.

"I'm fine."

He ignores me.

A moment later, we're seated on a huge rock facing the ocean, and Rainn runs over and hands me a sweaty plastic bottle. "Sorry it's not colder."

It's lukewarm orange juice, and it's gross. But I chug half of it and feel better almost immediately.

"Thank you," I say to Rainn.

His gaze sweeps across Ethan's arm, which is still firmly around me.

"Natalia? You okay?" Mr. Beckett calls.

I nod and do my best to smile. "I'm fine!" I yell back. "Just a little winded!"

Mr. Beckett shoots me a thumbs-up and turns his attention back to the group, who are now talking shit, with Janelle demanding a rematch.

"Rainn! You touched the net on that last one, it shouldn't have counted!" She's red-faced and gesturing for him to come back so she can yell at him more.

He rolls his eyes. "Need anything else?" he asks me, his tone concerned.

"I got this, Rainn," Ethan says.

They have a silent exchange, and Rainn nods slowly, betraying no sign of discomfort. He flashes me a grin. "You don't have to wait until you swoon next time. Just tell me when I'm being too sexy."

I laugh, and Ethan glares, and Rainn jogs back to the group, smiling to himself. Now it's just me and Ethan, our sides pressed firmly together. I want to stay here, tucked beside him, where I feel safest. I want to get even closer, skim my nose across his collarbone and drink in the ocean salt on his skin.

Instead, I pull away from him, and his arm falls. The comfort bleeds away in an instant.

"Didn't eat again?" Ethan asks.

I stiffen. *Again?*

"It was just a dizzy spell."

He gives me a loaded look. "You always do this when you're stressed. It's not healthy."

That gets my hackles up even more. "I don't *always* do anything. I'm fine."

"If you didn't almost just pass out, I'd be a little more convinced."

I stand up quickly—too quickly—and rock on my feet a little. "I didn't almost— You're being an ass."

"Because I'm trying to help?"

This makes me angrier. "Yes! You keep being around, *helping.*"

I don't know what has gotten into me, why I'm so angry that he's being wonderful. This isn't the first time he's gotten concerned that I didn't eat all day, which is, admittedly, something I forget to do from time to time. When I get so focused on everyone else, I ignore my own needs. He's being a friend.

But after this summer, I know all too well the agony of his absence. Just because he's around today, doesn't mean he'll be around tomorrow.

Especially if my letter is out there.

The panic surges through me anew. I take another long sip of juice.

"Talia, seriously, *what* is going on with you?"

I dig my fingernails into my palms. "What do you mean?"

"You're being meaner than usual, you're not eating, you stole the letters—"

"I didn't *steal* them."

He keeps going as if I didn't speak. "You can't even look at me."

My gaze, which was fixed on the ocean, snaps to him. And there's the tug, the impossible yearning that hits me like a tidal wave whenever our eyes lock.

"I know things are . . . weird between us," he says, softer, "but it seems like something more than that."

Weird between us.

It's the first time either of us has blatantly acknowledged it out loud—the weirdness. The kiss. The rejection.

I have to sit down again. The jagged edge of the rock digs into the backs of my thighs through my leggings. I finish the rest of the juice instead of answering him. Because I don't know what to say.

When it's clear I'm not going to answer, he sighs. "How are you feeling? Do you want to go home?"

"Trying to get rid of me? This summer wasn't enough of a break?" I meant for it to come out as a joke, but it's too harsh to be funny.

Ethan stares at me, his face slowly clouding over. "You always assume the worst of me."

"No, I don't."

Do I?

He looks . . . hurt. *Hurt?* Shit.

"Sorry, I—I don't mean to," I amend. "It's just . . . I can't go home right now."

He catches the fragility in my response and frowns. "Why not?"

"I mean, I could if I wanted to. I just don't want to." I stare at my hands. "My mom is moving out. Today."

He lets out a low gasp. "For real?"

I nod and swallow down the ache in my throat. "She's been doing it in shifts, but she's taking the last of it today. Then she'll really be gone, and it'll really be over between them."

"Fuck. I'm sorry."

I cross my arms around myself, curling my hands into fists. "You know how they fight. It's for the best."

I say it simply, but there's nothing simple about the fabric of your family tearing apart. Each fight, each conflict, each confusing conversation another unraveling stitch.

He doesn't say anything but puts a warm hand on my arm and squeezes. We sit in silence, but I want to tell him the rest. That it's so much more complicated because she's not staying in town but moving to Sacramento, where my aunts live. Three hours away. I want to know what he thinks I should do. I'm longing for his best friend reassurance that everything will be okay no matter what happens.

But I don't know how to lean on him as a friend and let him go at the same time. Because opening up to Ethan again would feel too much like giving him permission to break me.

Ethan leans back slowly. "Hold on. You organized this entire camping trip so you wouldn't have to be home today, didn't you?"

Of course he knows. The admiration in his voice makes me smile.

"It sounds crazy when you say it like that."

He laughs. The rolling, thunderous Ethan laugh that fills a room and my entire chest with light.

"God, I've missed you," he says, almost like he doesn't realize that him saying those words with his hand on my arm will tighten all the knots we just loosened. Will make me hope that I matter to him the same way he matters to me.

"I'm right here," I say, echoing what he said to me in the tent.

But it doesn't land in the sweet way it did when he said it. His expression is filled with doubt. He doesn't believe me. The realization stings, but I can't even blame him. He knows me well enough to sense that I'm not telling him the full story.

Just then, a burst of laughter grabs our attention back on the group. Rainn is currently showing off with a handstand, his hands deep in the sand, his shirt riding up and revealing his toned tan stomach. I guess they've resolved the point spat. Mason hits him square in the stomach, and Rainn falls immediately, laughing harder. I would have kicked Mason in the balls if he did that to me. But that's Rainn. Easy.

Ethan's gaze lingers on mine, his brow low, his mouth a thin line. "How long have—" He stops because his voice breaks. He clears his throat and tries again. "I mean, when did you and Rainn, um, get together?" he finally manages.

But I'm frowning. Deeply. "We're . . . not."

He blinks. "You're not?"

"No."

"But—he told me—I mean, you've been all over each other today."

I tighten my ponytail so hard it pulls on my temples. "What do you mean all over each other?"

He rolls his eyes. "You're touching, like, all the time." His voice is hard-edged. Angry. *Jealous.*

My own anger flares to join his. Wind carrying fire. "So what?"

"You obviously like him," he states.

Right now, I don't want to tell him I don't because it's beside the point. All I care about is the catch in his voice, the anxiety all over his face. It's so unfair. "Why does it bother you?" I challenge.

He leans back, jutting his chin toward the sky. "It doesn't."

I shake my head slowly. He's lying. It sends a shocked thrill through me. "So it's okay for you to be with Claire, but I'm not allowed to like or touch anyone ever again?" I ask.

"I didn't say that."

"Then what, Ethan?"

We're glaring at each other, inching ever closer to the perilous territory of prom night and the kissing and the chaos of after. I don't know why we are both so *mad.* Maybe because it's so much easier to be mad at him than to face the blunt hurt of his rejection.

He quickly runs his palms across the top of his shorts. "Does it bother *you*?" he asks, turning my own line of questioning back on me. "Me and Claire?"

Instead of meeting his gaze, I look over at her on the sand with the group. She's dancing around, singing loudly. Her voice is annoyingly good. She keeps turning to look at us but trying to act like she isn't. She's graceful and fun in a way my barking, bitter ass could never be.

Bother me? I want to set her cool blue hair on fire.

Before I can respond, Prashant calls my name, waving his arms frantically, his face full of stress.

"I have to go." I sigh.

"Wait." Ethan grabs my arm as I walk by. His hand is warm, his strong fingers closing gently around my wrist. "Can we—" But he stops, his eyes growing wide at something over my shoulder. He releases me and runs.

When he returns, his face is triumphant. He's holding a yellow piece of paper that was skittering across the sand. My heart stops.

One of the letters.

"No way!" I exclaim, breathless. I can't help myself, and I slam my arms around him. If he's surprised, he covers it well. He loops his arms around my shoulders, pressing me against his chest. The anger between us fades into the background. Still, I release him quickly.

"One down," he says, grinning. "I'll return it as soon as we get back to the campsite."

"How?"

We didn't get to this part of the plan.

"I have my ways," he says. He runs a hand through his hair and flashes me that flirty smirk that kills anyone within a one-mile radius. I don't know why he does it, or how to keep my traitorous stomach from fluttering.

But I do know, as if someone flipped a switch, that the ground beneath us is dangerous again.

CHAPTER THIRTEEN

Ethan

Senior Sunrise, 11:45 AM

I DON'T KNOW WHAT the hell I'm doing. Okay, I do know. I'm flirting with Natalia. It's automatic, my default state when I'm with her. Being close to her after all those weeks apart, getting to touch her even a little bit? It's like windows opening all around me; breathing is easier.

I can still salvage this in a real way, just like I put in my Lion Letter. If that's what she wants.

It might not be. Even though she said she and Rainn aren't together, *something* is going on there. I'm still not sure how she feels about him.

Or me.

I think back to prom night. Our kiss. It was fucking intense. It promised so much more between us. But I can't shake the fact that she only kissed me because of the pact. Did she stop speaking to me because she regrets it? Because I panicked? Or because she's into someone else?

We need to have a conversation that doesn't end with me being more confused than I was at the start. I have this pressing feeling that if we don't open up to each other before this camping trip ends, we'll have missed our chance.

At least now that I know what's going on with her at home, her extra-spiky edge makes more sense. No wonder she's been so upset. Her mom is leaving? Natalia's dreaded that exact thing for years. We've talked about it, joking in our dark way that if our parents split up at the same time, they could swap. It's not funny to think about now that it's actually happening. Now that my dad is an actual cheater and my mom has no idea.

I probably should've told Natalia just now, but I didn't want to make it about me.

I shove those depressing thoughts away and quickly change out of my sweaty volleyball clothes back into my jeans. There are too many people hovering around to be able to put the letter we found back in the jar yet. I'd rather have it on me, so I transfer it from my shorts to my jeans pocket. That's when I see a peek of blue ink. Not mine, since I used a black pen, but my pulse picks up.

Natalia was using a blue pen.

I squeeze my eyes shut. *But so were a lot of other people, Ethan.*

No matter my curiosity, I could never read it . . . could I?

I shove the note in my pocket and do my best to forget that it's there. Which is pretty fucking close to impossible.

I settle into a camping chair among the group on the beach, and my leg bobs with anxiety. I scan the sand for the twentieth time, looking for any more rogue yellow papers.

No others. Dread feels permanently lodged in my stomach.

Out of nowhere, Claire appears and promptly plops down on my lap. Oh . . . kay, this is jarring.

I feel like a serious asshole with everything I'm thinking about.

Claire deserves better than my confused ass. But if I push her off me, especially in front of the group, that would be rude, right? So, I just . . . sit there. It's not like it's the worst thing to have a cute girl in my lap.

Her coconut sunscreen stings my nostrils, and I'm super unsure where my hands should or should not go. I opt for leaving them on the arms of the camping chair as she leans into me and says, "Listen—you're missing the best part!"

"What?" I focus on the group conversation I'd been ignoring.

"There's ten seconds on the clock, we're down by two, there is nowhere to go on the court—we are in do-or-die mode!" Mason exclaims.

Oh god.

"I'm watching like, c'mon, you asswipes, pull out a miracle. This is the *Showdown*!" Mason yells like he's back on the sidelines. He's describing the basketball game from last season when we played our sworn rivals, Havenport Prep, at the annual "Showdown" game.

I know what to do with my hands now. Bury my face in them.

"And then this guy"—he slams his meaty fists on my shoulders and shakes me like I weigh four pounds—"*this* guy does a pump fake—"

"Creates hella separation from—what's his name?" Rainn asks. "The defender they always put on you?"

When I don't say anything because I'm too busy trying to melt into the sand, Rainn swats my calf.

"Delgado," I mutter.

"Right! Huge guy. Easily six four," Rainn exclaims.

I snort. He's barely six feet, only an inch taller than me.

"Oh, Delgado! I know who you're talking about. He's *so* hot," Claire says. She leans against my chest and, into my ear, says, "Not as hot as you, though."

Okay, that is just an outright lie, but my cheeks warm anyway.

"And then—" Mason exclaims, taking over again. All eyes are on him. He mimics a three-point shot, arms poised in the air as he watches the invisible basketball arc toward the net. Everyone seems to hold their breath, even though we all know what happened. After another silent moment, Mason pumps both fists in the air. "Sinks it! Buzzer goes off! Lions win by *one*! Showdown fuckin' champs! WOO!"

The small group listening cheers. Actually cheers. My face feels beet red.

I mean, it was an awesome game. An unbelievable moment. But the second the ball left my hand, all I can remember thinking is what a bad idea it was. I had never *once* sunk a shot like that. I could have easily driven to the basket for a layup to tie the game into overtime. I don't know what I was thinking.

"I shouldn't have taken the shot," I mutter. It was reckless. So reckless, I was expecting a full dressing down from Coach, who was always calling me out for making wild, panicked shots. But he only sort of gave me one.

I look around and, besides Natalia, who flicks an unreadable look my way, no one is listening to me anyway. I can't help thinking about it, though. If I had missed, I'd still be in my obscure corner of the social landscape of Liberty where I belong. That's how precarious popularity is.

But I didn't miss the shot. So instead of remaining in my place as the dorky gamer, or the baseball star's less athletic younger brother, or the disappointingly boring son of a celebrity, a few weeks after that game I was voted prom king out of *nowhere*. And now I guess I've crossed some invisible gulf where Claire is sitting on my lap and Mason is treating me like some sort of god. It's . . . weird.

I tell Claire I need to go get some water, but really, I just need a minute to breathe.

Sienna appears at my side while I'm grabbing a bottle out of the cooler. "The probability of making that shot was thirty-three percent. Two-pointer to tie was definitely the safer bet. You shouldn't have taken that shot."

I let out a shaky laugh. "You get it."

"Wouldn't the odds change again in overtime if they had made the two-pointer, though?" Prashant asks, eerily appearing out of the shadows.

Sienna frowns, squinting one eye and bobbing her head back and forth. Her math face. "Duh, of course. Fifty-fifty at that point. So going for the three *was* actually the advisable move."

My face falls. "Now you're just hurting my brain."

The two of them start talking about their mathletes team, the Variables, and their upcoming season against Havenport. Even though it's slightly mind-numbing, it's a relief being back on the outskirts with the other weirdos.

Natalia is setting up the pizza boxes for lunch, and our eyes catch across the table. As she studies my face in that disarming way of hers, her expression turns thoughtful. "You're doing that thing, aren't you?"

"What thing?"

"Mentally scanning for bruises to push so you don't actually feel good about yourself."

It's so shockingly accurate, I clutch my chest like she just shot an arrow into it. "Dang. Way to call me out."

She shakes her head slowly. "Only you would take a good thing and turn it into an existential crisis."

God, she gets me. "What can I say? It's a gift."

"Well, if it makes you feel any better, you will literally never do anything that cool ever again. A winning three-point shot at the buzzer? You've totally peaked. It's all downhill from here. There, go be miserable now."

I can't contain my smile any longer. "*Thank you.* That's all I was looking for."

She laughs, and my chest expands with pride and a feeling way too big to examine closely. As if pulled by magnetic force, my eyes fall to her lips. Lips that I know are soft and hungry.

God.

Then her face goes dead serious. "For the record, Luca Delgado is *way* hotter than you."

My own laugh escapes me from a place that almost never unlocks. "That's maybe the only thing I know for sure."

She laughs again, too, and it's the first time in a long time we feel like us.

The first time in a long time I feel like me.

Suddenly, Janelle's sharp voice cuts into the moment. "Hey, what did everyone write in their letters?"

Our laughter dies. I turn slowly to look at their group, and many of them exchange uncomfortable looks.

Mason scratches the back of his neck. "Uh, aren't we not supposed to talk about it?"

Janelle rolls her eyes. "Why? It's not like anyone would write anything good. And if you did, you should tell me now and actually make this day interesting."

No one meets Janelle's eyes, though. My heart is thundering in my chest.

"C'mon, you guys, I'm *bored*."

Prashant chuckles to himself when nobody else responds, and Janelle narrows her focus on him.

"Hey, Prashant!"

He pauses setting up the other lunch table and turns on his heel. His raised eyebrows are his only response.

"What did yours say? Anything freaky go down at chess camp?" she mocks.

"I don't play chess." Prashant folds his arms slowly, lifting his chin until he's looking down his nose at her. "Why don't you tell us what *yours* said."

Damn, nobody challenges Janelle. Everyone's attention turns to her expectantly, waiting to see how she's going to handle it. But after a beat, she just rolls her eyes before slumping back in her chair. "Ugh, you're no fun."

Prashant shrugs as if completely unbothered. But I notice he lets out a long exhale when he thinks no one is looking. Yeah, I'm definitely not the only one who wrote personal stuff in my letter.

All humor has drained from Natalia's face. She's wide-eyed, her breaths too shallow.

"It's fine," I say, my voice low. "Only six to go, remember?"

I think of the piece of paper heating up my pocket and shove my hand in there instinctually. It's so tempting to open it, to read it. I curl my fist around it, forcing myself to think about anything else.

Natalia stares at me and nods, but she's still too pale.

"You should eat," I say.

She's a grump about it, but as everyone descends on the food, she stacks her plate with pizza, too. Sienna pulls her into a conversation while they eat. As I'm making my own plate, my head whirring with how we can find a way to look for the other letters, Prashant sidles up beside me, muttering under his breath about Janelle.

"She's the worst," I agree.

"She has no idea what kind of pressure we're under." He grabs an apple out of a bowl and takes a huge stress bite. Cheeks bulging, he says, "Senior Sunrise sets the tone for the entire year. If everyone decides student council events are a waste of time, everything we plan this year is doomed. Homecoming, senior parking spots, spirit week, the poster contest, prom. Those are all our big moneymakers—a lot of it goes to the Lion Scholarships. Imagine someone like Natalia not being able to come to Liberty because we don't have enough money for all the scholarships next year."

My eyebrows spring up at that. I never think about the fact that Natalia is a scholarship student. Money is another one of those murky subjects between us. In a stunning display of ignorance and unchecked privilege, I told her once I don't get why money has to be such a big deal. She stared at me and with a shaking voice told me that's because I have it. She was so fucking right; I still burn with embarrassment whenever I think about that conversation.

But she especially doesn't like to talk about her scholarship, not once she found out my parents are some of the top contributors to the scholarship fund. The one thing their money is actually good for.

I try to imagine Liberty without Natalia, and it's impossible. The scholarships are vital. I look at Prashant in a new light. "I thought you and Natalia didn't get along."

"We don't." He looks like he's swallowing glass when he says, "But she has vision. And she's an excellent president."

I kind of want to hug Prashant. He's right. Even though I know a part of her would be happy forever painting in a dark room, listening to sad music all day, she dedicates herself to our school. Fundraisers, events, helping people preregister to vote, and organizing beach cleanups. She made a huge mistake with the letters, yes, but she's a good leader. A *great* leader. I feel even more determined to protect her now. She has too much to lose.

Prashant sighs. "Half the seniors polled are considering leaving after lunch."

"How did you poll—"

Prashant cuts me off. "You need to do something."

"Me?"

"You've got sway."

I snort. "No, I don't."

He gives me a long look. "So you're not a star basketball player? Prom king? Hanging with the hottest girl in the school? Hello?"

I turn to look at Natalia. She's wolfing down a massive slice of pizza, listening to one of Sienna's meandering stories.

Prashant freezes mid-bite. "I meant Claire," he says flatly.

I blink. "I know."

"What are you girls whispering about?" Tanner asks, appearing out of nowhere.

Prashant doesn't respond and instead backs away slowly, while gesturing between me and Tanner, like this is my opportunity. As if I have any interest in talking to Tanner Brown.

Tanner reaches down and pulls a water bottle out of the cooler next to my feet. He loses his balance, and I catch his shoulders before he falls. My lips curl back at his exhale. He still smells like booze. I know from all the times Adam stumbled home, it's not just a hangover anymore, either.

He takes a long swig of water, his eyes finally focusing on the ground behind the cooler. "Bro, why does that paper have my name on it?" I whip my head to see where he's pointing.

Shit.

CHAPTER FOURTEEN

Natalia

Senior Sunrise, 12:17 PM

I FORCE DOWN ANOTHER bite even though my stomach is taut with tension. While Sienna talks about how she, as an Aquarius, isn't sure she should go to college because the confining rules are in conflict with the rhythm of her innate being or something, I keep scanning the sand, thinking every little piece of trash could be a letter. I'm at once relieved and more nervous that we haven't found another one. That might mean they're all gone.

Or it could mean that they're lurking somewhere, in exactly the right place for the wrong person to find them.

Doesn't help that Prashant is leaning way too close to Ethan at the moment, and I can't stop wondering what the hell they could possibly have to talk about. If Prashant knew just how badly I messed up, I wouldn't have to face my choice about leaving or not. I'd get kicked right out of Liberty. Maybe not officially, but definitely by popular vote.

Would Ethan tell him what happened?

No. No matter how rocky things get with Ethan, I trust him more than anyone.

And when he does something, like, say, ponder the implications of popularity, it reminds me all over again why I freaking adore him, and it makes it impossible to think about anything or anyone else.

He looks at me across the campsite, as if reading my mind.

Those eyes.

Ethan's eyes are the hardest to paint. They're the most complex hazel, deep brown in the center, rimmed with a halo of green and lined by inky eyelashes. But it's not just the color. It's the way they hold the memories of our friendship. It's too easy to want to tell him everything when I look into them.

Then there's his warm smile, his arm around me earlier. His concern about the ways I sometimes forget to take care of myself. The way we immediately fall into laughter and understanding. The canvas in my mind swirls in azure blue, with swipes and slashes of fuchsia. My happy colors.

Terrifying.

Sienna successfully cuts into my thoughts then. "Like, as an Aries, school makes sense for *you*. Trying so hard is in the literal stars for you."

"More like, if I didn't try, I wouldn't remotely survive this school," I say.

She frowns, and her glasses slide down her nose a little. "What do you mean?"

My eyebrows meet. "Just . . . that I've had to earn my place here, you know? Everyone else belongs." I gesture to the cliques and groups gathered together, laughing and relaxed. "I mean, have you heard people talk about what they did this summer? I worked at the YMCA day camp, and Janelle Johnson went to freaking Bali."

Sienna puts her pizza on the grease-stained plate in her lap. "You belong."

I shake my head. "I don't. I never have. But it's not just the money. I've been thinking a lot about it lately and . . . what's the point of going to a *prep* school if you don't want what you're preparing for?"

Sienna nods slowly. "So you don't want to go to college?"

I swallow. "No—that's not what I'm saying. Never mind."

I don't know why my heart is racing, but I do know I don't want to talk about this anymore.

I've always struggled to translate what I'm thinking into words. That's what art is for. The glide of the brushstrokes, the shine of the wet colors bleeding from my tangled mind through my steady hand says more than I ever could.

But the only time I can push paint around is in the dark of night. When my dad can't remind me that art doesn't pay the bills. When I'm alone and everything's quiet.

That's also when my panic attacks happen. But I don't tell my parents about those.

I tried once, and Dad called it the "pressure cooker effect" of Liberty and told me that I'd get used to it. It was his idea that I go to Liberty in the first place, just like he did. To get the education he did, be president like he was, run track like he did. Sometimes I wonder if he forgets I'm a whole person instead of his chance at a do-over.

If I move with Mom, things could be different. She might give me the space I need to pursue art in a real way. Then again, it's always been important to her that I *achieve*.

She's proud that I'm a Latina presence in a predominantly white school, even though I'm not sure what difference it makes sometimes. Because I look only white, my classmates often treat me like I am. It feels like this abject denial of my roots. Half of them, anyway. They'll say offhanded remarks, not necessarily racist, but sometimes they are that, too. It proves just how invisible that side of me is to them. To the world, really.

Maybe it's not Liberty. Maybe I don't fit anywhere.

"Well, you could always take a gap year? I've been looking at this farmstead in Idaho where you learn to grow your own food—here, let me."

Sienna's cool, practiced fingers comb through the tangles of my messy ponytail while she talks. Soon I can feel the beginnings of two complicated braids forming.

"Won't you get bored farmsteading without math?" I ask, grateful for the change in topic.

Sienna stops braiding long enough to bend over my shoulder and give me a pitying look. "Please, I'm always doing math." She resumes braiding. "I've been reading up on life insurance mathematics, which is this fascinating combination of calculus, probability, and statistics—"

I cut her off. "This is what you do in your free time, but you don't think you should go to college?"

She huffs out an annoyed sigh. "Point taken. Anyway, so using those equations, you can figure out the odds of anything happening in real life. Math can actually predict the risks and probable outcomes of human behavior. It's so wild!"

She threads a hair tie around the end of one braid, then she starts on the next one.

"Like what?" I ask, fascinated by the way her mind works.

"Liiiiiiike the odds of me and Leti hooking up by the end of the night."

I burst out laughing. "Okay, what are they?"

She's silent a second, and I can imagine her math face: one eye closing, her head slightly bopping back and forth while she works it out in her mind.

"Twenty-six percent chance based on known factors. Too many unknowns to be fully accurate."

"That sounds way too low," I say. Math didn't see the way Leti looked at her this morning.

"Like I said, unknown factors," Sienna says, but I can hear the smile in her voice. "I promised myself in my letter that I'd finally talk to them today, so who knows what could happen."

Guilt sinks my stomach. If Sienna's letter is out there, the crush that she's been safely guarding for a year could be exposed. I'm not just a bad president, I'm a bad friend.

She finishes with my braids, and I turn to look at her. I should tell her what happened with the letters. She might understand—she might even help. But then her hopeful gaze drifts to Leti over my shoulder, and I lose all courage. I can't face the thought of her hating me for letting her secret out. I've already lost one friend this summer.

I grasp for anything else to say. "Is this insurance math a job? Like something you could do?"

She rolls her eyes. "Yeah, they're called actuaries. I could not remotely commit to that career path, though. It's way more fun using this math for chaotic good." Then her grin goes sly. "Like how I figured out the odds of you and Ethan hooking up tonight. Want to hear it?"

"Sienna!" I hiss. "It's *zero*."

She side-eyes me. "It's not zero."

I haven't told Sienna anything about prom, but she knows something's off. She has this way of watching people, and I'm not surprised she noticed whatever it is going on with me and Ethan.

"It's high," she says in a singsong voice.

I chew on my lip. "How high?"

"I'd bet money. *Good* money."

My stomach drops. I don't know if it's a good drop or a bad drop. We *need* to stop talking about this.

And we do because Tanner yells out loud enough for our campsite to hear, "What the hell, Forrester?"

MISSING LION LETTER #2

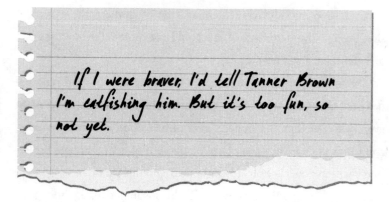

If I were braver, I'd tell Tanner Brown I'm catfishing him. But it's too fun, so not yet.

CHAPTER FIFTEEN

Ethan

Senior Sunrise, 12:33 PM

"WAIT—" I TRY TO snatch the yellow paper up first, but Tanner's closer and grabs it before I can, lurching a bit as he pulls himself upright. If he reads it, the rest of the day will descend into chaos. Tanner will talk about the letter; his whole group will find out and ask questions. Bored Janelle will spend every second hunting for more.

I can't let that happen.

I glimpse over his shoulder at the paper that *impossibly* says his name.

I don't think about the fact that he has forty pounds on me or that he throws people around on the football field like they're twigs. I don't think at all. Before he can read it or register what's happening, I snatch the letter out of his hand and run for it. It's his word against mine.

"What the hell, Forrester?" Tanner yells.

Everyone stares at him, then me.

Janelle's eyebrows spring up as her eyes drift to me. "Oh, this just got interesting."

I need a diversion and fast. I look around. Before I know what's happening, my legs carry me over to where Rainn and Mason are talking. I yank Rainn up by the shirt, making a few people gasp.

"Whoa, dude, what're you doing?" Mason exclaims.

I don't know. I don't know what I'm doing other than relying on one of my best friends for help the way I always have before things got so fucking complicated. I drag Rainn closer to the water. He's staring at me wild-eyed and confused.

"What the hell, Ethan—"

I let him go, and in a low voice I say, "We need a diversion. Hit me."

He sees my hand curled at my side, takes in Tanner charging toward me. Rainn's eyes immediately flicker with excitement. "For real?"

I nod and raise my arms to shield my face.

Without hesitation, Rainn punches me in the side, harder than I expect.

I clench my jaw against the impact. I lower my hands and glare at him.

He jabs at me again, this time connecting with my chest. It forces a cough out of me.

He raises his eyebrows at me, grinning. "You told me to hit you."

"Not that fucking hard." I rub at my chest.

"Aw, c'mon, Prom King, show me what you got," he taunts. His eyes flash with something then, a real anger that he's hiding under his smirk. He's not *actually* trying to fight me . . . is he?

We both notice Tanner catching up, and Rainn lunges again. I barely manage to swat his fist from hitting my face.

That fucker.

I hit him back on instinct. Rainn rolls his arm at the last second to protect his face, and my knuckles crunch into his shoulder.

Tanner skids to a stop as my blow lands. Before he can decide what to do, Mason yells out, "Fiiiiiiiiight!" I knew I could count on him. Tanner hangs back as people look up and run across the sand toward us.

Diversion achieved.

Everyone starts yelling, including Mason, who, for some reason, keeps screaming at us to spill the tea. He clearly has no idea what that means.

I dodge all of Rainn's hits at first. With a brother like Adam, I've learned to be quick.

Adam's a strong guy, a baseball player until he blew out his knee last spring. He's made of tough stuff. Granite. Steel.

Me? Rubber. Jelly maybe. But he never let me win; he never gave an inch. He took it as his job to teach me once I started coming home with bloody lips and black eyes in middle school. There was no such thing as the ironic emo vote in sixth grade. You were either skinny and sensitive or big and mean. Guess which one beat up the other?

But thanks to Adam, I have pretty good stamina in a fight. Rainn doesn't know I spent my summer with Adam running around Green Lake and lifting weights in his garage. I'm stronger than ever. Stronger than Rainn thinks. And his sharp jabs to my ribs are starting to piss me off.

I duck another one of his punches and shoot a quick blow toward his chin that he barely manages to knock aside.

"I'm getting Mr. Beckett!" Leti Mitchell yells.

Shit. I hadn't thought of that.

But I can't stop now. Rainn has length on me, and he smacks me on the head while bouncing on his feet like a boxer. He looks ridiculous. And he wants Natalia. She thinks he's so sweet and easygoing, but being on the other side of his fist, there's more to him than that.

I rush at him, but my fist only finds air. He laughs, and every humiliated nerve in my body springs to life.

"You can do better than that," Rainn says, raising an eyebrow.

I see my shot and go for his legs, but he takes me down with him. We crash spectacularly into the surf, the freezing shock of it cutting my breath short. My skin is covered in goose bumps and salt water. Rainn is scrambling under me and manages to kick me off him. I fall flat on my back on the wet sand, a rope of slimy seaweed tangled around my leg. It's hard to tell, but I think a couple of people are using their Polaroid cameras to take pictures of this.

My knuckles are raw, my eyebrow stinging and hot like it got cut open. But I can barely feel anything with the adrenaline coursing through me, the freezing water crashing against my feet and shins, making my jeans heavier.

Rainn wrenches me up, but I throw his hands off me and take a staggered step back.

"What're you doing?" Natalia yells.

I don't know if she's yelling at me, Rainn, or both of us. But as soon as I look at her, her eyes wide and pissed, I get even angrier.

Fighting over you, I think.

Rainn is coming for me again. Showing off for her. He's too fast. His fists keep making contact with my forearms, my ribs. I distantly note he's kind of beating the crap out of me, but I've been hit enough to know when to back down and when to keep going. I have to keep going.

"Fuck him up, Anderson!" Tanner yells at Rainn.

At least my plan is working. Tanner is distracted by his own bloodlust, and the letter he found is safely tucked away in my pocket.

This might've started fake, but neither of us is holding back now. Facing Rainn, I only see the guy who keeps wrapping his arms around Natalia. He tries to grab me in a pathetic excuse for a choke hold that I squirm out of easily, but not before punching him in the kidney. He grunts heavy at the impact.

Our audience cheers. Prashant has his arms crossed over his chest, and he's got this evil villain smirk on as he's surveying the excited group around us. He thinks I did this because of what we talked about.

"Ethan, look out!" Claire yells.

Rainn's elbow connects with my nose.

It wasn't a purposeful knock, more of a side effect of our flailing. The warm taste of copper fills my mouth where I bite my tongue. I spit it into the surf, my mind silent, my pulse wild.

I don't know how many more blows we both land before I hear Mr. Beckett yelling at us to break it up, Ms. Mercer not far behind.

The crowd steps back, lots of wide eyes and hands over mouths. A very slow, deliberate click of one last Polaroid.

Mr. Beckett has his hands on his hips, glaring at us. "What is going on here?" he cries.

He's pissed. He's never pissed. We're in deep shit.

"Liberty has a zero-tolerance policy for physical violence!"

"We were just joking around," Rainn says, slinging an arm around my shoulders. His smile is so light I almost think I hallucinated the whole thing. "Right, Ethan?"

Natalia won't look at me, her cheeks flaming pink. I realize then we could actually get in real trouble. I shrug his arm off me.

"Yeah, we were just messing around. Got a little carried away," I say.

"A little? You're bleeding." Mr. Beckett gestures to my forehead. I touch my eyebrow and wince with the stinging of salt water in the fresh cut, but my fingers come away with only a small trickle of blood. Nothing major.

"I cut it on a rock," I say. Though I think it was actually Rainn's knuckle.

Mr. Beckett looks at Ms. Mercer and throws his hands up. "We have to send them home for this, don't we?"

My stomach plummets to my feet. I didn't even want to come to Senior Sunrise in the first place, but now I don't want to go home more than anything. I need more time to figure this out with Natalia. We need to find the other letters. This can't end here, now. Because of *Tanner*.

But really, because of me.

Ms. Mercer studies us. "Of all the students who I thought might cause trouble today, you two were the last on my list."

Rainn and I exchange a look.

"Sorry. We just do this sometimes—we thought it'd be funny," I say. I prod him with my elbow.

"Yeah. Same."

Mr. Beckett lets out a long sigh and squeezes the bridge of his nose. "Friends, physical violence is *never* a joke."

"We know. It won't ever happen again," I say, my voice pleading.

Ms. Mercer and Mr. Beckett have a silent conversation. She takes a large step toward us, looking at us closely. After she stares into my damn soul she inhales deeply.

"Okay. This feels settled. I don't think we'll have any more problems."

My shoulders release.

"Anything else out of line, not only will you be going home, you'll be looking at suspension. Got it?" Mr. Beckett says.

We both nod furiously.

"As it is, the two of you are on cleanup duty. Rest of you! Now that it's warming up, free time on the beach. There are extra skimboards and towels lined up over there. Have fun. Don't go past the buoys," Mr. Beckett announces.

He rubs more sunscreen on his pale nose and adjusts his large straw sun hat low over his face. Clearly he's relieved he won't have to interrupt his beach time with the paperwork a real fight would cause.

Prashant stage-whispers "Nailed it" to us as he walks by, and even though he looks confused, Rainn shoots him a grin.

Now that the show is over, the rest of the class scrambles to grab boards or settle into sunbathing. Rainn and I have to watch them strip down to their suits and dive into the water while we follow Mr. Beckett to the tables in our wet clothes. I pull off my dripping shirt, and it lands with a slap against the sand.

As soon as Tanner walks away, distracted by the lure of free time on the beach, I shove my hands into my pockets. They close around the letters, one in each pocket: the first letter with the blue ink and the one Tanner found. One is soaked and pulpy. Destroyed. The other managed to stay dry, since I hit the water on my opposite side. I sneak a peek at the dry one and immediately see a hint of blue through the folds.

I should want them both ruined to better rid ourselves of evidence, but I'm oddly relieved it's intact.

It's not like I'm going to read it . . . but I can't deny that I want to. Only to see if it's Natalia's. It's a thought I haven't let in too deep because it'll eat away at me. I'm dying to know what hers said, what she was so desperate to get back.

It must've been delicate. Sensitive. She's always been so private, I could see her panicking about that.

Mr. Beckett hands us both trash bags and paper towels to clean up lunch. "You should start with that eyebrow," he says. "Where is that first aid kit?" When he wanders off, tapping his chin, I get the feeling he'd be pretty worthless in an actual emergency.

It's just me and Rainn then.

"Hey, um." I clear my throat. "Sorry for dragging you into that. Tanner was being a dick and I needed to . . . distract him."

We both look at Tanner, who is lying in the sun like a starfish, snoring. Well. At least it worked.

Rainn says nothing. I press a paper towel to my eyebrow, and we start to clean up the pizza boxes and soda cans in strained silence. I want to ask him why he's so pissed at me. But he beats me to it.

"I saw the way you held her after the volleyball game."

So it is about Natalia. Somehow it always is.

"She almost passed out."

He stops cleaning and glares at me. "I like her, Ethan."

"You don't even know her." I meant to only think it, but I definitely said it. Shit.

He takes a half step back, getting ready to posture up again. "Of course not. No one knows her like you do. You don't want her, but no one else can have her, right?"

Who says I don't want her? At least I don't say *that* out loud. "What are you even—"

"You told me to go for it," he says.

I close my eyes, guilt coursing through me. "I know."

"Do you like her?"

Do I like her? It wouldn't be lying to say no, I . . . *everything* her. But I can't say that to him. For one thing, I don't want to get my ass beat again. But also, I don't want to tell him what I should say to Natalia first. So I say nothing.

After a full minute of silence, Rainn scoffs. "That's a yes."

The silence extends until I lean over to pick up a piece of trash and a grunt escapes.

"I won't go so easy on you next time," Rainn says, his eyes darting to where I'm skimming my rib cage with my free hand. He's sort of smiling.

"You're a dick," I say, grimacing. "Since when can you punch like that?"

"I've been working the bag in our garage all summer," he says, jabbing the air a few times. "Thanks for noticing."

As if I could do anything but notice. I won't be surprised if the side of my rib cage is covered in bruises later. And even though I didn't mean it as a compliment exactly, at least he's not looking like he wants to punch *me* anymore.

"But you got some good ones in, Prom King," Rainn says. He's back to that chill Rainn smile, and I throw a can at his head that he dodges easily. "But seriously, dude, what now?"

Natalia walks up then with a first aid kit, cutting off my chance to respond.

Rainn clocks the way she walks straight to me. How she goes a little pink as she scans my bare torso, then wordlessly pushes my hair off my forehead to look at the cut there.

I clench my jaw against the sudden closeness of her—the heat of her sun-soaked skin, the jasmine scent of her hair. Her tiny freckles are darker from being outside all morning, dusting her nose and cheekbones. So pretty. As if I don't want her. Who wouldn't want her? All she has to do is exist near me and I have a thermonuclear meltdown inside.

She turns to glare at Rainn. "*What* was that?"

"It's my fault," I say. "Um, Tanner was being a dick, and Prashant said we should do something to get everyone excited and . . . yeah." I can't tell her about the letter in front of Rainn. It's as good an excuse as any.

She closes her eyes in frustration and takes a long inhale. "I don't even know where to begin with that. You're all children," she mutters.

"I'm fine by the way," Rainn says.

Natalia shoots him a leveling look before returning her attention to my eyebrow.

"This doesn't look too bad," she says. She delicately grazes her fingertips across my forehead again, and it sends goose bumps along my scalp. *God*. Rainn's still watching us, though, so I flinch away on instinct.

Her expression closes over, and she drops her hand. Cheeks burning brighter. "Sorry, I won't touch you again."

Um, what?

Rainn seizes his opportunity. "It's just because you're like a sister to him. Right, Ethan? Isn't that what you said on prom night?"

That asshole. Guess he had to get one more jab in after all. God, that is not how it went at *all*. My heart is sprinting as I spin to face him. "*You* said that."

He shrugs. "The memory is hazy."

I turn back to Natalia, whose face has gone blank. Bad sign.

"Hey—"

"It's fine, Ethan. I get it."

She offers me the saddest smile in the history of smiles. Before I can throw Rainn into the fucking sun, Natalia shoves the first aid kit against my chest harder than strictly necessary, making me wince.

She walks off quickly, her flip-flops slapping against the sand. I don't move fast enough, and Rainn takes off after her before I can.

CHAPTER SIXTEEN

Natalia

Senior Sunrise, 1:00 PM

I WILL NOT CRY over Ethan. I will never cry over Ethan again. For the love of god, someone tell my tear ducts to calm the hell down.

I pull off my flip-flops, which are slowing me down, and throw them hard into the sand. They land dully, unimpressed with my tantrum.

The sand is hot under my feet, forcing me to the cool water. When will I get the message that he just doesn't like me like that? He *flinches* at my touch. I take a deep breath in. Except, our kiss wasn't like that. The most confusing thing about that night is that he was into it; that much was clear.

Well.

Maybe he was into *it,* just not with *me.* That's the whole problem. The girl who makes boys do bad things but isn't the girl anyone actually wants. Isn't the girl Ethan wants. *Which I already knew,* so I'm not sure why my traitorous eyeballs are filling with tears.

I trudge down the shoreline as fast as I can, canvas in my mind going deep gray. I mentally add thick globs of white and forest green, taking a brush to them, spiking through the other colors. I add more and more until the canvas is leaden with it. Weighed down by the pressure of it all, too heavy to lift.

"Hey, Natalia, wait up!" It's Rainn.

I stop walking and quickly scrub the tears from my eyes. The surf crashes against my bare feet while he runs up. "Can we talk?"

This agitated, very non-Rainn vibe is rolling off him. I nod, and we start along the shoreline. The sun is beating down. I can feel the light sting of a sunburn forming already. I adjust the neckline of my tank top higher, waiting for Rainn to say something.

"I'm sorry. About the fight. We were just screwing around and—it wasn't cool."

I shoot him a side-eye. I don't believe for a second that they were only messing around. I just don't know *why*. There is nothing more confusing than boy drama.

"You don't have to apologize," I say.

"Still," he says, shrugging. He clears his throat. "It's just . . . I forgot how you and Ethan get sometimes."

"What do you mean?"

He pushes his shaggy, sun-bleached hair off his forehead. "You know Ethan's my bro, but . . . he acts like no one could possibly get you the way he does, or something."

I frown, though my heart knocks once against my ribs. I steal a glance at Ethan under the lunch canopy. He's still cleaning up—*shirtless*—and manages to look moody and windswept while he does it. I think of the letter in his pocket that he's concealing for me. All the secrets between us. The history between us. Rainn may not like it, but it's true. Whatever it is that Ethan and I have, it's special.

Then Claire walks up to him in a bright red bathing suit, and my fingers curl into fists. I bet he doesn't think of her as a sister.

I force my attention back to Rainn when he says, "I know we're all friends, but . . . it was cool to have you to myself this summer."

My pulse picks up, sensing something in the hopeful lilt of his voice.

He squeezes one eye shut and lets out a nervous sound like *gragh* before he puffs up his chest and says, "Okay. I'm just gonna say it: I like you, Natalia. Like, a lot."

I blink rapidly. Oh.

The ocean rushes for our shins, but I'm too stunned to move.

I've only ever thought of him as a friend . . . but maybe that's because I've been so wrapped up in Ethan? He's definitely surfer cute, and he's always so easy to be with. We *did* have fun this summer.

If Ethan doesn't want me, if he thinks of me as a friend or a sister or whatever, is that supposed to ruin me for everyone else forever?

Looking into Rainn's bright, nervous eyes, I will my heart to open to the possibility of him. I try to envision spending more time with him, learning him in new ways, really relaxing into him. Maybe this is how I get past what happened with Ethan and we all move on.

Rainn's gaze drops to my lips, and before I have time to think, he kisses me.

I wish I was brave enough to finally talk to him. What does it mean when you can't stop thinking about someone you shouldn't want? Because I HAVE to let it go. He's straight. At least I think he is. But if I were braver, I guess I'd actually talk to him. Ask him if the way he looks at me means... anything.

It's probably all in my head. I hate that coming out isn't something that happens once. It's exhausting doing it over and over. To wait for it to be right. But it has to be right. It has to be safe. Every single time. I haven't kept it a secret exactly. My family knows and I just haven't wanted to make a big thing of it at school. But I'm sick of nobody getting me and I guess I wonder if senior year might suck less if someone... did.

If Rainn did.

CHAPTER SEVENTEEN

Ethan

Senior Sunrise, 1:00 PM

I KEEP STEALING GLANCES at Rainn and Natalia walking down the beach while I finish cleaning up the lunch stuff. First, he kicks my ass, then he leaves me to clean up this mess by myself. Dick.

What are they talking about? Why didn't I run after her before he did? She keeps storming off without giving me a chance to say *anything.*

"There you are!" Claire's voice infiltrates my internal storm.

She's running toward me up the beach, a skimboard under her arm. Her blue-black hair is falling in wet ropes across her shoulders. She's wearing a bright red bathing suit that's, uh, cool. I force myself to keep my eyes on her face. Pops of pink brighten her cheeks. "The water is way too perfect. You should come in."

"Um. Maybe later," I say. I really want to be alone. Free of . . . confusing red bathing suits.

Claire drops the skimboard on the sand. "You okay?"

I shrug to mask my surprise that she could tell I'm in a mood. After that fight, fake or not, I know things with Natalia have shifted again. But

Claire gently runs her fingers near my cut eyebrow, and I realize she meant my injuries.

"Oh, yeah. Fine."

"What was that all about, anyway? I thought you and Rainn were friends?" she asks.

"Just messing around," I say automatically.

But I don't know what that was. The fight was my fault, obviously, but then he made that fucking comment to get under my skin. To drive a wedge between me and Natalia.

Claire chews on her lip like she wants to say something. Doesn't take her long to work up the courage. "He thinks you're into Natalia, doesn't he?"

Is there any point in denying it? "Yeah," I sigh.

Her eyes narrow. Not in an angry way. Like in the way guys on the court do right before tip-off. "Are you?"

Something about the way she asks makes me think she already knows. Or suspects.

"We're friends." It's not a lie. But it is the shield I hide behind.

"Why is she so mad at you?" Claire asks.

Huh. She's . . . observant. I don't want to be a dick or anything, but god, it really feels like none of her business. So I must be on the brink of truly losing it when, for some reason, I find myself answering her. "Um. We had this pact that I, um, broke, I guess?"

Did I break it? Because I wouldn't go through with it? And *is* that the reason she's so mad at me? I'm not even sure anymore.

"A pact?"

I shrug and try to laugh it off. Even though I didn't say anything specific, a wave of anxiety swells through me that I said anything at all. The pact was always a secret. Just between us. Not even Rainn or Sienna knows about it.

"Sort of . . . it was . . . never mind."

I can't even be sure Claire's listening anymore because she's looking past me at something over my shoulder.

"Well, she's obviously into *him*," she observes.

I shouldn't look. But I'm a jackass with a masochistic streak. When I do, I see Rainn and Natalia down the beach wrapped in a kiss.

No.

It's wrong. It's all wrong.

The way her hands press against his chest, the way his cup her jaw. The jaw I've grazed with my own lips. Kissed the soft underside of and pulled a sound out of her I only think about when I'm alone. If their flirting all day was a slap, this is a bludgeoning. A painful tightness constricts my throat.

Even when I fight for Natalia, I lose.

But I get the message now. It's loud and fucking clear. I can't keep doing this to myself. So what that I want to be braver and talk to Natalia about everything that happened? Everything I'm feeling? She obviously doesn't want to talk to *me*. She doesn't want to figure this out. If she did, she'd stop running away. She'd stop believing the worst in me. She wouldn't *kiss Rainn*.

I turn to Claire. Cute and uncomplicated. I like the way she scrunches her nose when she smiles. Maybe I could be uncomplicated with her. I could stop torturing myself with questions about what I'm supposed to be doing and who I'm supposed to be. Who I'm supposed to be *with*. I could just fucking decide. Then maybe breathing wouldn't hurt so much.

I hold her gaze an extra beat. "You know what? I *do* want to go in the water."

Her entire face lights up. I run back to my tent and strip down to my board shorts, leaving my clothes in a heap. Forgetting all about the letter in the pocket of my jeans. Forgetting all about my promises to Natalia.

My heart is pulp in my chest as I let Claire grab my hand and lead me into the waves. But maybe this is what Prom King Guy would do. Maybe Prom King Guy wouldn't have a shitty, cheating dad, and wouldn't keep secrets from the entire class, and wouldn't ruin everything with his best friend over one kiss.

Since it's getting more intolerable by the hour being me, maybe I should really try being him.

CHAPTER EIGHTEEN

Natalia

Senior Sunrise, 1:07 PM

RAINN'S KISS IS A complete shock to my system. His sunbaked shirt warm against my chest, his thumb brushing against my jaw, his lips that I've never once thought about on mine. Instead of opening, my heart retreats, slamming all the doors and locking them. This is all wrong.

I press my palms against his chest and gently push him away.

"Oh—sorry. I thought—did I not read the room right?" he asks. His cheeks are flushed crimson.

"You surprised me," I hedge, laughing awkwardly.

"Gotcha. Okay." He laughs, too. "I'll give you fair warning next time."

Next time?

All I feel is panic. And dread that I have to be honest with him.

"Rainn . . . ," I start.

That golden smile begins to fade at my tone.

I hate even the thought of hurting him, putting him through what I've been through. I know what rejection feels like, and it *sucks*. But if

I've learned anything, it sucks worse when everything is murky. I just have to be clear.

Clasping my sweaty hands, my heart in my throat, I cut straight to it. "I'm sorry, but—I don't think of you like that."

He blinks. Once. Twice. It's a long and strained ten seconds. "Oh. Um. Okay . . ."

Sweat forms under my shirt, and one single drop breaks away to travel down the length of my spine. Another torturous pause while he surveys me intently. Then he lets out a knowing sigh. "Forrester?"

"No, it's not about Ethan," I say quickly.

Rainn gives me an incredulous look and, okay, I don't want to make this worse by not being completely honest. I exhale. "Fine, it's not *only* about Ethan."

He nods like, *There it is.* "I knew it."

I struggle to find the words to say it all out loud. I haven't told a soul. Whenever I even think of it, it's sandpaper on broken skin. But I force myself to be honest, open. "I might not even be here this year."

That catches him off guard. "What? What do you mean?"

"My mom got a new job and is moving to Sacramento. I might go with her."

He blinks slowly. "Wait . . . Sacramento? That's like, three hours away."

"Yeah."

"When?"

I kick at the frothy wave nudging my ankles. "She leaves tomorrow."

"But school starts next week," he says.

"Yeah. It's kind of down to the wire," I say, pulling on the end of one braid.

He's quiet a minute, his frown heavy. "Okay . . . you said you *might* go. So is there a chance you'll stay?" he asks, that hopeful tone returning.

I shrug slowly. "My parents are cool with me staying if that's what I decide, but . . ." I trail off because my throat closes.

Saying it out loud doesn't make it any easier. The choice remains impossible: choose my mom and leave my life or choose my dad and lose my art.

Rainn lights up. "Oh, so you could just live with your dad, then?"

As if it's so easy to let a mom go. As if it's so easy to make a call that will alter the course of my life.

As much as she pisses me off, as much as she's ruining everything by leaving, I don't blame Mom for moving. Not really. As a comptroller, she has the opportunity to be the financial director of an entire department. The first woman of color to do so at her office, she told me proudly. She deserves it.

But kind of understanding the situation doesn't make the choice any easier.

I have so much more I want to do at Liberty, so much more I want to accomplish. I'm finally in a place where I could make a difference for future scholarship students, have some influence. If I'm finally brave enough to let Ethan go, and nobody finds out about the letters, and I manage to actually survive this day, I could really make something of this year.

I even wonder if living with just Dad could be kind of good.

I don't know if it's because he doesn't understand art, doesn't understand girls, or doesn't understand me. Or maybe because half of me is of a race and culture he can never be, but we've always struggled to connect. It's possible living together just the two of us might . . . help us.

But getting a chance at a real do-over, at going to a school that doesn't demand perfection, where I could paint without hiding it and where everything with Ethan won't follow me? I'm not going to lie; it's getting more tempting by the minute.

"Yeah. Maybe. I don't know."

Rainn nods slowly. "Okay, well sorry, for, you know, kissing you," he says, flushing again.

I want to sink into the sand. Let it swallow me up, so I don't have to continue with this conversation. But I shake my head and rush on. "No—it's okay. You know I love you as a friend—"

"Oh, please don't do that," he says, grimacing.

I swallow the rest of my words down and wrap my arms around myself, feeling horrible.

We look at each other, and the frown slips off his face, revealing the embarrassment beneath.

I want to reach for him. The friend I care about inside the guy I'm hurting. "I'm sorry. Are you . . . okay?"

He won't meet my eyes. "Yup." He pushes his hands deep in the pockets of his tie-dyed sweatpants, still soaked from the fight, looking everywhere but at me. He's shutting down, and I hate it.

I usually fix problems. But today, all I've done is make them.

"How can I make it better?" I ask.

He laughs a little. "Um. Try to be less cute?"

I bristle. I know he thinks it's a compliment. I know he's trying to make a joke to ease the awkwardness. But it hits me all wrong. As if I forced him to like me. As if I seduced him on purpose.

A siren. The kind of girl who makes boys do bad things.

Peals of laughter carry across the beach. Everyone else in the class is enjoying the water. I spot Ethan no longer cleaning up but hip-deep in the ocean, Claire on his bare back. She shrieks every time a wave hits them.

"Ethan! Don't you dare!" she yells.

He pulls his hands up above his head, and she drops straight into the water. She pops up laughing and shoves him back into an oncoming wave. When he emerges from it, he shakes the water out of his hair.

"I'm so going to get you for that," he yells, grinning. Playful.

When she climbs onto him again and he wraps his hands back around her strong dancer thighs, I'm as close to homicidal as I'll ever get.

All I know is that it hurts. Everywhere.

But no, this is good. It's better this way. Even if I can't breathe. Even with this hollow feeling in my chest. It's totally better. This is how I let Ethan go.

I return to the present when a cold wave crashes against my shins, soaking my leggings from the knee down. I keep my eyes on the frothy tide slowly crawling up the shore.

"Does anyone else know about Sacramento?" Rainn asks. He's watching me intently.

There's a different question within his question: *Does* Ethan *know?*

"No, just you," I say.

Rainn flashes me a sad smile. I almost cry again when he holds his arm out, a clear and friendly offer for me to tuck beside him.

I don't deserve the comfort, but I take it anyway.

Because if I believed in signs, I might have just gotten the one I needed to finally make my decision.

CHAPTER NINETEEN

Ethan

Senior Sunrise, 2:00 PM

I DO MY BEST. I let Claire climb all over me, even though her skin against mine feels strange. I splash water on her and laugh when she pushes me over. We flirt and joke, and I try to relax. I try to have fun.

After we get out of the water, we still have some time before the obstacle course activity, so we go back to the campsite to change. When I climb out of my tent, Claire's waiting for me and . . . wearing my jacket. Which, okay. I don't mind or anything, and the winds are picking up again, so I guess it makes sense if she's cold. But there's this wrongness to it that I can't quite shake.

"Want to go for a walk?" she asks.

"Okay."

She grins and glues herself to my side. I flinch. My rib cage is tender and bruising all over from Rainn's punches. I slowly peel myself away from Claire as we start wandering down the walking trail between the campsite and the beach.

"I've been dying to get you alone all day so we could talk," she says.

We had fun in the water. She's hot. Prom King Guy wouldn't care about the unease rolling through him, so I'm trying not to, either. "Yeah? About what?"

She shoots me a flirty smirk. "You know how I'm applying to all those theater schools?" she asks.

I nod.

"I was wondering if I could, like, pick your dad's brain about what I should include in my application. Or maybe he even knows some of the faculty . . . ?"

When I don't say anything, she keeps going.

"No pressure! It's just, after *Mamma Mia!*, he told me I could ask him anytime, but I didn't know how to do that exactly. Like should I call him? Email? Go through his publicist? I know he's not home a lot, so I thought *you* could tell me. Now that we're, you know, together."

And there it is. The fucking punch line, *finally*. Of course, Claire doesn't like me. She's been using me to get closer to my dad. Ta-da! All the flirting, the compliments, the touching—it was all to lube me up.

This is one of my worst fears realized. Well, after a girl being paid to date me or needing rules to kiss me, so I'm three for three. What prize do I win?

"Sure," I say, my voice devoid of emotion. "I'll have his publicist reach out."

She squeals and squeezes my arm.

Okay, I can't do this. Prom King Guy's life sucks just as much as my own. I stop walking and face her. I summon as much fake confidence as I can when I say, "But . . . we're not together."

Her eyes fly wide. "What? What are you talking about?"

"Um—just that I don't want to be your boyfriend?"

I hate that I say it like a question. She's glaring at me like I'm a jerk. And, sure, I guess I am. I'm not so innocent in all this. I know I was exploring this thing with her in part because I'm nursing wounds about Natalia, which isn't fair. Even if she hadn't shown her hand about my dad, after everything that's happened today, it would be seriously shitty to let this thing with her go on with my head such a mess over another girl anyway. I shouldn't have even let it start in the first place. It all just spun out of control too quickly to grasp on to.

"Why?" she asks, her tone legit aggressive.

"I think it would be . . . better? To be friends." Though honestly, at the moment, I want to run as far and fast as I can in the other direction.

"Not for me." She crosses her arms. "I don't want to just be friends."

I frown. I've never really done this before, but I'm pretty sure when one person wants to end things the other can't . . . refuse?

"Okay, well . . ." I scratch the back of my neck, entirely lost for words. "I do?"

"What did I do?"

I let out a long exhale. "Nothing. Well—I mean, I don't like people talking about my dad like that—"

Claire's gaze sharpens. "Like what? Calling him talented and nice?"

Gah, I'm not doing this well at all. I rub my eyes.

"No—and it's not—" I was going to say it's not *her*, but I can't finish that sentence because as much as it's the other stuff, it's also definitely her.

Natalia walks by then, carrying a giant box of bandannas on her way to the obstacle course. I refuse to look at her. Which lasts all of three seconds.

"Oh," Claire says, pulling my focus back to her. She's followed my gaze, and her eyes close slowly.

I don't have to say anything because when she looks at me, both our cheeks get redder. Mine from embarrassment, hers from red-hot fury.

"It's not—"

"Fuck off, Ethan."

She storms away.

I guess it wouldn't be a good time to ask her for my jacket back.

MISSING LION LETTER #4

It doesn't even matter that I'd die to sing with Claire because I can't make myself step onto that stage to even TRY. I'm not remotely capable of auditioning for the spring musical, which is the only thing more bravery would afford me. I doubt Claire would even want me to be onstage with her anyway after I drunkenly gushed about how talented and hot she is at that party this summer. When every thought I've ever had about her just spewed out of my mouth until she kissed me—probably just to shut me up since she never spoke to me again. Humiliating.

I imagine standing up right now and belting out a song just to see the looks on their faces. On her face. It's impossible. How could I ever stand on a stage when the mere thought spikes my pulse to an unhealthy level? Let alone the one time I actually tried to sing in public and I puked all over my shoes. Classic.

I'm never happier than when I sing. But I should do anything else before I ever pursue musical goddamn theater. I was put in this body with this brain. I have so many other goals and so many other options. Singing is not what I've been preparing for during my entire time at Liberty. So, what does it mean, then, that I'm really good at it?

But when I imagine leaving Liberty without stepping on that stage...there's an actual pang. This is my last chance. Fine. If I were braver, I would try to forget Claire and audition for the spring musical this year. If I were really brave? I'd never stop singing.

CHAPTER TWENTY

Natalia

Senior Sunrise, 2:30 PM

UGH. IT'S TIME FOR the dreaded trust obstacle course. What if I get paired with someone heinous? Like *Claire*. I fought Prashant and the entire student council on this game when we were planning this summer, but I was outvoted. Apparently being blindfolded and led through a course by someone else is "fun" instead of "my worst nightmare."

"It's because you have trust issues," Prashant says when I complain to him about it one last time.

"Your mom has trust issues," I mutter.

"She does. Which is why she became a psychiatrist and why I know so much about them." He smiles beatifically, and I burst out laughing. He does, too.

Mr. Beckett cups his hands around his mouth. "Time to partner up! Everyone grab a bandanna! This is a bonding exercise, so whoever has your same color is your partner. No trading!"

There's a scramble for the bandanna box. There have to be at least thirty colors of various shades in here. I pull out the one closest to me, a bright coral. People start comparing and pairing off. I look around, and Mason Hartman is high-fiving Rainn, his cheeks flushed.

"Bruh! No one ever picks me! This is *awesome*!"

"I mean, I didn't," Rainn says, holding up his yellow bandanna. "But that's grim, so yeah, man, let's do this!" Rainn grins.

They high-five again with their yellow bandannas. Rainn shoots me an apologetic look that we didn't get paired together. Me too.

Time to check Sienna's bandanna and hope she chose coral. But when I spot her, she's sidling up next to Leti with a maroon one in her hand. Leti has the match and gets all rosy and flustered. The two of them stand side by side and sneak smiles at each other, and it's not possible to feel any way but excited for them.

Well, that's my two friends out. A small bud of fear starts to blossom. I can name every person in the entire senior class in alphabetical order, but I don't really *know* any of them that well. I'm always too busy working to participate in the activities themselves. Ms. Mercer insisted I join in on everything today for that very reason. Highly annoying.

I go over to Prashant, who looks miserable standing next to Janelle, navy-blue bandannas dangling from their hands. Yikes. I keep wandering looking for coral. Whites, hunter greens, sky blues, oranges, fuchsias. But no coral.

Just as I'm about to look in the box to see if anyone even grabbed the other match, Claire and Ethan materialize in the crowd. My stomach plummets for two reasons: She's wearing his basketball jacket and in his hand is a coral bandanna.

I want to turn my face to the bright afternoon sky and shout, *Why are you doing this to me?*

Every time I want space from Ethan, we are forced back together.

Claire notices me first, her eyes darting to the fabric in my hand.

She shoots me a withering glare, and as she walks by me, she bumps my shoulder with hers.

What the hell was *that* for? Another territorial warning shot like the tagged picture from earlier?

A lot of people let out a low *ooooooh* and look toward me, waiting for my reaction. They're whispering behind their hands or shooting knowing looks, their eyes flying between me, Ethan, and Rainn. Now Claire. Ugh, that ridiculous fight must have made them think there was drama. I straighten my spine and keep my expression neutral. They won't get any from me.

This is exactly why I've been so stressed about someone finding the letters. All anyone needs is a sliver of information to create a whole narrative about you. Whether or not it's true. If they find out what I did today, it won't matter what I've done at Liberty over the past few years—the story they create will be the only thing they believe. I just know it.

Which is really why I'm so scared *my* letter might be out there. Without context, it's a tinderbox of gossip about Ethan. As confused as I am about our friendship, I don't want anyone to have any more fodder to use against him. He's been through enough bullying to last a lifetime.

I've been lucky so far no one else has found a letter today, but I'm too aware that my luck could run out any minute.

When Ethan finally notices the bandanna in my hand, he lets out a long sigh before walking over to me, obviously as annoyed as I am that we're paired up.

He doesn't meet my eyes and stops a full arm's length away. Neither of us says anything.

Ms. Mercer announces the rules. "One partner is blindfolded, and the other leads them through the obstacle course only with words—*no touching.* Do not remove the blindfold, or you'll be disqualified. This is about learning how to communicate and trust each other, which are vital skills, both at Liberty and in life. Choose who will be the leader and who will be the follower now."

Ethan turns to me, his expression empty of feeling. Like we're strangers. He pushes his curls off his forehead, still damp from his water flirting with Claire. Images flash again of her twined around Ethan's body, their wet skin glistening in the sun. Why does she feel the need to warn me off when she already has him?

I'm not allowed to care; I shouldn't care; I don't *want* to care. But I do. I really, really do. A thousand possible starts of sentences die on my tongue.

Mr. Beckett cups his hands around his mouth again. "C'mon, people, let's move it along!"

Finally, Ethan says, "Obviously you're the one who's going to be blindfolded."

My eyes pop wide. "Hell no."

"If anyone needs help with trust, it's you."

"Why does everyone keep saying that?"

"Because it's true?"

When I don't respond, Ethan's eyebrows float up expectantly. Ugh, we don't have time for this.

"Fine." I ignore the bandanna in his outstretched hand and use my own. Not because he's right, but because I don't want to look at his perfect face anymore, anyway. The world goes dark, and we get started.

I can hear everyone else laughing and stumbling and being silly. But Ethan is basically monosyllabic.

Turn. Step. Bigger step.

When I ask clarifying questions, he sighs heavily like this is the biggest waste of his time. He's obviously upset about something bigger than being paired up together, but I have no idea what.

Ethan sullenly directs me through lots of turns that feel like they're taking us farther and farther away from the main beach area, and quickly the other voices start to fade away. His directions get more detailed the farther we go.

"Turn right and walk straight for, like, twenty paces," he says.

"Twenty? How big is this course?"

But I do what he says. After another few minutes, I'm completely disoriented. I don't hear anyone around us anymore. Are we that far ahead, or that far behind?

"Is anyone close to finishing?" I ask.

"Uuuhh." The squeeze in his voice makes it sound like he's leaning far forward or back to see. "Looks like Claire and Tanner—take a large step over a rock."

I do. Then I almost trip when Ethan says, "Tanner found a letter by the way."

"What?"

"He picked it up because it had his name on it, but he didn't read it. I took care of it."

"When? How?" My voice is shrill, disbelieving.

"You were there. Turn left."

I turn left slowly, and it dawns on me. "So *that* was the reason for the fight with Rainn?"

He hesitates before saying, "More or less."

Even though I can't see him, I know he's holding something else back. But I don't ask because frustration is still rolling off him in waves.

Ethan saved me . . . again. By letting himself become a literal punching bag.

"Thanks for doing that," I try.

"You don't need to thank me. It's my ass on the line, too."

Right. It probably has nothing to do with me. He was in the wrong place at the wrong time when I sent the letters flying. He's only been protecting himself all day—not me.

As we walk on in this strained silence, I don't know what possesses me other than the fact that I feel bolder with the blindfold on. "You and Claire seem closer."

"Natalia," he says, his tone laced with warning.

"What?" I exclaim.

"Just don't, okay? You have no right."

I scoff and throw my arms out. "What does *that* mean? Why are you so mad at me?"

In the dark of the blindfold, his sharp inhale is my only clue something wild is about to break free. "I don't know, maybe because you left that night? Or because you ghosted me all summer? Or maybe because you just kissed one of my closest friends? Pick one!"

My hand flies to my blindfold to rip it off, but his warm fingers wrap around my wrist to stop me. "Don't, we'll be disqualified."

Everything he said is pulsing between us, and it's *torture* not being able to look at him. All my other senses are on fire, though. I hear his rapid breathing, feel his tight grip on my wrist.

"We're not supposed to touch, either," I breathe.

"Right," he says quietly. But he doesn't let go. I don't have to see him to know he's looking right at me.

To know he's even more upset than I thought.

I grab hold of the last thing he brought up. The kiss with Rainn.

"You saw?" I ask, my voice shaking.

He drops my hand as his bitter scoff rips a jagged edge between us. "You were standing in the middle of the beach, Natalia, everyone saw."

There's something in his voice I haven't been able to pick up on until now, but it's not just jealousy. It's pain. I've hated how powerless I've felt watching him with Claire all day. I can't do anything about his feelings for her, but maybe I can start to be honest about my own.

My voice is gentle when I say, "Ethan. I don't like Rainn. I thought we were flirting for fun. I didn't know he felt like that. But I don't feel the same way."

There's a stillness then. Another tremendously long silence filled only by the crashing tide. My pulse pounds a riotous rhythm through me.

"You don't?" he asks finally, his voice spiking with something I can't identify.

"No. I don't."

I take a wide step back to get some air that isn't filled with his scent.

"Wait—" he calls.

Too late.

My ankle turns on a patch of slick seaweed, and I fall backward into a volleyball net. Before I can hit the sand beneath it, Ethan's strong fingers grip my wrist again and snap me upright, crashing me against his chest in one swift motion.

With the blindfold on, everything else is heightened. His heart pounding against mine, his warm breath ragged on my cheek. My lips dangerously close to his throat.

I try to step away from him, but there's a sharp yank on my scalp. "*Ow.*"

Ethan moves behind me. "Oh, damn. Your hair is stuck in the net."

He's so close I can feel the rumble of his voice in my back. Then his hands are moving, his shoulder rubbing against mine while he works out the snag.

After several seconds he says, "I have to undo your braids."

"Fine, do whatever, just detach me from this net before I—" I stop when I feel his fingers in my hair. I'm grateful he can't see the way my eyes fall closed.

Another moment, another several heartbeats with his warm fingers working through my hair, and it's done. I'm free.

Still, neither of us moves.

I don't mean to, I don't even tell myself to, it happens as if I'm pulled by magnetic force—I lean back. The slightest press of my shoulders against his chest, the faintest arch of my neck. His breathing changes. Faster.

Ethan's fingertips drift out of my hair and slowly glide down the length of my arms, so whisper soft it could be a breeze. But it's him.

"Are you cold?" he asks, voice low.

I'm covered in goose bumps, but I couldn't be less cold right now if I tried.

"I'm fine," I say, my voice weak.

I'm past thinking. When his soft touch travels to my wrists, my trembling fingers spread wide on their own, inviting his to thread with mine.

But they don't. He drops them abruptly and steps away.

I frown, the blindfold slipping down my nose a bit as I do so. I finally wrench the thing off, tired of this game—tired of *these* games—and turn around to face him. The sunlight is shockingly bright, I have to blink several times before I can see anything clearly.

"Great. Now we're disqualified," he says. But there's something in his expression . . .

I look around. The obstacle course is gone. No one else is on this part of the beach. Not just from Liberty; *no one*. We're completely alone.

Momentarily distracted, I say, "Where the hell did you take me?"

He presses his lips together in amusement and shrugs. "As far away as possible. I wanted to see how long you would listen to me before you did that." He gestures to the blindfold in my hand. "You lasted way longer than I expected."

"Ethan!" I smack him, but I have to bite my lip to keep from laughing. "You're so—"

"Clever? Cunning?"

"Contemptible."

He shakes his head slowly. "Damn. You went for the alliteration, and I've got to respect that." He extends his fist for me to bump. Which I do *not*.

The mirth fades from the air the longer we look at each other.

"We should get back," he says, looking away.

"That's all you're going to say?" I ask.

Is he just going to ignore whatever this is between us? Because I don't think I can anymore.

"What do you want me to say, Talia?" he asks, still not meeting my gaze.

It takes me twelve rapid heartbeats to find my voice. "Just . . . tell me what we're doing," I whisper.

Then he looks at me in a way that makes me wish I had kept the blindfold on. Squarely. Boldly. Like he's narrowed in on the eye of my storm; into the only place where stillness exists inside of me. His voice comes out rough and quiet when he says, "I *can't*."

He pushes a hand through his hair, his eyes sweeping across my mouth before looking back to me. "But we *have* to talk about it. Because I'm going fucking crazy."

I don't understand any of this. I'm so bad at these kinds of conversations, but now that he's opened up a little about why he's so mad and hurt, I'm desperate to know more. I want to know *everything*. Like why did he reject me? Why does he sound jealous one minute yet back away the next? What about Claire?

And why does it look like he wants to kiss me, when he's made it clear he doesn't want me for real?

He's right. It's time to talk about it. All of it. I take a deep breath and nod. "Okay."

He nods slowly, too, his shoulders relaxing. "Okay?"

"Okay," I repeat.

A shrill whistle carries across the beach, followed by a panicked Mr. Beckett running toward us. His cheeks huge around a football whistle, flailing his arms. I guess we've been gone awhile.

Once we return to the obstacle course and cross the finish line, everyone is waiting. But the only one I see is Rainn, holding a yellow piece of paper in his hand.

CHAPTER TWENTY-ONE

Ethan

Senior Sunrise, 3:35 PM

HE KNOWS.

I stand at the finish line of the obstacle course as if hammered to the spot. I stare at Rainn, the yellow paper in his hand. He blinks down at the letter, and his face falls until his relaxed smile is replaced by bafflement.

When he looks up, his eyes dart all around, as if looking for the source.

Is it my letter? Natalia's? Someone else's?

My hand shoots into my pocket to be sure the first letter is still in there. It is. Taunting me.

Natalia and I exchange a look. Her eyes are wide with shock. I keep my hands low at my sides, fanning the air slowly. *Don't panic.* I fixed it with Tanner. I can do it again.

I finally move, but not too fast. I don't want to draw attention. We need to get to him before anyone notices what he's holding. To explain.

Natalia keeps pace beside me, the panic rolling off her.

Rainn watches us approach, and when I shoot him a desperate look, understanding crosses his face. He may not have details, but now he knows Natalia and I are involved.

I get to him at the same time he tries to covertly push the letter into his pocket. I grab his arm and tug. "Hey, man, can we talk?"

He nods and starts walking with me. But in my desperation, I pull on his arm too roughly, and he fumbles—accidentally dropping the paper in the process.

Janelle turns at that exact moment and watches as it flutters to the sand. "What's that?" she asks.

Akira Kurosawa was the first director to use slow motion as a turning point in his movie *Seven Samurai*. Somehow, he figured out before anyone else that there are moments in life when time slows down just long enough for you to realize that nothing will be the same once it speeds up again.

Janelle swipes the paper up with her long, fake nails and reads it before any of us can stop her. I have no breath in my body.

"Oh my god," she exclaims. "This is someone's Lion Letter!"

A few people hear her and look over.

She spins on her heels. "Claire!"

Claire walks over, my jacket gone, eyeing me warily.

"Yeah?" Claire asks.

"Look at this," Janelle says gleefully, shoving the paper in Claire's face. I should grab it and run and save whoever wrote it. But I have to know what Janelle knows first. I have to know exactly how bad this is. I stand behind her, my pulse racing so fast I feel it in my temples, and read the letter quickly over her shoulder.

I don't really get the point of this. What could everyone else be writing about? Are they seriously pouring their hearts out to a piece of paper that's just going to become litter? People are actually crying.

Man, I hate this place sometimes. I'm not like Natalia, who needs a pact to do something that scares her. I don't need games to be braver. I'm brave every day. When I see a problem, I deal with it. When I want something, I go after it.

Jackson Ford was a problem, and now he's gone.

I like Sienna, so I'm going for it today.

Done. Simple. There's nothing to cry about.

My face feels impossibly hot. It's not mine, but . . . it's not good. Natalia told someone about our pact? But . . . we swore we never would. This letter was written before I mentioned it to Claire today. Someone else must know. Is this Rainn's? Is that why he got so flustered?

But no, he doesn't like Sienna, too. *Does he?* I study my friends, wondering if I know them at all.

"Someone got Jackson fired," Claire says, her voice simmering with unspent rage.

"That guy sucked," Rainn says.

I eye him with suspicion. God, is this really his?

Claire snaps him a withering gaze.

But why? Rainn's not wrong, Jackson did suck. He only managed one semester of theater school before coming back and working at

Liberty. Maybe Claire likes him as a director, or whatever, but he was the kind of guy I would never leave a girl alone with.

"Do you know who wrote this?" Claire asks Janelle.

"Whoever likes Sienna," Janelle says, her lips twisting with excitement. After a pause she adds, "And doesn't like Natalia."

Rainn's gaze slides to Natalia's, and it's full of sympathy. Right. Rainn wouldn't say something like that about Natalia. Then whose is it?

Natalia comes out of her daze at the mention of her name.

"What?" she asks, voice tight.

I reach for the paper, "Wait, don't—"

But it's too late. Claire hands it over, her gaze boring into mine.

I watch as Natalia's face contorts with the dismissive cruelty of the note. I can tell the exact moment she reads the part about the pact because she goes pale. Why did they have to name Natalia in it? Why did they have to mention our pact? Well, I guess because it was supposed to be private.

God, I don't know how this day could get any worse.

"What pact?" Janelle asks no one in particular.

"Probably the same one Ethan told me about, huh, Ethan?" Claire asks.

Oh. That's how.

Natalia's mouth drops open as she stares at me with this look of utter betrayal.

Janelle plucks the letter out of her limp grasp, looking back and forth between us as she shoves it in her pocket.

"Talia, it wasn't like that—" I try.

But she shakes her head and rushes away. Without looking at anyone else, Natalia drifts past Prashant and his held-up clipboard, past Ms. Mercer, who tries to ask her a question.

That look on her face . . .

"Natalia!" I call.

She doesn't stop. She doesn't turn. She runs. Like she always does.

"What is happening?" Rainn hisses in my ear, uncharacteristic agitation in his voice.

What . . . do I do? Do I admit what I know? Do I say anything about how the letters got out? What happened to me and Natalia being in this together? To this being her mess that she swore to clean up? If I thought I was confused before, this thing with her has quantum mechanics looking simple.

Before I can answer, Sienna calls over to me. "Ethan? Is Natalia okay?"

Simultaneously, we all turn. Sienna and Leti Mitchell are walking toward us from the group they were standing in. *Holding hands.* I'm psyched for Sienna, who's had a crush on Leti for*ever.*

Then Claire's eyes narrow, and it clicks. It's Leti's letter.

I should do something to warn them.

What Leti wrote about Natalia wasn't cool, but it was supposed to be private. It's not like Leti was trying to hurt her feelings, and I can't help but think that if Natalia hadn't messed with the letters, she never would've known. Plus, Ford is an oxygen thief who likely deserves everything that happened to him. If Leti had something to do with that, then they deserve a parade.

Move, Ethan.

But I can't. Janelle has terrified me since sixth grade, and apparently, I'm having flashbacks. My feet are fused to the sand, my voice stuck in the space between what's right and selfish: self-preservation.

Janelle doesn't waste a second when Leti and Sienna join our group. She says, "You both sure got cozy during the obstacle course. You really *went for it today*, Leti."

Sienna shoots me a *Why is Janelle Johnson talking to us?* look.

Before I can respond, Claire speaks. "Did you get Jackson Ford fired?"

Leti's eyes pop wide, and they let out a surprised laugh. "What?"

"We know you did something," Claire accuses.

Sienna frowns. "Didn't you see that gross stuff he posted? *That's* what got him fired."

"It didn't help, but that wasn't the only reason," Leti says, squaring their shoulders.

Sienna's eyebrows spring up, and Claire's wringing her hands as if she were wringing Leti's neck.

"I mean, I didn't have to do much. I only told the administration what I know," Leti says.

Janelle inches closer and asks, "Which is?"

Leti hesitates and looks at Claire a beat too long before sliding their attention back to Janelle. "Doesn't matter."

Claire exhales slowly, her posture relaxing a little. "Tanner's gonna freak when he finds out."

Oh right, they're friends. Didn't Janelle say Tanner went to a Jackson Ford party last night? God, I can't believe Natalia thought Tanner was *remotely* good enough for her.

Leti then turns to Sienna to explain further. "Mr. Ford's the guy I told you about—the one who posted nudes of my sister after they dated. I had to do something."

"That asshole," Janelle says. She looks at Claire. "I always tolerated him because he's the booze hookup, but you never said he was gross like that."

Claire's shaking her head quickly. "No, no, he wasn't," she insists. But I'm not sure who she's trying to convince.

"Why are you defending him when Leti just told us what he did?" Sienna asks, her face furious.

Claire folds her arms around herself. "I mean, it's not like he's here to defend himself! There are two sides to every story, and a lot of us relied on him and cared about him—" She cuts herself off and stares at the sand.

The silence is cloying. Rainn and I exchange a confused glance. We're both a step behind until Janelle says to Claire, "You said nothing ever happened."

Ohhhh.

"*Janelle!*" Claire exclaims.

Janelle grimaces. "Oops."

Holy shit. Claire and Jackson Ford? But he's a legit adult with a beard and, like, a vacuum. And he was Claire's director besides. What a scumbag.

"Claire—" I start.

She whips to face me, eyes narrowed to slits. "Don't you dare pretend to care about me now, Ethan."

Whoa. Oh . . . kay.

"I—"

Prashant appears then, mercifully cutting me off. He taps on his clipboard. "Hello? Did any of you hear me? We're relocating back to the campsite for free time."

Claire uses the excuse and storms off.

"Sorry. We're coming," Janelle says, smiling.

Prashant narrows his eyes at the sweet tone in her voice. As he backs away slowly, keeping a side-eye on Janelle, he points to me. "We need Natalia back soon. Can you go"—he rolls his wrist as if searching for the right word—"Ethan her?"

Heat shoots up my neck at the way he says that. I don't miss Rainn's eye roll, either. I swallow down my anxiety about all of this and nod. I was going to look for her anyway. The only time I've seen that look on her face was when she had a full-blown panic attack during finals. It was awful.

When Prashant is out of earshot, Leti asks Janelle, "How did you find out about what I did?"

Instead of answering, Janelle exclaims, "Wait—there's another one!"

Apparently, all it does is get worse.

My muscles finally connect with my brain, and I step in front of Janelle to block her. As if that'll do anything; it's not like I'm going to restrain her. She scoffs and pushes past me and snatches a letter stuck high in the ice plants that line the bluffs along the beach. Janelle is tall, a volleyball player, and reaches it easily.

She scans the paper and slams a hand over her mouth.

"Oh my *god.*"

She comes running back over here, waving around the new letter. Leti's and Sienna's eyes grow wide.

"What does it say?" I ask.

"Oh, Ethanpedia, always desperate to know." Janelle *tsks.*

I glare at her, fuming. But I don't have time for this bullshit. I'm getting more worried about Talia by the second. I have to find her. *Now.*

"*Please*, Janelle," I try one more time.

Janelle's pitying grin rises slowly. "Can't." She tucks the second letter into her pocket with the first. "Someone's been stealing from the cookie jar. And I'm going to find out who."

CHAPTER TWENTY-TWO

Natalia

Senior Sunrise, 3:47 PM

I WALK AS FAR as I can go before my lungs compress like there isn't enough oxygen in the world that could save me now. I gulp in the salty ocean air in tiny, urgent gasps. Each breath stretches my lungs wider, my ribs expanding as I try to pull more of it deep into my abdomen. I can't get enough.

Pushing my heavy legs, I run faster toward the retaining wall separating the beach and the bike trail. I slump down against it, hiding behind it, facing the wild expanse of the ocean. The solidness of the stone keeps me upright as my vision clouds, then darkens. The black pushes in against every nerve. My pulse is a jackhammer determined to break open my chest while the rest of me grows numb.

How can I be sweating so much when I'm this cold? If I could think straight, if I could *breathe*, I'd figure this out. I could fix this. But all I can hear is Claire's smug voice when she said, *The same one Ethan told me about.* All I can see imprinted in my mind are the words from the letter: *I'm not like Natalia, who needs a pact to do something that scares her.*

That's how someone sees me. Maybe how they all see me. They all know Nice Natalia doesn't exist. She's just a front for terrified, weak Natalia. And now they know the letters got out. It's only a matter of time before they discover it was me. It's over. Everything I've built at Liberty.

I press my hand against my eyes and sink further into shame.

Footsteps scrape against the sandy concrete. "Natalia?"

Ethan. His strong, firm hand curls around my arm, pulling my hand away from my face. Warmth flows through his touch like a patch of sun on a cold day. Our eyes lock. His steady gaze is its own deep breath. It fills with so much concern, so much *understanding*, I let out a small, strangled sound.

"Go away," I croak out. "*Please.*"

"Not a fucking chance." Without hesitating, he crouches down until he's square in front of me, his long legs bent beneath him.

I don't have any fight in me, and I crumple into him.

"Okay. Okay," he soothes into my hair. "I think you're having a panic attack."

I nod. It's a bad one. Like all the things I've been trying to keep inside today are finally free to wreak havoc. My eyes dart around, and my lungs refuse to expand. My pulse is everywhere. Too fast, then too slow. I'm dying. When your heart stops working right that definitely means you're dying.

"Hey? Look at me."

I do.

"You're safe. Follow my breaths." He looks deep into my eyes and takes a long, slow breath that I try and fail to mimic. But he nods, encouraging, never taking his eyes off mine. Breathing in. Breathing out.

He's a lighthouse in this storm, his presence my safe harbor. I don't look away as my thoughts dash in a hundred directions. The letters, my parents, moving, Ethan with Claire.

Secrets and heartaches and uncertainty and never, ever doing *anything* right. I only make things worse when all I ever try to do, all I ever want to do, is make things better. To *be* better. But no one sees the trying. They don't care about the trying.

They want perfection, then they want it better. The goalposts always moving, the standard always changing. It's suffocating and impossible, and yet again and again and again, this is what's expected of me. What I expect of *myself*. But it's never good enough.

I'm always letting someone down.

Will everyone be okay? Will Ethan and I?

Will I ever, *ever* be okay?

I reach for a deeper breath.

"Good," Ethan says. His voice is so warm and calm, I feel the pressure of tears behind my eyes again. He keeps nodding and breathing, nodding and breathing.

But this boy, he's never pushed me. He's never, not once, asked me to be anything but exactly who I am.

The thought is an anchor, and I cling to it for dear life.

My own breath comes in, shaking and shallow, but after another few minutes it's a little slower. I keep following his rhythm, focusing on the sun-soaked scent coming off him, and the air in my lungs going in and out. Slowly, slowly, my vision clears.

A few minutes more, and I no longer feel like I'm being squeezed from the inside out. The roar of the ocean consumes the roar of my pulse, and I'm back here, on my favorite beach, with my favorite person.

Ethan can sense the shift and settles beside me, wrapping an arm around my shoulders. He presses the entire side of his body to mine. It feels so good.

"Better?"

I nod. "Better. But . . . I need to ask you something."

"Anything."

"How did Claire know about the pact?"

He stills. It didn't seem real, like something he'd really do, until this moment when the guilt is etched all over his face. At least he doesn't try to deny it.

"I didn't tell her anything specific," he says. "We were talking and . . . it just came out."

I want to believe him. I want us to be okay so desperately I force myself to stay calm. "Okay . . . but why are you talking about it to her and not *me*?"

He sighs. "Natalia, please tell me when I could've come up to you today and said, 'Hey, real quick, can we talk about that time we almost had sex?'"

I bury my burning face in my hands. "Oh my god, Ethan."

"See? This is what you do when I try to talk to you about it. You . . . *dissolve* and run away. It happened. *Please* stop acting like it didn't."

And there it is. It happened. I press my cheek to the tops of my knees and our eyes meet. "Okay. I'm sorry."

We both relax in a way we haven't all day.

"Why did you tell Leti?" he asks.

I frown. "I didn't. Why would I tell Leti about it?"

He shrugs. "Then why was it in their letter?"

"It was *Leti's*?" I think back on what the letter said and realize they must've been referencing our deal about art school. I tell Ethan as much, and he lets out a humorless laugh.

"God, this day is so fucked."

When I ask what else happened after I left, he fills me in. He tells me what Leti did to get creepy Jackson Ford fired and that he's pretty sure Jackson and Claire had a thing. That's a secret that never would've come out if I hadn't let the letters loose. As much as Claire bugs me, I feel really bad about that.

Finally, he tells me that Janelle found another letter, but she didn't reveal what it said.

"I feel so bad for whoever's it is," I say.

"Me too."

We exchange an uncomfortable look.

"It's only a matter of time before she figures out what happened."

"Yeah, maybe," Ethan mutters thoughtfully. "Do you think . . . it might be easier if you just tell everyone what happened? You said it was an accident—"

"It *was*."

He presses his lips together and nods. "But what if they find more? We're lucky that Tanner won't remember and Leti's wasn't more personal. The other missing ones might be and . . . I don't want someone else getting taken down by Janelle. I think we should tell them."

I expect my pulse to spike again, but it doesn't. I'm drained of panic at the moment. What am I hiding for anyway? It *was* an accident. If I tell everyone, they might understand. At the very least, if I come clean, no one else will get hurt.

"Yeah . . . you're right," I say.

His shoulders sag in relief.

When I tuck closer to him, he winces as if in pain. He shifts, adjusting me against him gingerly.

I sit forward so I can swing around to look at him. So close I can see the dark stubble on his jaw. "You okay?"

"Yep," he says, wincing again. I scan his torso where his other hand hovers and put it together.

"Did Rainn—he didn't *actually* hurt you during the fight, did he?"

He shakes his head. "I'm fine."

I narrow my eyes. When Ethan took an elbow to his nose last year during a game, he had blood rushing down his face and he shrugged, said he was fine. Even when it turned out his nose was broken and he had a black eye for a week. He's only "fine" because he doesn't want to be a burden to anyone.

"Let. Me. See," I say, tugging at his shirt.

After a taut beat, he releases my hands and nods. I push his shirt up slowly and holy effing hell. Half of his rib cage and the muscles winding around his back are covered in red welts and early purple bruises. I lightly run my fingers down Ethan's side, and his warm skin ripples into goose bumps.

"He didn't mean to. You know how easily I bruise," he says, loyal as ever.

I want to pull him into a full-body hug. To comfort and soothe him the way he just did for me. To let his Ethan-y scent hit my bloodstream again. But something in his rigid posture stops me.

His shirt falls, pooling on my wrist where my hand is still on his bare rib cage. We both seem to notice at the same time that my thumb is absently stroking small circles against him. His eyes lift slowly to my face.

I stare at him, and this rush of emotion crashes through me. He's giving me the kind of look that dissolves all my defenses, as if I have any left. I'm being less and less careful with Ethan by the minute. We both have this way of really zeroing in on each other, knowing when the other isn't okay.

But I don't want whatever is going on between us to be out of some obligation. Like the way he treats me when I don't eat right. I don't want him to feel like it's his job to fix me, or something.

But I do want us to open up to each other again.

I drop my hand quickly and say, "You know, Rainn asked if it was because of you."

Confusion flickers across his features. "What?"

"If I didn't want to be with him . . . because of you."

I watch Ethan's throat work on a swallow. "What did you tell him?"

Before I tell him everything, I have to take care of myself and figure out what I want. For real.

Adrenaline soaked and exhausted, I hold his eyes with mine and say simply, "The truth."

CHAPTER TWENTY-THREE

Ethan

Senior Sunrise, 4:12 PM

IS SHE TRYING TO kill me? *The truth.* God, what does that mean?

I wait for her to elaborate. She doesn't. It's like she's intent on keeping me burning with uncertainty. But I shouldn't be surprised. She hates talking about feelings. That's always how she's been. And now that she's barely on the other side of this panic attack, it doesn't seem like the right time to push the issue.

But she's usually chattier when she has food in her system. It's not a scheme if it's *true*. Right?

"One last meal before the firing squad?" I ask, gesturing with my chin to the small beach general store at the top of the hill near our campsite. "My treat."

She grins. She already seems lighter than she has all day. Telling everyone will be good. Even if they hate us, it'll be better than someone else getting hurt.

We climb up the hill and head into the shop. It's got all kinds of kitschy beach stuff, along with a standing freezer of individually wrapped ice-cream cones and Popsicles. Natalia chooses two Drumsticks, and we approach the counter. The checkout guy is watching a television behind the counter tuned to an entertainment show with Dad's face plastered all over it.

Of course.

A pretty newscaster with long blond hair announces in a perky voice, "Roger Forrester, known for his iconic role in the popular political drama *The Beltway*, opened up about the new season."

I stiffen. This interview again. It's been on loop everywhere, since the new season premieres next week. My dad comes on, and they obviously filmed this at *our house* over the summer when I was in Seattle visiting Adam. The last time he was home.

Natalia shifts beside me, and I notice she's watching it with a narrowed gaze. Dad's seated at the dining room table, the very same place where just this morning I shoveled a bowl of cereal into my face and where Mom pretended she hadn't been crying all night.

In the show, the table is clean instead of covered in mail, and it has some bullshit plant on it I've never seen before. Dad's wearing a button-up shirt the color of burlap. His face is covered in that perfectly curated stubble of his that makes it look like he's a guy who, like, gardens, or something. He smiles warmly and comes off as the epitome of the approachable, down-home family man. His bullshit brand.

I'm mad all over again.

He's asked where he draws inspiration for his character, Jonathan Reid.

"My family," he answers. "No matter what political schemes he's working through, Jonathan Reid's number one priority is his family."

I almost crush the cones in my hand. The show cuts then to a picture of the four of us from our trip to Tahoe last year. We look like an enviably happy family.

But in truth, that was the only full day we were there. Mom got paged back to the hospital for an emergency surgery so we had to go home early, and Dad left right after New Year's Eve for a two-month shoot in Europe. And when he came back, he was . . . different. That's when I started suspecting.

"No matter what roles I've played on-screen"—the camera zooms in for a tight shot on Dad's face as he tears up—"'Dad' is the only one that matters to me."

I laugh out loud.

Wow. I almost want to applaud; his performance is that outstanding. I slap the money on the counter, bringing the cashier's attention back to me. His eyes go wide as he points at the television, then looks back at me. "You're not . . ."

"Nope. He's not," Natalia says, pulling me out of the store.

Back in the ocean air, I let out a long-held breath. My dad. My lying, cheating *asshole* of a dad.

I tear open the plasticky paper around the cone with so much force I almost drop the whole thing.

Natalia puts a steadying hand on my arm. She's asking without asking. But what can I even say?

That somehow the world kept spinning like everything was normal when, in fact, my own had collapsed inside a text message?

Natalia is looking at me. Waiting. I should be helping her figure out how she's going to tell the class about the letters, not stuck in a spiral of my own self-pity. But she's got that stubborn look in her eyes again, and I know she's not going to let me avoid it this time. I run a hand through my hair.

"It's been . . . a really shitty summer," I admit.

Concern breaks across her face. "Really? Did something happen with Adam?"

I shake my head. "He's doing great actually."

She nods, relieved.

It's like I have to physically force the next words out. "My dad moved out. Right after prom."

Natalia goes utterly still. "What happened?"

"He cheated," I say, looking at my dirty shoes.

I don't say more, I can't. I can't tell her about the texts, the ultimatum. How heavy that silence was when Dad told me he was leaving. How I felt a fury building inside me so strong, I could've beat the house to dust with my bare knuckles. But I didn't. Because if I fell apart, Mom wouldn't be able to keep it together. Adam wouldn't. Doesn't matter what I need if they're not okay.

Mom still doesn't know about the affair. I *hate* that I do.

"Oh, Ethan . . ." She says my name like a whisper in the dark. I almost buckle then and there.

I sniff, shrugging her kindness off. I don't deserve it. "I'm fine."

She cocks her head to the side the way she does when she's seeing right through me. "You're *not* fine."

She doesn't suggest it or wonder, she *knows*. And that alone makes the backs of my eyes burn. Because of course she's right. She sees me.

All I can do is hang my head low and say, "You're right. I'm not."

Natalia takes a step toward me and places a hand on the middle of my chest, palm flat on my sternum. The touch, as gentle as the fading sun, pulses through me. It's so unexpected, her touching me at all, but touching me like this. It's . . . deep. She waits for me to meet her gaze.

When I do, her voice is quiet and determined when she says, "You will be."

I want to believe her so badly it hurts. I nod and grab her hand, holding it against me. She blinks, surprised, but she doesn't pull away, either.

We just stand there like that, looking at each other. She's put her hair back in a messy braid, and it makes my fingers twitch to undo it again.

Instead, I gently tug on the end of it as if ringing a small bell. "Cute."

I don't miss the soft flush along her cheekbones, which lifts my mood more than it has any right to.

The longer we stand there, the harder I have to bite back the urge to bring her mouth to mine. God, I want to.

But Natalia squeezes her eyes shut, breaking the moment when she says, "I'm *such* a jerk. I should've been there for you this summer, but I was so caught up in my own head . . ." She looks at me. "I'm *so* sorry."

I can see that she is. But frustration rolls through me because, yeah, she disappeared exactly when I needed her most. I try to push that feeling away because it's not all her fault, and she was also going through family stuff I didn't know about.

"Me too."

There's more to say, so much more, but "sorry" is a good start. I squeeze her hand, and we break apart to walk on in companionable silence awhile, wandering back toward the group.

When we get there, Natalia suddenly asks, "Uh, why is Claire looking at you like she wants to stab you?"

I follow her gaze. Sure enough, Claire is glaring at me from the campsite like she would relish a good prom king regicide.

"I broke things off with her before the obstacle course," I say.

I watch Natalia's profile closely, but she gives nothing away. All she says is "Oh."

"Yeah." I want to state the absolute obvious out loud—that it feels like finally, the universe or timing or the fates are on my side. Our side. But that could be wishful thinking. Especially when she hasn't told me what "the truth" for her is and if it's the same as mine.

"Why?" she asks.

I scratch the back of my neck. "I'm not into her like that. And I think she was only into me because she thought I had connections or something."

"To . . . ?"

I can feel my face heat up. "Um . . . Hollywood, I guess?"

"How?" she asks, her eyes widening to saucers. She's being purposely obtuse to make me feel better, and I grin, more than game to play along.

"Oh, I wasn't sure if you knew this—yikes, this is kind of awkward." I drop my voice to a whisper. "My dad is Roger Forrester."

"Never heard of him," she deadpans.

"He's *very* famous," I say, nodding seriously, really playing it up. "So, you see, I have many admirers whose intentions are potentially . . . nefarious."

"If only they knew your most embarrassing moments. I could tell them about your Star Wars pajama set—oh! Or your existential crisis about dragons when you got your wisdom teeth out," she suggests.

"Hey, now, I was never more devastated than when I realized I was never going to ride one."

"Oh, I know. '*Childhood lies! Did you know that, Natalia? It's all a lie!*'" she cries, quoting my drug-addled meltdown.

We both crack up. Her laugh is throaty and big, releasing the last fragments of her panic attack. The sun is hitting her hair just so, and god, she's pretty. Who could look at Natalia laughing, ice cream melting all over her fingers, and not want to remember? I quickly reach for one of the Polaroid cameras sitting on the picnic table nearest us and snap a photo of her.

"*Ethan*, I look disgusting," she says, covering her eyes with her free hand.

Disgusting? I've seen Natalia throw up on the side of the road from car sickness. I've seen her grow loopy and pale through countless all-nighter study sessions. I've seen her peel off flakes of skin from a sunburn and white-knuckle exactly one hangover. And she has never once looked disgusting.

"Not possible," I say. I show her the small picture. It's gorgeous. Like her.

Her teeth sink into her bottom lip to hold back her smile. She is unsuccessful, which I count as a major win.

I slip the photo into my pocket, and my fingers graze the edge of the first letter we found. I wonder for the millionth time if it's Natalia's. And for the millionth time, I tell myself I can't read it.

When we shift so effortlessly from hard topics to inside jokes, when I make her laugh, or when she touches me like her hands alone could heal my deepest cuts, I get this overwhelming feeling that we could work together. Like, *really* work.

But she doesn't know I'm the liar who turned on his own mom so that his dad could have his affair in peace. Would she look at me like that ever again if she did?

I'm okay not knowing for a little while longer.

CHAPTER TWENTY-FOUR

Natalia

Senior Sunrise, 4:49 PM

WHEN WE GET CLOSER to the tents, everyone is huddled in their friend groups, and it's obvious they're on edge. Ethan and I walk by one group whispering to one another and looking around. I slow my pace when I catch what they're talking about.

". . . someone's Lion Letter."

"Where did they find it?"

"On the ground. Apparently, it's not the only one."

"Oh my god."

My stomach sloshes as we walk by another group.

"I heard Leti got Mr. Ford fired. I think it was a revenge-porn thing."

"I heard it was because he and Claire Wilson were hooking up—that's what one of the letters Janelle found said."

"Well, now we know how Claire got the lead."

"Stop! She was good."

And another group:

"How did Janelle read their letter?"

"She *found* it. Someone is scattering them everywhere where *anyone* can find them."

Ethan and I exchange uneasy glances. This is spreading fast. My mind is crowding again, the embers of panic lighting anew.

A few people are starting to walk around together, like they're searching for something. Under benches and brush. They're on the hunt for more letters, which means I'm running out of time.

The wind blows then, pushing my hair back and shooting goose bumps down my arms.

"Freezing," I say, gesturing to my tent. "See you in a bit?"

He nods like he knows what I really need to do is collect myself to figure out what I'm going to say when I confess. My words can get so jumbled when I'm nervous. I need to be alone and think. Just for a minute.

But when I duck into my tent for a sweatshirt, I pause. What the hell? My sleeping bag is crumpled and pushed to one side instead of smoothed in the center. My clothes and pens and sketchbook are all spilling out of my bag when I distinctly remember putting them away before the volleyball game.

Someone's been in here.

Another wild gust of wind rattles the tent as I go through my bag quickly. But I don't find anything missing. If they didn't take anything, what were they looking for?

I pull in a deep breath. Maybe I'm overreacting.

Maybe it was Sienna, who is chronically underprepared for sleepovers and has rifled through my stuff for toothpaste or a tampon on more than one occasion. The thought calms me somewhat, but I'm not convinced.

I need to tell everyone what happened before the gossip gets worse and things spiral out of control. I know that. But I can't face them like this when I'm still on edge from my panic attack. Ethan helped—*so* much. But there's only one thing that pulls me all the way back to myself.

With a nervy inhale, I put my sweatshirt on, tuck my sketchbook under my arm, and slink off to the cliffside alone. I find a spot by the rocks and settle on the bench, where I can bleed some of my worries out through my pen.

I open my sketchbook and poise my Micron pen over the blank page. It starts moving into a sketch quickly. The scratching sound of the pen on the paper, the sharp scent of the ink, settles my mind.

At first, I'm simply sketching what I see. The rolling waves of the ocean. The cooling sand. The long and hazy horizon. But slowly, my brain shuts off, my hand takes over, and I'm not thinking at all anymore. Just feeling.

Sea spray. Honey-gold radiance. Effortlessness. Laughing and talking and nearness. Holding and sharing and whispers. Fingers tracing down my skin. Warmth and want. Acceptance.

Lines curl, becoming whipped, tangled hair. Curves become shapes, shoulders and elbows and hands. I go to another place as my pen moves, moves, moves as if on its own. Deepening grooves in the paper until the edges curl slightly with the pressure of the lines, the weight of the ink. I don't know how long I work on it, but eventually my hand stops when it tells me it's done. I blink down at the image.

In the background, a temperamental ocean swollen with waves. In the foreground, the torsos of two people, a boy and a girl, in an embrace as wild as the sea behind them. Her arms hooked tightly around his neck; his arms wound around her back. Bodies pressed together, faces buried into each other's necks. There's no space between them, clinging as if crashing into each other from running a great distance.

I don't need to see their full faces to know how they're feeling. Safe. Relieved. Soothed.

Like they fit.

If I were to paint it, I'd choose soft watercolor. Warm tones. Golden yellows, rich ambers, burnt siennas, and hints of the faintest pinks. Heart colors.

As it is, it has good movement, and is decently shaded, but it's far from perfect. Why, then, are my eyes burning?

Ethan has always made surprise appearances in my sketches over the years. Like when I was learning to draw hands, his showed up again and again in my sketchbooks. The strength of them, the mole beside his thumb, the crooked angle of his pinkie that didn't heal right after he broke it playing basketball. And I've drawn myself too many times to count.

As I learned life drawing—proportion and shading and shaping—I was the closest subject to use. I turn the pages of my sketchbook now and see them with new eyes. There are endless pages where I'm on one, and Ethan is on the other.

But this is the first time I've ever drawn myself *with* him. Us, together. I've never gone there.

I run my fingertips across it, my heart racing. This is my real Lion Letter. It says everything I could never find the words for. How I've always seen my future: with Ethan, a vast horizon before us. Beginnings instead of endings.

Before I learned that there is such a thing as different worlds; before men started determining my worth for me; before our kiss unearthed a yearning so acute, I haven't been able to think straight since, I've wanted Ethan by my side.

Earlier today, I told Sienna I don't know where I fit. But now it's clear.

If I belong anywhere in this world, it's with Ethan Forrester.

Because no one makes me feel more like myself than him. And no matter what he feels for me, I can no longer deny that I feel *everything* for him.

I close my sketchbook carefully and take a deep breath.

Soft footsteps behind me. I turn, and Sienna is there.

"Heeeey. Thought I'd find you hiding here."

She plunks down on the bench beside me and folds her legs under her. I pull my sketchbook closer to me, stashing it under my leg. I know she's going to ask me about the letters. I gather my strength.

After a long pause, Sienna says, "Are you going to tell me what happened with you and Ethan during the obstacle course?"

Oh.

Flustered, I say, "Nothing." My cheeks turn hot even though I'm telling the truth. Nothing like *that* has actually happened between me and Ethan all day.

She doesn't believe me for a second. "Fine. Don't tell me. But you could at least ask me what happened on *mine.*" Sienna shoots me a significant look.

"You and Leti?" I ask. Guilt sits heavy on my chest. Before I fess up to the class, I need to tell her. And apologize to Leti.

She flushes crimson and nods. "Blindfolds are hot."

I giggle. She's not wrong.

"So um, Ethan told me . . . about Leti's letter," I say. "And I—"

Sienna rolls her eyes and flicks a dismissive wrist. "Yeah, Janelle is up to the same mean-girl shit messing with the letters. She wouldn't even give Leti's letter back. But Leti didn't back down for a second. It was epic."

She thinks Janelle took the letters? I twist my lips and hesitate. I could play along . . .

But I'm done pretending. About everything.

"Janelle didn't mess with the letters," I say, grimacing. "I did."

And then it all spills out. I tell her about my parents and Sacramento and Ethan and New Year's Eve and prom night and how I wrote it all down and wanted to take it all back because I got scared someone would read it.

"Ironic, I know," I mutter.

Sienna's quiet as she takes it all in. When I'm finished, she lets out a heavy "Whoa."

"I'm sorry. If your letter is out there, I'm so sorry—"

"Natalia. The chance of mine being out there is improbably low. I'm not worried. Even if it is, I wrote about wanting to be a better queer advocate at school and liking Leti, which, spoiler alert: worked out. Nothing too ground-shaking," she says, shrugging.

My eyes fill with tears. "Why aren't you mad at me?"

She frowns. "Because it was an accident. You're not perfect. I used to think math was the only thing in life that was. But the more I read up on Gödel's incompleteness theorems, the more I'm convinced nothing is."

She wraps her arm around me, and I slump into her sunscreen-scented shoulder. "You're pretty damn close," I say.

"That's true." We both laugh a little.

We watch the waves, then she speaks again. "I knew something happened at prom, since you guys got *so* weird afterward. But dang, you barely even kissed, and Ethan fled the state. What would've happened if you had actually gone through with it?"

I laugh with her, which feels so good after holding all this in for so long.

"I really don't want you to go to Sacramento," she says.

"We're all leaving next year anyway." But that reasoning sounds hollow even to me.

"But you've been working your butt off creating all these bonding opportunities for our class. Do you ever include yourself in that?"

I dig my toes into the warm sand where it's cooler. "I try to."

"You say you don't feel like you belong at school, but—and don't hate me, but it seems like you keep yourself apart sometimes. Like this is your job instead of your *life*."

I swallow around the knot in my throat. "It's just . . . I feel out of control all the time. And I guess I figure if I'm in charge, if I stay busy enough, I won't feel as bad, I won't be as . . . weak. But the harder I've tried to control things, the more I've messed everything up."

The letters, Rainn, avoiding this choice about Sacramento. Running out on Ethan, ghosting him for months to protect myself, without sparing a thought that he might need me. I was so sure I was making things easier for us both by staying away. By keeping our worlds separate.

I was wrong.

I scrub my hands over my face. "Ugh. What am I going to do?"

Her face goes serious again as she shakes her head. "I don't know, but at least go easier on yourself. I'm stressed out sitting next to you. It's going to be okay."

"How? When?" I ask miserably.

She's quiet a long beat, then says, "Probably the minute you and Ethan stop pretending you aren't in love with each other."

My heart slams against my ribs. "We're—that's—not even—"

She pulls away, her expression implacable. "Natalia. You need to tell Ethan how you feel. How you *really* feel."

My shoulders sag forward. "I don't know if I can."

"You can."

"And if he doesn't feel the same way?"

She smiles. "Zero chance."

I think of Ethan's soft touch and blazing eyes. The way he's been by my side, has had my back all day despite everything. I think of his flirty smile and gentle hands in my hair. How strained he looked when I asked him to tell me what we're doing and he said, *I can't.*

Is it remotely possible we can't for the same reason?

As the tide creeps in, I dare to let hope do the same.

When we head back to the campsite, I remember what I wanted to ask Sienna. "By the way, did you go into my tent at all today?"

"Nope. You'll be so proud; I actually brought my own toothbrush this time! Why?"

Apprehension crowds my body. "No reason."

Just then we hear a raised, angry voice down by the bathrooms. Sienna and I exchange a look and pick up our pace, following the sound. We round the corner, and my stomach drops when I see Tanner Brown, his face a mask of fury, looming over Leti like he was waiting for them to be alone.

CHAPTER TWENTY-FIVE

Ethan

Senior Sunrise, 5:30 PM

I PULL ON MY hoodie and walk around, looking for Natalia. I don't see her, but I do see Rainn on the periphery of some football players and Janelle holding court. They're all laughing and darting glances over their shoulders.

Oh no.

As I get closer, the laughter becomes more unsettling, a taunting and ugly sound that I remember all too well from middle school. I really don't want to know what, or more likely *who*, they're laughing at.

I hover, considering my options, when Janelle's voice floats over toward me. She's holding something in her hands and reciting from it. "'If I were braver, I would have *begged* you to stay that night.'"

And I go cold. Ice fucking cold. No. *No.*

"'Because you have no idea how much I wanted you.'"

Fuuuuuuck.

Janelle lowers the letter, *my* letter, her eyes wide. "Oh my god!" she exclaims. "It's totally about sex!"

Holy fuck, kill me dead.

My heart is a hammering, angry fist punching me from the inside. How is it possible that out of the seven letters lost today, mine was found by Janelle fucking Johnson? *I should ask Sienna the odds*, I think, a hysterical laugh building in my throat.

"Not necessarily," Rainn says philosophically. "Just because it talks about staying the night? That could mean literally anything."

Janelle scoffs. "That's only the beginning. 'Never in my wildest dreams did I ever think you'd be topless in my bed.'"

The group hollers again. I might actually puke. Rainn gestures for it, holding his palm out. Then I'm forced to watch in helpless horror as Janelle, with a gleeful *See for yourself* expression, offers the paper to the person who has already kicked my ass once today.

I want to lunge for it and rip it out of her hands, crumple it, burn it, anything to get half the senior class from hearing the rest. But I can't because everyone will know it's mine if I do.

Rainn scans down the page, frowning. He reads aloud, "'I only barely know what it's like to have you in my arms . . . to lie next to you like that and think you might want me, too.'" His eyebrows spring up. "Damn."

The group whoops and laughs.

"We should stop, it's obviously private," Rainn says, looking worried.

If I could move or speak or do *anything*, I'd throw my arms around him in gratitude. But as it is, I can't. I'm frozen staring at them, willing my body to react, willing my words to come. They don't. Now of all times, I need to be Prom King Guy. Charming and dismissive and aloof.

But, of course, that guy doesn't exist. He never did. And so, my slow-ass brain is all I'm left with. I completely disassociate.

I think about how the eighteenth century was known as the "Great Age of Letter Writing" and that some people would use cryptography to code their letters so this exact fucking thing wouldn't happen. So that their secret, private thoughts couldn't be dismembered and put on display by bored assholes with nothing better to do.

So that no one but the person it was intended for would be able to decipher their heart on a crumpled piece of notebook paper.

So that if they got too scared to send it, it could never be used against them.

Janelle reads over Rainn's shoulder. "'I couldn't finally have you in my arms to only lose you again in the next breath. Because I know now what I was only piecing together then. It would change everything for me. It already has.' Oh my god, this is so cringe. We *have* to find out who wrote this," she says, her voice giddy.

Claire's voice chimes in. Her eyes are locked on me when she says, "I know who wrote it."

CHAPTER TWENTY-SIX

Natalia

Senior Sunrise, 5:30 PM

"I HEARD ABOUT WHAT you did to my boy Jackson," Tanner says, staring down at Leti.

Leti doesn't even flinch.

"Did you also hear that 'your boy' is a wanted sex offender?" they ask wryly.

"That's a fucking lie." Tanner crowds Leti's space further.

"Oh my god," Sienna gasps.

I look around for Ethan or Rainn. Some backup in case we need it, but I don't see them. The bathrooms are a short walk from the campsite, partially obscured by a long line of oak trees. We're on our own.

Leti may not like me, but I don't even think twice. I won't let them face this douchebag alone. Sienna and I run over and stand beside them.

"Leave them alone, Tanner," I say.

He glares, and it takes a second for his eyes to focus on me.

"You mean *her.* Leave *her* alone. She's the same Letícia she's always been. A butchy haircut doesn't change that."

Fury pulses through me. Leti laughs, but I can hear the edge to it. The armor that it is. That it has to be.

"You are so small-minded, bro," they say, shaking their head.

"You're a bitch," he says, his nostrils flaring.

"*Hey!*" Sienna exclaims.

"And proud," Leti says, shrugging.

Leti hasn't even taken their hands out of their pockets. Their letter was right. They're brave every freaking minute. I don't know how they're staying so calm when my own temper is flaring. I hold up my hands, and they're shaking.

"Tanner? Go back to your tent."

He rolls his eyes.

I shake my head, my breath coming faster. "C'mon, let's go talk to Ms. Mercer," I say to Leti and Sienna.

"*No.*" Tanner steps closer to me like I hoped he would, and that's when I smell the booze on his breath. *Gotcha.*

"She's not going anywhere," Tanner snarls.

A chill cracks down my spine, forcing my posture straighter. "Back away now, and I won't tell the teachers you've been drinking all day." It goes against every fiber of my being to break such a big rule, but I'll do it to keep my friends safe.

He rolls his eyes again. "Psh, my parents just bought Liberty an Olympic-size pool. I'm *goooood*." He drops me a pitying gaze. "I know that's not something you understand."

My god I can't believe I *ever* dated this guy.

Sienna pulls on my arm, but I shake her off. My pulse is frenzied, my lip quivering. I keep my eyes hard on Tanner's when I say, "Thank you."

His smirk falters.

"Thank you for helping me understand that no matter how good the education, some people are doomed to be ignorant. You're such a lost cause, I bet your parents change the subject when their friends ask about you."

Sienna bursts out laughing.

"What did you say to me—" He lunges for me and grips my arm.

"*Get off her!*" Sienna yells. It catches the attention of a group of girls from our soccer team who are walking by. I hear their fast footsteps as they run toward us.

"Tanner, seriously—let go of me!" I exclaim. I try to shake him off, but he's too strong. He digs his fingers deeper into the soft flesh of my arm, hard enough to bruise.

The group of furious girls fast approaches, but before they reach us, a skinny arm crosses my vision as it cracks a fist into Tanner's jaw.

"Get away from them!" Prashant yells.

Everyone gasps.

Tanner staggers back, clutching his jaw. He lets out a garbled "Whah thwa *fwuk*?"

"*Prashant?*"

Prashant pulls a whistle out of his shirt and starts blowing it until Mr. Beckett runs over, a novel in his hand.

"What's going on?" he pants.

"Tanner's bleeding," Prashant says evenly.

"And drunk," I add.

The soccer team is gaping at their president and vice president with thrilled, shocked expressions on their faces.

Mr. Beckett looks around this strange group and lets out the longest, most disappointed sigh I've ever heard.

"Tanner, this is strike three. You know what that means. Come on, let's get you some ice and call your parents. I feel as though you've taken advantage of my leniency today . . ." He starts lecturing Tanner as they walk to the parking lot.

My pulse hasn't calmed down. Sienna folds Leti into a hug. The soccer girls pat Prashant on the back and cackle at seeing Tanner get taken down like that. Then Mason Hartman comes strolling out of the bathroom and takes in the scene. Prashant still clutching his hand. Leti on the verge of tears. Half the girls' soccer team plotting Tanner's demise.

"Dude, what happened?"

We fill him in quickly about Tanner's gender-phobic comments, and Mason looks homicidal. He's all quarterback when he grabs Prashant's hand and inspects it with his athletic eye.

"Not broken, but you need ice," he concludes. "I'll go grab some."

Prashant nods, a rare flush to his cheeks.

Mason takes off with the soccer girls, and now with Tanner gone, too, Leti is visibly upset. Their eyes are red when they say, "Thanks, y'all. Just . . . thanks."

"I don't think I did anything but make it worse," I say. "I'm sorry he said those awful things."

Leti shrugs. "Used to it."

"You shouldn't have to be," I counter.

They try a smile, but it's wobbly.

"Do you . . . want a hug?" Prashant asks warily.

Leti laughs and hits him on the arm. "Nah. Killer right hook, though."

I turn to Prashant, my eyes wide. "Seriously. You just punched Tanner Brown."

"You were in trouble," he says.

The small smile slips from my face because suddenly I want to cry. I slam my arms around my vice president. He stays stock-still, arms at his sides while I hold him in a grip of gratitude.

"Ow. You done yet?"

I shake my head against his chest.

He lets me hug him a few seconds longer, then I take a step back.

"Thanks for having my back today."

He nods once and adjusts his glasses. "Well, when I'm president, I'm sure you'll do the same for me," he says, smiling a little.

I roll my eyes.

Sienna loops a comforting arm around Leti, and the silliness bleeds away. This could've been so much worse. If we all hadn't shown up when we did, Leti could've gotten hurt. And it would've been all my fault.

It's time to come clean before anything else happens.

Mason runs up with the ice then, one of the soccer players laughing with him about how entertaining Senior Sunrise has turned out to be.

"First the Jackson Ford thing, then Prashant Shukla punches Tanner Brown, now the drama with the sex letter," she says, laughing again.

My stomach fills with dread.

"Sex letter?" I squeak out.

She nods with her chin toward the eucalyptus grove. "Janelle's reading it now over there."

I jog up the small hill and sure enough, there's a group gathered on the other side of the campsite, but all I see is Ethan standing in the center of it, white as a ghost.

I run.

CHAPTER TWENTY-SEVEN

Ethan

Senior Sunrise, 5:33 PM

CLAIRE FLICKS ANOTHER QUICK gaze my way. Her expression is hard and hurt—she's prepared to burn it all down. I don't know how, maybe she recognizes my handwriting, or she can read the panic on my face, but she knows it's mine.

She's obviously upset with me for the way I ended things, but she wouldn't really do this. Would she? No one is that cruel. Time stretches as I plead with her silently.

She makes a decision and locks her eyes on mine as she says, "It's Ethan's."

I think there's a massive, rumbling reaction, but I can't be sure through my tunneling vision and the pounding in my ears.

Rainn's voice. "*What?*" He whirls on his heel to face Claire. "How do you know that?"

Her face gets pink. "Look at him."

And they do. Every single pair of eyes settles on me. Everything I've ever feared is true: We are all one fragile confession away from getting cracked open.

Rainn's eyes narrow at Claire. "What is wrong with you?"

"Don't get mad at *me*. It's obviously about Natalia."

Oh, this is just getting better and better. There's a low murmur in the crowd. Everyone around us might as well be reaching for popcorn.

Rainn's expression falls as he slowly puts it together and turns back to me. "Is that true?"

My words clog in my throat.

But I guess it's obvious that it's true, because Rainn shakes his head slowly. "You told me nothing ever happened—"

Breathing is too difficult to speak coherently. "It didn't—we hadn't—"

A football bro mutters in a high, affected girly voice, "'I would have begged you to stay.'"

"*Pussy*," another coughs into his fist.

They laugh. A *lot* of them laugh. And like Rainn's punches earlier, I absorb it with a clenched jaw. The bruises will form later.

Rainn glares at them, and they shut up. The command he has that I don't, the same my brother did. The same thing every dude who's never poured his ardent heart into a letter has.

He takes a giant step toward me. He holds the letter up, and I want to snatch it back and squeeze it so hard in my sweaty palm it'll dissolve the ink. But I keep my hands balled into fists at my sides, my breath coming too fast.

"Were you going to give this to her?" Rainn asks.

My brain finally kicks back online as the miserable, lonely kid who was thrown against lockers launches into survival mode. Also known as sarcasm. "Yes, that was exactly my plan for this anonymous, private exercise."

He stares at me hard, but there isn't really malice in it. It seems more like . . . frustration. Confusion. Disappointment?

I hear her before I see her.

"What's going on?" Natalia pants behind me, as if she just sprinted over here.

Some in the group gasp, others make a collective *ooooooh* again.

I can't make myself look at her, but I can imagine that her face is that practiced cool, with a small fake smile that doesn't reach her eyes.

This is bad. Like, really fucking bad. It's not just that she could read my pathetic letter and that half the class now knows she was *topless in my bed*. God.

It's that we didn't get ahead of this. She didn't admit to what she did in time and now everything is out of control. When things get too chaotic, Natalia runs away.

I can't let that happen. Not when we're so close to figuring out this thing between us.

Rainn looks at me another few torturous seconds, then slowly slides his gaze to Natalia. "This is for you."

My mouth falls open. Wow. I guess at this point I shouldn't be surprised that Rainn wouldn't even think about having my back, but I am. And it sucks.

"What is it?" she asks, staring at the yellow paper, knowing exactly what it is.

Someone else cough-says "*sex letter*," and half the group laughs.

"It's nothing," I say, my voice hollow and weird.

"It's definitely something," Rainn says, shooting me an exasperated look.

"Just—give it back—please," I splutter.

"I can't do that, dude. She needs to read this."

Why is he doing this to me? Does he hate me that much now? Natalia looks back and forth between us.

"Give it to me," she says, her eyes laser-focused on Rainn. She's using the same uncompromising, stubborn-ass tone she used on me when she wanted to see my bruises. Rainn knows that tone, too, and offers it to her without hesitation.

She reaches for the letter. The sad, wrinkled paper that holds the kind of soul-baring words only poets and guys with tattoos can get away with. I'm neither of those things and Natalia knows it. I'm a loser with an aching heart and nothing to offer her but humiliation at the hands of our entire senior class. She can't read that letter.

I step forward, and I gently grab her arm. I plead with my expression, *Don't*.

She tells me something, too. *I never would.*

Our own cryptography.

She grabs the paper out of Rainn's hand and doesn't even look at it before she folds it and hands it to me. Relief floods through my entire system.

Prashant walks up then, a large, dripping bag of ice on his hand. Small dots of water darken the dirt beside his feet. What the hell happened there?

Natalia shakes her head slowly, barely contained rage rippling off her in waves. She turns to face the group. "The Lion Letters are *private*."

That's when I notice the *Gotcha* look between Janelle and Claire. This was a setup.

Before I find my voice, Claire says, "If they're so private, why was Ethan's letter in your tent?"

"What?" Prashant exclaims. His expression is as shocked as I feel. My pulse roars in my ears.

Natalia's eyes are wide and red, mascara smudged under her lids. She presses a hand to her chest and takes a step toward me. "I didn't know—it must've fallen out when we were putting them back in the jar—"

Gasps from the crowd.

"Wait, you *both* stole them?" Claire asks, looking genuinely surprised.

I take a step forward. "Yes—"

Natalia steps in front of me, her back ramrod straight. "No. Ethan didn't do anything."

Only I can see her hands clasped so tight they're drained of all color. Natalia, the most private person I know, who is terrified to be seen as anything but controlled and together, is admitting her mistake in front of the entire class.

For me.

"It's my fault. Everything is my fault," she continues. Her voice comes out shaky. "I didn't steal them. It was an accident. I—the wind scattered them. I didn't mean to. I was going to tell all of you, but I wanted to find as many as I could first—"

Panic rises in the group.

"You *lost* them?" Mason asks, his voice spiking with anxiety. He pushes an agitated hand in his hair.

"Only a few," she says weakly.

"She's lying. She obviously dug Ethan's letter out because she wanted to know what it said," Claire says.

"*No*—"

"Yeah right," Janelle scoffs, rolling her eyes.

"I swear," Natalia says only to me.

"I believe you," I say immediately.

And I do. I've seen all sides of Natalia today. Stressed, squirrelly, controlling. Also, the loyal, respectful, and trustworthy parts, too. If she says she didn't, she didn't. She holds my gaze a moment, her eyes softening.

She turns back to Janelle. "I would never do what you just did." Her voice is low and shaking with anger now.

Janelle laughs, cold and sharp. "Oh my god. You literally stole our letters and you're still acting like you're better than everyone."

Natalia's face goes red. "I didn't steal them. And I'm not— I don't think I'm better than *anyone*," she says quietly. "But no matter what I did, you shouldn't have read Ethan's or Leti's letter out loud."

Janelle slides me a pitying look. "Yours *was* pretty pathetic. And surprisingly smutty, *Prom King*."

She says "prom king" ironically now. A lot of them laugh then, catching up to what I've always known. I hate that it makes my eyes hot. But you can't fight or flee yourself, so I just stand there like the loser I've always been.

Natalia's shoulders stiffen, but she smiles at Janelle. Sniper smile. "Would you want to read yours, then? I'd love to hear your confession. Maybe it's wishing you weren't so lazy, considering how smart you are? Or maybe it's wishing you were kinder, so you could actually change the boring-ass narrative about popular mean girls? For someone so pretty, you have the ugliest personality."

The group *ooooooh*s and Janelle's cheeks flame in response.

I allow myself to think this will all be okay for exactly four seconds before Claire steps forward.

"She's obviously lying! If it was actually an accident, you would've told us. But you chose to hide it. Why?"

"Because I was scared this was how everyone would react," Natalia says.

A few people exchange glances of sympathy, but mostly the faces in the crowd are angry, hurt, or panicked.

Claire rolls her eyes. "Or you're *still* lying because you totally read them and are going to use our secrets as blackmail. We all know you need the money."

Natalia looks like she's been slapped. I'm not sure what's louder, the thundering blood in my veins or the deathly silence that falls over the group.

Claire blinks several times, her cheeks popping pink. "I just meant—"

That's when I find my voice. "We all know what you meant," I growl. "Obviously, that's what *you* would do. But Natalia would never. She has done nothing but take care of our class."

"Yeah, she's been a killer president," Mason chimes in. "I vote for her every year. I know I never have to worry about school shit because Natalia takes care of it. Everyone fucks up sometimes, Claire."

The tip of Natalia's nose turns red like it does before she cries. She bites her lip and shoots Mason a small smile.

"So, *what*?" Claire exclaims. "Because she's the president she's allowed to do whatever she wants without any consequences? That's an abuse of power!"

"You would know." It's Sara Lui from the theater crowd. "We all know you and Mr. Ford hooked up, Claire. He totally abused his power."

I notice several people nodding.

Claire's mouth falls open. "You have no idea what you're talking about."

Sara keeps going. "That's why you got cast as Sophie over me in *Mamma Mia!* How could you do that for a part?"

Claire looks like she might cry and gets cut off by Janelle. "Hold up, let's at least refrain from slut-shaming."

"Says the bitch reading the sex letter," someone else says.

The crowd murmurs their agreement, but Janelle just rolls her eyes.

Claire spins around to look at everyone, her eyes wild. "People, focus! All of this personal shit got out because *Natalia* messed with the letters!" She has an arm outstretched pointing directly in Natalia's face.

The group goes quiet as the blame lands again at Natalia's feet.

"I— I didn't mean to—" Natalia starts.

"But you *did*. Those letters were supposed to be private, and—" Claire shakes her head. She's red-faced and glassy-eyed when she says, "I don't trust you as our president anymore. I'm calling for an impeachment, effective immediately."

Color drains from Natalia's face.

"Who's with me?" Claire asks the group.

Almost everyone raises their hand. Everyone but me, Rainn, Sienna, Leti, Prashant, and Mason. It's a devastating blow.

Prashant steps forward. "Okay, this is not how it works at all," he says. "First of all, you don't have the authority to impeach."

Claire's face goes sour.

"But"—he fans his non-iced hand out toward the raised hands— "you do have the numbers to support a formal consideration of impeachment by student council. Is that how you would like to proceed?"

Claire nods, the gleam in her eyes shining.

Prashant sighs. "Then I, as vice president, must now take it to student council for a vote on the first day of school. If it passes there, we'll conduct a reelection for the position the first week of school. And in the meantime"—he shoots a pained look at Natalia—"I will act as interim president."

Natalia takes a staggered step back. "Seriously, Prashant?"

He shrugs, though he does have the decency to look like he feels bad. "It's protocol, Natalia. We're a democracy."

Natalia's chin quivers, but she doesn't argue. The integrity of the position matters to her as much as anything.

Our eyes catch. Remorse laces every feature of her beautiful face. This ugly moment all around us, happening to us, and *still* my heart expands looking at her. And that's when I know. I hate this school; I hate most of these people.

But I am so fucking in love with *her*.

CHAPTER TWENTY-EIGHT

Natalia

Senior Sunrise, 6:45 PM

I'VE BEEN UNSEATED. OR I will be if student council votes in favor of almost the entire senior class. The only thing I've had to distinguish myself at Liberty is now over. I make one mistake in four years and it's enough to erase every good thing I've done.

In my mind, I'm wrist-deep in the paint, scooping it into my cupped hands as if from a stream. With sharp swinging movements, I'm flinging it as hard and fast as I can against the wall of canvas. Over and over and over the colors splatter and collide with one another. The paint crawls higher up my arms until I'm elbow- then shoulder-deep. Raining paint. Thundering. A torrent of color until it becomes nothing but mess.

Nothing but disaster.

I keep waiting for the panic to crash through me again, but I'm only numb. And I have a best friend to check on.

I approach Ethan now that the larger group of jerks has scattered to eat dinner before the bonfire. "Want to talk?"

He shakes his head, not meeting my eyes. "I think I need a minute," he says, shoving his hands in his pockets and walking away.

I watch him go, wishing I could hit reset on this whole freaking day. I wouldn't blame him if he hated me forever for what just happened. I'll probably hate me forever.

Rainn and Sienna approach me then. Rainn's eyes are full of frustration. Sienna and I share a knowing look, and she silently urges me to tell Rainn.

"I should've told you about the letters," I say to him. "I'm sorry."

"What were you doing with them?" he asks.

"I was just trying to get mine back."

"Why?"

I snap my gaze to his. "So that exact thing wouldn't happen, Rainn." My anger catches up to me. One of the soccer players filled me in that Rainn read part of Ethan's letter, too. *Out loud.* "So that no one would ever have the chance to do to me what you just did to Ethan."

Now I kind of understand why Mom gets so intense when she's mad. If you don't hear the words, at least you hear the tone. And my tone is knife-at-your-throat hostile.

"How could you do that?" I ask him.

My entire being is on fire with the need for him to find a way to explain it—how he could hurt his best friend like that. Please let him say something, *anything* that could possibly excuse what I did to Ethan.

He shakes his head. "I was trying to get Janelle to give it to me so I could figure out who it belonged to. After the obstacle course it was obvious you and Ethan had something to do with the letters getting out. I was trying to help."

My heart softens. "Oh."

"But I still read it out loud," he says miserably. "He's gonna hate me now. I screwed up."

No, *I* screwed up. My anger twists inward, and my words come out accusatory instead of apologetic. "We all know what he's been through with the bullying shit."

He juts his jaw forward. "Jesus, Natalia, I said I was sorry!"

"No, you didn't."

Sienna watches us shoot back and forth like a tennis match.

"Oh," Rainn says, frowning. "Well. Shit, I'm not the one who let them out! Why are you getting so mad at *me*?"

Sienna elbows Rainn, but he's right. I'm not being remotely fair.

I release a breath and wrap my arms around my middle. "Exactly! It's my fault. I'm not mad at you," I say, unable to meet his eyes. "I'm mad at *me*."

The eucalyptus trees shiver in the breeze, and we all take a long pause before Rainn says, "Maybe it's not the worst thing that I read it."

He and Sienna share a quick look that I can't identify. I scoff, remembering the mortification on Ethan's face.

Rainn's tone softens. "Don't you want to know what it said?"

Everyone is calling it the *sex letter*—of course I want to know what it said. I hate that Rainn knows, that freaking Janelle Johnson knows, and I don't.

"If Ethan wanted me to know, he would've given it to me," I say, trying to hold on to my resolve.

It's Rainn's turn to scoff. "It takes that guy fifteen minutes to order a sandwich; he has no idea what he's doing. Especially with you." There's rough affection in his tone and it melts some of my anger away.

It really does take Ethan freaking decades to make a decision. It's one of the sweetest and most infuriating things about him.

Rainn and I share a quick glance, and I realize that even though we're in awkward territory, we're quickly falling back into the rhythm of friendship. The flirting thing between us is as easy to shed as a cardigan.

A couple of guys walk by us snickering, and it's obvious they're talking about Ethan and us and this whole mess.

I glare at them, then look at Rainn and Sienna and say, "I need to fix this."

"How?" Rainn asks.

I shake my head. I have no clue. But I refuse to let Ethan be the butt of the joke again. I will not let him be the center of a scandal at school the way he was when his dad's career took off or when Adam went to rehab. He hates the spotlight he's been under because of his dad. It's only one more year, and he may say he's "fine," but I know better. No one whose privacy is violated like that would be fine. Leti isn't. Claire isn't. I wouldn't be.

I hurt them as much as Janelle did. It's up to me to solve this.

"We could do what you said back there and steal Janelle's letter? Read it aloud?" Rainn suggests, dead serious.

"I said that in, like, a hypothetical vengeance way. We can't actually do that." As tempting as it is . . .

"Janelle went too far this time. People obviously felt awful for him," Sienna says. Her expression turns thoughtful. "Wait. I have an idea. You check on Ethan and make sure he's okay, and Rainn and I will take care of it."

I look between them. Rainn nods.

"No, I should fix this—"

Sienna cuts me off. "He's our friend, too, Natalia. Let us help."

My eyes burn again, and I hug my friends. "Thank you."

We agree to regroup later, and they walk away while Sienna excitedly fills Rainn in on her plan.

Before I can start looking for Ethan, Prashant approaches with his hands shoved in the front pocket of his sweatshirt. The temperature is dropping now that the sun is starting to dip.

Prashant eyes me warily, his voice careful when he says, "We, um, have to set up the s'mores and songs station for the fireside chat tonight."

"You can't do it yourself?" I ask.

"It's opening boxes and pouring out marshmallows, of course I can," Prashant says flatly. "But that is literally the first time you've ever suggested I was capable of such a thing."

I plaster on a smile. "Well, as the interim, it's probably time for you to actually do something on your own besides stab me in the back," I say, sarcasm lacing my words.

He gives me a long look. "You seriously expected me to go down with your ship?"

I can't meet his eyes. Maybe that's exactly what I expected. Especially after he punched a guy for me.

"I shouldn't have expected your loyalty," I say, attempting neutrality and missing by a mile.

He narrows his eyes. "I *am* being loyal. To the presidency, to the class, to the school. Do I personally think losing a few Lion Letters is an impeachable offense? No. I get that it was an accident. But Claire's not wrong, you had no right to mess with them. You're better than that. *We* have to be better than that."

Prashant gestures between the two of us, and there's a deeper meaning to his words. He doesn't just mean those of us on student council. As one of the few people of color at school, he knows all too well that the expectations are different for us. He's the only person at Liberty to ever acknowledge that side of me out loud. Even as shame burns my cheeks red, I want to hug him again.

His tone softens a little when he says, "You messed up, Natalia. You don't get to act like you didn't."

He walks away then, and I stand there stunned for a moment. Of all the people I've let down today, this one cuts deep. There's so much more to Prashant than I ever gave him credit for.

How could I do this?

I've let the stress and pressure I feel back me into corners until I see no way out. But I'm starting to wonder if I mostly do it to myself. Even though my parents expect a lot of me, I've grown to expect more. To head off even a whiff of their disappointment with preemptive perfection. To keep anyone from getting to know the real me. Because unless I'm perfect, I don't like the real me.

But if Sienna's right and nothing is perfect—not even math—then what hope do I have?

I trudge across the campsite to try to find Ethan. He doesn't deserve anything that's happened to him today, and it's all happened because of me. When I cross through the eucalyptus trees, I see blue-streaked hair. My insides start burning all over again.

Claire hears my footsteps and shoots me a furious look. Her eyes are red-rimmed like she's been crying. She walks past me, picking up her pace.

I follow her. Without thinking, I call out, "How could you do that to Ethan?"

"Leave me alone, Natalia," she says, her voice tinged with warning.

"I know I screwed up, and I'm sorry, okay? But—"

Claire stops so suddenly I crash into her back. She spins to face me, her eyes flashing. "You must be joking," she says, laughing. "I've had, like, the *shittiest* day possible because of you, and you think I would accept your apology?"

I squeeze my eyes shut, my heart hammering. "No, I guess not—but

I *am* sorry. About the letters and everyone finding out about you and Mr. Ford."

She looks like she's going to cry again. "Everyone is being so judgmental."

I wince with remorse.

She goes on. "I'm not some victim or something, he's only four years older than me."

When I don't say anything, she narrows her eyes.

"What?"

"Only you get to say what happened to you," I say slowly, "but he *was* your teacher."

"He was my *director*. And I don't remotely care what you think."

My nostrils flare. "Okay, whatever. Hate me forever; I deserve it. But you already got your justice. I'm probably going to lose my presidency. So, from now on, leave Ethan out of it. He's been through enough."

"We all make mistakes, don't we?"

I get her meaning. She's saying what happened to Ethan is as much my fault as it is hers. And I hate that she's right.

"Besides, I didn't think Janelle would, like, humiliate him," she says.

Humiliate? My stomach turns over on itself. I don't want to ask her when I could've learned it from my friends, but now I'm so hungry to know, it's a sharp craving on my tongue. "What did the letter say?"

Claire tries and fails to cover her delight when she asks, "He didn't tell you?"

"No."

When her eyebrows shoot up like *That's interesting,* I rush to say, "Not yet."

She looks around and knots her fingers together. "Well, basically, that he feels really bad for breaking your pact and—"

I put up a hand to stop her. "Wait. What do you mean he broke it?"

Because he wouldn't go through with it? Or because he's no longer a virgin? Oh my god, is that why everyone's calling it the "sex letter"?

I stare at Claire, and she's blushing.

Wait. Did he and Claire . . . ? Is *that* what Ethan has been keeping from me all day? My throat constricts. It's not the virginity thing. But thinking of Ethan with anyone else like that—with Claire like that—is a fist around my windpipe.

Claire is watching me very closely. "I don't usually kiss and tell, but . . ." She arches a suggestive eyebrow and shrugs coyly. There's my answer. He really had sex this summer. With *Claire*.

My heart—oh god, my heart.

Now I finally know that the way he looked at me that night, the way his featherlight touch traced my collarbone, my neck, the curves of my hips was nothing. That the way his voice came out husky and jagged when he said my name in the moonlight was nothing. That the way our breath and hands shook meant *nothing*.

Ethan called it stupid that night and no wonder. It was all in my head. Just like the paintings I'll never make and the future I'll never have.

Of course it was Claire. Their worlds are the same. She's exactly the kind of girl Mr. Forrester would want for Ethan. She says what she means, goes for what she wants. Has money. They live on the same freaking street. Their worlds couldn't be more compatible.

She doesn't need a pact to do things that scare her.

No one does but me.

Stupid. I'm so, so stupid.

The corner of her mouth curls up slightly. "He was too scared to tell you all this, but there shouldn't be secrets between friends."

Without another word, I walk off.

The sky is fading to pink, the beginning of a gorgeous sunset. When I return to the campsite, a small fire is growing in the firepit.

The scent of it is filling the air with memories. So many trips with my parents when the woodsmoke clung to my hair, my clothes, as if stuck to every layer of my skin. Trips I'll never take with them again. Memories that are dead and gray just like the ash under the flames. How long have they been unhappy? How much of my childhood were they faking it?

How much of my life is a lie?

Sienna shoots me a thumbs-up then and nods toward the farthest point of the campsite. I follow her gaze, and my breath chokes.

Ethan, eyes on the ground, sitting by himself on a bench that overlooks the water. It's such a stark contrast to the start of the day when everyone couldn't get enough of their prom king. These people.

But I can't make myself go over to him. I don't want to say something I'll regret. Or not be able to say anything at all. He's free to do what he wants. He's never owed me anything. But I can't be around him when I feel this deeply for him.

Why am I even thinking of staying at Liberty when I could leave, cut it and all these people out forever? I'd get a *real* do-over instead of just a symbolic one. At a new school where no one knows me. Where Ethan *isn't*. Where I don't have to face this every day. Where losing my presidency, losing him, doesn't follow me.

I make sure the teachers are occupied, then I walk over to the box of phones. Huddling behind the table where no one can see me, I dig mine out and turn it on. Within a minute, it lights up with too many notifications to count. I ignore them all and, heart pounding, I send a quick text to my mom.

I want to come with you to Sacramento.

I slam my eyes closed and let out a long exhale, pushing the panic away. My phone buzzes. I expect it to be a response from my mom, but it's a notification, a headline from a gossip site.

I read it once. Twice. Look at the photos. Oh *no*.

Despite all the reasons not to, I run toward Ethan one last time.

CHAPTER TWENTY-NINE

Ethan

Senior Sunrise, 7:30 PM

THE CAMPFIRE IS STARTING soon, but I'm not ready to face everyone yet. I'm sitting on the bench at the overlook, head leaned back, eyes closed.

I love her. Holy shit, I *love* her.

What if she doesn't feel the same way? And she just might've lost her presidency because of Claire. Because of *me*.

I don't care what any of these dickholes think of me. But I do care what Natalia thinks. I always have.

Yet I stood there, pathetic and frozen and weak. I didn't stick up for myself, and I hardly stuck up for her. I didn't defend the letter with the same confidence I felt writing it. I didn't hit Rainn or confront Claire when it mattered. *I let it all happen.* Like how I let bad things happen to the people I love.

First my mom, now Natalia.

Fast, crunching footsteps and then a presence at my side. I don't have to open my eyes to know she's standing next to the bench, hesitant. Watching me. My heart begins to pound.

Without opening my eyes, I say, "Did you know about twenty percent of students between ages twelve and eighteen experience bullying?"

Her feet scrape across the dirt, and I feel the warmth of her as she perches beside me on the cold bench. Delicate, like the whole thing might break. Like *we* might break.

"That sounds way too low, honestly," she says. "Are you okay?"

I could lie, but I don't. "Not really." I open my eyes and look at her. "You?"

She shakes her head. "Ethan . . ." Her voice quivers. But she doesn't say anything else and pulls out her phone.

My eyebrows spring up in shock. "*You* stole your phone back?"

"*Borrowed*. And, um, I— I got an alert from that gossip site."

Her eyes are planet-wide. Nervous. Then the dread hits me deep in the stomach because it's got to be about Dad.

"I won't show you if you don't want to see it right now. But I don't want to keep any more secrets from you."

I take a steadying breath and hold out my hand. With a look like she swallowed a slug, she gives me the phone. I can actively feel the blood draining from my face as I read the headline:

CAUGHT! ROGER FORRESTER AND COSTAR SOFÍA SANCHEZ SMOOCHING IN SOHO

I read it again. And again.

Nausea climbs up my throat while I read the article that cites several "sources" saying the *love affair*—cool way of saying *adultery*—started on the set of the movie they filmed in Italy. There's no comment from either camp. I read it all, every nerve deadening.

I swipe through the photos. Dad in a button-down shirt that *Mom* gave him for his birthday last year, arms wrapped around a woman barely older than Adam. They're kissing in broad daylight on a busy New York City sidewalk where they're on location for the show. The photos are grainy, but there's no denying it's him.

So that's done, then. Hollywood cliché transformation complete.

I guess . . . this is why Dad was calling me all morning. To warn me the story was going to break.

Or, more likely he wanted to know if I was the one who leaked it. If only. It's not like I hadn't thought about it the past few months. But I could never do that to Mom.

God, *Mom*. She's barely survived my dad leaving, but at least she didn't know about the affair. Now she does. Everyone does.

And what about Adam? A jolt of panic goes through me. Will it set him back? Will he start using again? I should use Natalia's phone to call him. Check in.

But I don't move. I can't. I live on this bench now.

"What's the point of having a new mommy if she's not even old enough to buy you beer?" I say, trying to make a joke. It falls so pancake-flat at my feet I wish I were tumbling off this bluff with the eucalyptus leaves. I guess I might be in shock.

"I'm so sorry," Natalia says.

I bury my face in my hands. She puts a soothing hand on my arm, and it feels good, comforting. For some reason, it also annoys the hell out of me.

"Hey. Talk to me," she urges.

"Now you want to talk?" My tone is hostile even to my ears. "You had all summer to talk to me! When all this was actually happening. When I was *alone* with it."

She nods, chastened. "I know."

All the bitterness I've pushed down for months and maybe even years is seeping from every scabbed wound that never healed right. My brother abandoning me for pills, my mom disappearing into her work, my dad caring more about himself than anyone. The bullying that didn't stop until family-ruining fame tumbled into my life and demolished it.

"I'm sorry," she says again.

"Stop saying that."

"Why?"

"Because it's not your fault. It's *mine!*" My voice echoes like a thunderclap.

Natalia's touch is soft, but her voice is firm when she says, "There is no way any of this is your fault."

I don't know if we're talking about this thing with my dad or us. But it doesn't matter. "I told you, I've known about the affair for a while."

"Still doesn't make it your fault," she says, steady.

She doesn't get it. I need to tell her the rest so she understands just how fucked up my family is. How fucked up *I* am.

Because when I caught my dad texting with Sofía after his trip, he asked me not to tell my mom. And I agreed.

I agreed.

I agreed.

Dad told me it was nothing. Then that it was something, but he was ending it. But a month later, instead of ending things with *her*, he ended things with us.

I'd like to think if prom night hadn't happened, Natalia and I would've been talking all summer and I would've told her by now. But I'm not sure that's true.

I'm guilty by association for the part I played in betraying Mom.

Every day for the past seventy-six days since, I am more convinced that all Forrester men are selfish and messed up.

Because if a man who used to read to me for hours, who never once rushed me through my favorite place on earth (the Space and Science Museum), who taught me how to play basketball and bought me my first gaming PC and has never once failed to tell me how much he loves me . . . If that man can become a stranger—can shift so dramatically from someone I admire to someone I loathe and am deeply disgusted by—what hope is there for me? I look just like him . . . What if I become just like him?

"I kept the whole thing a secret for a long time. When I couldn't take it anymore, I told him he had to tell my mom, or I would. The next day he moved out."

I pause, hoping the confession will make me feel better, but saying it out loud just makes me want to puke. If I hadn't given him the ultimatum, would he have stayed? Would he have ended the affair like he said he was going to? Would he and Mom have worked it out?

How could he do that to Mom? How could I?

"I couldn't tell my mom after that. She was a fucking wreck when he left. He would've stayed if I hadn't forced him out." I almost choke on the words. "He would've broken it off if I hadn't pushed him."

"*No*. You are the best kind of good. You should've never been put in that position in the first place. He's the one who cheated. He's the one who left. *Him*. Not you. Trust me, your dad is a fucking creep," Natalia says, voice shaking.

That stops me short. "What?"

Her eyes fly wide like she can't believe she just said that. "Sorry, um. I guess I'm just upset. For you. You didn't do anything wrong, and I'm so mad he did that to your family. To you."

I stare at my shoes. "That's the thing, Talia. I *did* do something wrong. I kept this huge secret from my mom, and I don't—" I swallow down the ache in my throat. "I don't even know why."

"I do," she says softly. "You were trying to protect her. You're really good at that. *Too* good at it."

I scoff. "What does that mean?"

"If I hadn't spoken up, you were going to let the class think you were the one who messed with the letters. Am I wrong?"

No. She's exactly right. I shake my head.

"You can't keep throwing yourself on the fire. All you'll do is burn."

My mind is swarming too fast to respond.

She scoots closer. "No matter how hard you try, you can't shield everyone from the pain that's meant for them."

My voice is rough when I say, "I don't do it for everyone. Just the people I—"

God, I almost say *love*. But I stop myself just in time. When our eyes lock, I want to grab her hand.

So I do. I thread my fingers with hers, gripping them hard, rubbing my thumb across the back of her hand. She looks down at them, now interlaced, and blinks several times.

"Ethan, I . . ." She trails off and slowly pulls her hand out of mine. *Oh.*

CHAPTER THIRTY

Natalia

Senior Sunrise, 7:43 PM

BEFORE THIS GOES ANY further with Ethan, I have to tell him about New Year's Eve. And Sacramento. I meant it when I said no more secrets.

But before I can say anything, he digs his heels into the ground and rockets off the bench. Surprised, I stand up, too.

He runs his fingers through his hair and finally looks at me.

If I had to draw his face with my eyes closed, I could. Easily. Every expression he's ever made. The curve of his top lip as it tilts into a smirk. The way one side of his nose lifts in a small snarl when he's rankled. His anger sharp between his eyebrows and joy brightening his eyes. I thought I'd seen them all. Until now.

This one, wide-eyed and stricken and hard around the eyes, but soft around the mouth is true hurt, sorrow.

It knocks me backward.

"Why do you keep doing this?" he asks.

I frown, genuinely confused. "Doing what?"

"Running from me."

The irony isn't lost on me that when he looks at me like that, all I want to do is literally run. As far and as fast as my track legs will carry me. Far down to the beach until my lungs are burning and my mind is no longer screaming.

But I don't. I keep my voice even when I say, "I'm not. I have nothing to run from."

The sky bears an explosive sunset behind him, making him glow golden as he crowds me. His piney scent mixes with the heavy salt air. My heart takes off on a gallop. Heat and hope building in my veins. I have to push it away. I have to stop. I'm leaving and I haven't told him. I have to tell him.

But then he rests his forehead on mine, and everything else falls away. "Then what is it?" he pushes. "Because you feel this, too. I know you do."

I inhale, overwhelmed. Why is this happening now? When we have no hope of being together? When I came over here to be his friend, then let him go?

The wind rustles against us, and he pushes a strand of my hair off my face. His eyes are tender and searching and open, like he knows there's a battle raging inside me right now.

"You can't say things like that," I say.

"Why not?" he asks. "Why do you keep pulling away?"

I can't answer him. I can't think straight when he's this close. My breath is coming faster and faster.

"I don't know," I breathe. "I only—" I stop.

"You only *what*?" he coaxes softly.

My heart is sprinting because his eyes are dark and beckoning. His chest is rising quickly against mine, and I reach for the truth inside me even though it'll shatter me to finally say it out loud. "I only ever want you closer," I near-whisper across his lips.

My eyes fall closed the second he crushes his mouth to mine.

CHAPTER THIRTY-ONE

Ethan

Senior Sunrise, 7:48 PM

THE KISS IS SAVAGE with urgency. Lips and teeth and moans. Hot breath and cool skin. My fingers disappear in the wild tangle of her hair as I pull her flush against me. Still, I want more, so much more. The delirious taste of her, the anchoring feel of her. Sunset on our skin, Natalia in my arms.

Finally.

I dip her chin with my thumb, deepening the kiss. She makes the same small sound that's already killed me once, and I devour it, starved for her. She clutches my shirt in response. Right on my bruises. I swallow the pain; I don't care. I won't let anything stop this. But when I pull her bottom lip between my teeth, she squeezes my sides again, harder, and I hiss against her mouth.

"Sorry!" She staggers back, chest heaving, flushed all over. She covers her mouth with the back of her hand.

"It's okay—holy—"

"Yeah," she breathes.

If prom night was fire, that kiss was an inferno. I shake my head, near laughing. I reach for her, desperate to get back to it, but she doesn't return my smile. She looks . . . terrified.

No.

"What's wrong?" I ask.

I expect her to say something like it's weird to kiss her best friend, or she doesn't want to do this at a school thing, but her glassy eyes meet mine and she says something impossible: "I'm moving. To Sacramento."

Everything skids to a stop. I shake my head, trying to keep up. "What? When?"

"I guess this week. My mom got a new job," she explains, wringing her hands together.

I blink, dazed.

She keeps talking. "I wasn't sure if I should go with her. But—after everything today I thought, okay, if I'm really going to be braver like our Lion Letters say, I should do the things that scare me."

That pulls my focus, and I let out a hollow laugh. "That's what your Lion Letter was about? Moving? God, I'm . . . *such* an idiot," I say, burying my face in my hands.

"No, it wasn't—what does that mean?"

She grabs my arm, but I turn and fling it off.

"Ethan, I didn't expect this to happen. I didn't know—please don't shut me out."

I spin on my heel, eyes blazing. "That's all you *ever* do to me."

Her tears spill over.

Damn it. The ocean breeze whips up to us on the overlook again, bringing the situation into focus. Somehow, we've gotten too good at pulverizing each other. I'm losing her. I'm really losing her.

"How could you not tell me?" I hate how broken I sound.

"I—I didn't know how."

She doesn't back away, but I'm braced for her to leave any second. That's what she does. It's what everyone in my life does. Not every problem can be solved. Not every broken thing can be fixed.

I shake my head slowly as my eyes fall closed. "Talia, I can't do this anymore."

She's silent. When I open my eyes, we look at each other a long time.

"Do what?" she asks, so quietly I almost miss it.

She's watching me, pale and scared and sorry. The girl I love and am so mad at right now I can't breathe. She's kept so much of herself from me. And now she's moving? Leaving. *Running*. The anger crashes against my longing and detonates.

"I can't watch you leave again. I just . . . *can't*."

I turn away. Even with my back to her, I can feel her practically vibrating with the need to fix everything broken between us. Within me. But it's too late for that.

It's too late for us.

Fire eventually turns to ash.

CHAPTER THIRTY-TWO

Natalia

Senior Sunrise, 7:52 PM

WE REALLY JUST KISSED. Like *that*. Not because of a pact or a dare or a game. But he kissed me like he wanted to. Like he couldn't *not*. And it was a new spectrum of colors I've never felt before. They were . . . otherworldly. Nothing has ever felt so right in my life.

But I panicked and ruined it, like I always do.

I can't watch you leave again.

The electricity between us evaporates in a snap. He turns his back to me, and it's obvious he's done with this. With me.

Watching him disappear inside himself, I know with sickening certainty that I played this *all* wrong. I should never have told him like this. Maybe never even done this. Why did I text my mom when I was so upset?

I let Claire get under my skin. I let what happened between them matter more than what is happening between us now.

My head is roaring with everything I need to tell him and ask him and explain to him. But the words are stuck like they always are. Because the fact remains that for all the secrets revealed today, mine is still buried deep.

I squeeze my eyes shut, trying to focus, to slow down the racing thoughts to give him the explanation he deserves. But it takes too long.

I run out of time when he says, "Just go."

His tone is flat, emotionless. Dismissive. He's never pushed me away like this before and that's how I know with gut-dropping clarity that of all the mistakes I've made today, not opening up to him was the worst.

Fresh tears heat my eyes, and I wrap myself around his back, pressing my cheek to his shoulder blades.

"Ethan—I'm so sorry," I whisper. "For . . . everything."

He doesn't respond. His body is rigid in my arms. I've never seen him like this, so wildly out of reach.

His voice is barely audible over the roar of the waves. "Talia. *Please*."

It's a plea for me to let go. Leave.

A tear does fall then, slipping down my nose and melting into his hoodie.

He's had enough. And I don't blame him. I drop my arms.

I ask if we can talk later, but he either doesn't hear me, or he ignores me.

I walk slowly back toward the campsite, tears streaming down my cheeks, my brain on fire with the need to understand what just happened. That fight, that *kiss*. We've crossed a new line. The pact was one thing, but this . . . What does this mean?

Ethan sees me more clearly than anyone else. Everything shines in shocking blues and vivid pinks when I think of him. When we touch, they shift into warm, golden tones and comforting forest greens. When we're apart, color drains and becomes hazy.

Then why have I been so closed off to him?

A chasm of loneliness opened inside me on that dark drive home on prom night thinking he didn't want me. Just when my heart was softening, when I thought he was going to kiss me again, he stopped.

Talia . . . I—I don't think I—this is stupid. I don't—with you—not like this.

That word echoed through me. "Stupid." The word he started using constantly after the popular crowd paid attention to him. The way my anxiety makes me feel. The way I *never* want to feel. Always controlled, measured, prepared. Never stupid.

When he said it, I immediately felt like I had done something shameful. That I had tricked him into touching me. Into wanting me. Using the pact as pathetic armor against all of my feelings.

I lured him to me, and he regretted it instantly. I did exactly what his dad said I would.

He staggered as I pushed him aside, looking for my shirt. Shame and want and sadness burning through me.

"Wait, whoa, Talia, hold on," he said.

He grabbed for my arm, and I wrenched it back. "It's fine, Ethan."

"You're pissed."

I wasn't pissed. I was devastated. Humiliated. Because I thought he only saw the siren that night, the trashy girl who was trying to coax him into doing something he didn't want to do, instead of the confused girl who was desperate to connect with him in a new way. I was ready to be as open with him as I know how . . . and he turned me down.

And then instead of us figuring it out together, I ran away and he went and gave himself to *Claire*.

Though I get now that he was hurting in a way I didn't even know this summer. Just like I was. And maybe Sienna's right. Maybe what he was doing with Claire was what I was doing with Rainn: trying to be okay.

But we're not only made of cracks.

Even if he didn't then, after that kiss we just had, I know he wants me now. Which might be even more terrifying. And thrilling.

Maybe I can still salvage this. Since he's right, and I'm the one who storms out, who leaves, who *runs*, it's up to me to mend it.

Rainn's familiar laugh carries all the way across the campsite then. It gives me an idea. I speed-walk toward the sound.

I don't know that Ethan will ever forgive me for the summer, for the letters, for all the disasters I've caused. I've had chances all day to fix it, and I've screwed up every single time. But I won't give up.

I can get this one right.

When I reach him, I covertly hand Rainn my phone.

His eyes fly wide, and he says, "You broke another rule?"

"Trust me, I wish I hadn't. Look at the article."

He does and he winces. "*Shit.*"

"Do you think you could talk to him? I tried, but then I told him about Sacramento and—"

I stop talking because my throat closes up. *And he kissed me like he loves me, too.*

Rainn nods and hands me back my phone. "Of course."

I tell him where Ethan is, and he takes off toward the overlook.

I can never, ever make it up to Ethan. But that won't keep me from trying. Because I *finally* get it. He's not someone I should ever be running from.

He's the one I should be running to.

CHAPTER THIRTY-THREE

Ethan

Senior Sunrise, 7:59 PM

I START PACING, AND I *need* to punch something. I could fuck up a mountain right now I'm so mad. She kissed me like that yet she's still willing to walk away?

It sucks the air from my lungs, and all at once the fight drains out of me.

I collapse back onto the bench and bury my head in my hands and cry. I cry like I haven't cried since seventh grade, when I got thrown against a locker so hard it chipped my front tooth. I cry wondering what is so wrong with me that no one stays for me. I cry from a place no one can reach.

I guess not even Natalia.

I can't keep chasing her. I can't keep waiting for her to choose me.

She's seriously moving to Sacramento? We haven't even— I thought there was more time. But if she's leaving, if she's going to be living three hours away and not even willing to try, what hope do we have?

But it's clear now that we never did.

If I had my phone I'd scroll for quotes or facts to make sense of this.

Some trivia to soothe my mind and remind me that I'll survive this. That I'm not the first guy in the history of the world to have his heart broken.

But it sure as fuck feels like I am.

And then quiet footsteps and a timid voice. "Hey, man. Can I sit with you?"

I scrub my wet eyes across my sleeve and nod.

Rainn slides onto the bench. He runs his palms up and down the tops of his thighs. His tie-dyed sweatpants are filthy from the dirt and sand, and he brings the scent of campfire with him as he settles beside me. "Natalia told me what happened with your dad. You okay?"

I don't say anything.

"Okay, duh, obviously, you're not." He scratches the back of his head. "Really sorry. Trust me, I know how it feels."

I frown.

He goes on. "Okay, not *exactly*. What went down with my parents was never all over the internet. But I never told you why they split freshman year . . ."

My expression must convey my question because he says, "Yeah. With his physical therapist."

"Fuck," I say, shaking my head.

Rainn nods. "I know."

We listen to the ocean awhile, and I like that he doesn't say it's going to be okay. He doesn't need to for me to know that he gets it.

After another few minutes I ask, "Does it freak you out that there are studies that have found a gene that possibly correlates to infidelity?"

His face screws up. "No. I saw what that shit did to my mom. I'm never going to cheat." He looks at me a long moment. "And, dude? You refuse to go to a different coffee shop even though the one by school literally never gets your order right."

"I like supporting local businesses. What does that have to do with anything?"

"Exactly. You're hella loyal. You aren't your dad. You're . . . *you*."

Whoever that is. But I finally look at Rainn, and I'm starting to feel less like I want to punch something.

He says, "I'm sorry. About reading your letter and not telling you about Sacramento. It wasn't my news to tell."

"I get it."

And I do. I don't blame him or Sienna. It's only that Natalia told them and *not* me.

His voice quieter, Rainn says, "For the record, I only tried to give her your letter because I know she feels the same way."

I roll my eyes.

He hits my arm with the back of his hand. "If anyone wrote a letter like that about me, I'd want to read it. I had no idea you felt that way about her."

"Yeah, well . . . doesn't matter anymore."

Rainn turns toward me, his knee jabbing the bench back. "You're not serious."

"I am."

He growls in frustration and holds up his hands in a squeezing motion, like he's miming wringing my neck. "You two are *so* stubborn. She is so into you, dude. Jesus, she turned *me* down because of you."

I laugh bitterly and shove away the lift of hope in my chest as best I can. "She turned you down because of *you*."

He rolls his eyes, but he's relieved I made a joke. "Do you love her?"

After a long moment, I nod. "But it doesn't matter—"

"Why not?" he asks, exasperated.

"She's cut me out of her life like I'm nothing to her. Why wouldn't she tell me about this?" I press.

He shrugs. "Maybe it has nothing to do with you."

My mouth opens, then closes again.

"It's hard to say the shit out loud that you don't want to face, you know?" He chuckles. "Natalia's even worse at that. If she could've painted you something, that probably would've helped. Like you with your facts."

I don't know how he does it, but it pulls a small smile out of me. He's right.

I look at him squarely. "Why are you doing this? You beat my ass up over her, like, eight hours ago."

He grins. "First of all, I beat your ass up because you asked me to, and it was fun. And yeah, I liked her." He's looking at his hands, and I can tell he's summoning some serious strength here. "But I'll get over it. As soon as I read your letter, everything just made sense. You two have always had this . . . snow globe thing. Like, your own magical world. Everyone else can see it, but you're so deep in it, you can't. I'm just shaking the snow for you."

I shoot him a side-eye. "Dude. Profound," I say. And mean it.

"Why does everyone always sound so surprised?"

After we sit in silence, listening to the waves for another minute, I slap a hand on his shoulder. "Thanks. For this. We're good."

His face lights up, and he pulls me to stand with him.

"What the—"

He slams his arms around me. The hug is so jarring, a laugh escapes out of me even though my bruises protest. When he releases me, he keeps his hands on my shoulders, staring me dead-on.

"Enough with this mopey shit. Your dad sucks, but that's not your fault."

I try to shrug him off, but he doesn't move.

"You'll talk to her before you go jumping off any cliffs?"

"Technically this is a bluff."

He smiles, and also looks a little like he wants to punch me again.

I shove my hands in my pockets, and my fingers curl around a crumpled piece of paper. The first Lion Letter we found this morning. My chest tightens.

I wait for Rainn to go, promising I'm not far behind him, before I pull it out. I know I shouldn't read it. But I can't resist anymore.

I open it, and the blue ink catches my eye first. My name next. But I wouldn't need to see my name, or the ink, to know who wrote it. Like her laugh, like her touch, I'd recognize Natalia's handwriting anywhere. In scribbles and crossed out etches, I see inside her head for the first time in months:

> If I were braver, I would tell Ethan everything. ~~I would tell him what happened on New Year's Eve and why things have been so weird between us.~~ Why I've been so off ~~since then.~~ I haven't known how to tell him because I didn't want everything to change between us. I know it has to and that once I tell him it will but ... I swear I didn't want any of this to happen.
> ~~If I were braver, I would tell Ethan why I ran off that night. What I really wanted. How scared I was that I ruined everything. I just feel so out of control when I'm with him—~~
> If I were braver, I'd accept that nothing

> can ever come from these feelings, no matter
> how big they are, or right they feel. His dad
> was right—we're in different worlds. I get it
> now, what everyone else seems to understand:
> I'm not good enough for him. I never have been.
> I'm not rich enough. I'm not pretty enough. I'm
> not smart enough. I keep waiting for a cure for
> this feeling, and I'm terrified...
>   If I were braver, I would let Ethan go.

I reread the letter, different phrases sticking out and burrowing into the center of me.

I just feel so out of control when I'm with him ... these feelings ... I'm not good enough for him ...

But the words I can't stop staring at are "His dad was right"; that mixed with the image of the way she looked when she called him a creep.

What the fuck did he do?

I check my watch. We've already missed the bonfire, and then it's going to be time for lights out. We're not going to have time to talk tonight, but I have to see her. I run to catch up to Rainn and tell him as much.

He grins, full of mischief. "Leave it to me."

CHAPTER THIRTY-FOUR

Natalia

Senior Sunrise, 9:40 PM

ETHAN AND RAINN HAVEN'T come back yet, and it's almost time for tent checks, then lights out. They missed the bonfire, which was just as well, since everyone looked at me like I was a walking STI. But I have to admit Prashant made a pretty respectable s'mores station and being ignored gave me time to think through what I want to say to Ethan. Though I probably won't see him until tomorrow morning at this point.

Sienna and I go to the bathroom together to brush our teeth and wash as much sand off as possible before bed. Side effect of beach camping. I catch a glimpse of my reflection in the scratched, warped mirror, and my bright red eyes are shocking. I'm not sure if it's Senior Sunrise or Ethan, but I've cried more today than I have all summer.

Is Ethan okay? Did I do the right thing by sending Rainn over? How—*how*—can I make this better? The one good thing is no one else has their phone, so no one will know about his family's gossip until tomorrow.

My feet are heavy as I walk back up to my tent from the bathroom.

Mr. Beckett cups his hands around his mouth and announces to the *entire* campground, "Liberty Lions, tent check!"

He starts with me and Sienna. He has dark circles under his eyes and seems ready to get this over with. He checks us off his list before we even have a chance to climb into the tent.

Once Mr. Beckett trudges away, Sienna turns and gives me a hug. "Okay, good night!"

"What? We just told him we're sharing," I say, confused.

She has this weird look on her face when she says, "Yeah but for now, I'm gonna chill . . . elsewhere."

"Oh, 'elsewhere,'" I say, my eyebrows rising. "That's what we're calling Leti's tent?"

She grins, saying nothing.

"Fine, I'll cover for you. How long are you going to be gone?" I ask, keeping my voice low.

She shrugs, her expression going sly. "I have a feeling you won't be in any rush for company."

With that she runs off. All I see is her lantern bobbing cheerily in the dark before disappearing into Leti's tent on the other side of the campsite.

Okay . . .

I strategically planted my tent as far from the group as possible, so having it to myself will be kind of nice. But I probably won't sleep. My head is a maze I can't even paint through right now.

With a lantern in one hand, I unzip my tent door with the other and freeze.

Ethan's sitting on my sleeping bag.

"Hi."

My pulse sprints at the sight of him. He's in gray lounge sweatpants and a black hoodie, his dark curls falling over his forehead. His eyes are red, too. The entire tent smells like his piney soap.

"What are you doing in here?" I whisper, my eyes wide. I quickly climb in and zip the door back up, so we don't get caught and promptly *expelled*.

"Sienna is sharing with Leti. Rainn is on teacher lookout."

"But—"

"We need to talk."

He pats the spot on the sleeping bag across from him, and I don't even hesitate. I've broken enough rules at this point, what's one more? I slowly fold my legs under myself. We're facing each other, knees to knees.

I feel the way I do before a hurdles race. Like my limbs are filled with springs and need to *move*. But I force that feeling away. No more running. Ethan deserves my stillness.

Ethan begins, "I'm sorry about before. I shouldn't have yelled at you like that."

"Yes, you should've."

A laugh escapes him. My heart picks up pace again at the sound. "I'm sorry, too. For today, the summer. The way I ran. The way I . . . run."

"Yeah. Sacramento."

My exhale skitters through my lips. "Yeah."

"Why are you going? The *real* reasons."

There's no point in holding anything back anymore, so I don't. I tell him how confused I've been. What a relief it would be to go to a new school, to stop trying so hard since I'm buckling under the pressures of Liberty more and more every day. How scared I am of messing up. How much I miss painting.

And he listens. He really listens, the way he always has—without interrupting or interjecting. Like he *wants* to understand. Just like all the times we never touched but still held each other through the worst.

Finally, I dive into the deep end of the issue. "I want to paint and . . . my dad won't even let me take studio art," I say. "He wants me to take *statistics*. If I go with my mom, I can do what I want. On my terms, you know?"

His hands clench and unclench. "Oh . . . kay. But what happens when he doesn't like the major you pick or the college you want to go to? Will you keep running? Things can change if you speak up. Eventually you're going to have to choose for yourself."

"That's what I'm doing."

He shakes his head. "Is it? You kept this a secret about moving. You hid this from me. From *me*." He emphasizes this point by hitting his own chest so hard I almost feel it in my own. "Why?"

"I don't know."

His eyebrows drift up. "You knew I would call you out."

I audibly exhale. "Maybe," I concede.

"You spend so much time closing yourself off so no one else ever sees the real you. You're making yourself miserable. Do you really think that will change in a new city?"

I bristle. "I—maybe! You don't know. I could go there and paint and relax and—"

"And hide."

My throat closes.

"Is this really what *you* want? Not your parents or me or anyone else—you?" he asks.

I comb my hands through my hair, pulling it over one shoulder, agitated. "I knew you'd do this. Ask me a million questions I don't have answers to."

His voice softens. "It's one question. Only one."

But it's the hardest question. And it sprouts a thousand in its wake.

What do I want?

Am I allowed to want something if it's selfish? What if what I want hurts everyone around me? And the worst of all: What if I want the wrong thing?

I squeeze my eyes shut searching for the canvas in my mind. It's there, but it's blank. Empty white space of nothing. I can't find the color. I can't—I *can't*—my breath is coming too fast.

Warm hands on my cheeks. "Hey. Come back."

When my gaze lifts, Ethan's deep eyes are inches from mine, staring straight into me. "Natalia, *what* are you so afraid of?"

The air in the tent grows heavy. Though he removes his hands, the invisible force that pulls us together time and again wraps around my heart, and the truest answer tumbles out.

"*This*," I breathe.

His fingers flex in his lap. "Why?"

The wind kicks up, vibrating the walls of the tent. Neither of us moves. I'm frozen under his piercing stare. I've pushed my jumble of feelings for him so far down, locked them so deep away, I don't even know how to access them anymore.

"What's happening between us . . . what happened on prom night was, *is* . . . so confusing," I answer truthfully.

He takes a deep breath, then waits until I look at him. When I do, he says, "For me, too."

"Really?"

He nods. We're close. So close.

I swallow down the knot in my throat. It takes several tries. "That night, it didn't seem like you wanted to."

"I did," he says quickly. "But not then. Not after you said it wouldn't change anything."

"I only said that because I didn't know how you felt. I didn't want you to think I was trying to force anything."

He lets out a sound like he got the wind knocked out of him. Color is high on his cheeks. His voice shifts low when he says, "Then—would it have changed things for you?"

Yes.

But I will make myself feel any way I need to keep him in my life.

"If it was nothing to you, it can be nothing to me," I say finally.

The space in the tent shrinks at the deep steadiness of his gaze, his voice. "It was something to me."

Chin quivering, I say, "Then why did you call it stupid?"

He yanks his head back as realization and horror hits his face. "Oh god, I was talking about the *pact*. I couldn't be with you like that because of some game . . ." He shakes his head. "I wasn't talking about you or us—"

I say the scariest, worst thing. "There is no us."

He grabs for me. Hands winding around my waist, fingertips finding the soft flesh of my hips beneath the hem of my sweater. I don't want to look at him so closely. So close but never close enough. But I do.

His gaze hard on mine, he says, "There's always been an us."

For one unsure, searching second, we pause. Then we collide.

Ethan's soft, urgent lips moving against mine. He tastes like minty toothpaste and ocean salt, and I melt against him. Every way I go, he follows. Strong and sure and solid.

I've had to shove all my feelings for him to the darkest corners of my heart to survive. But now? Now, my fists are in his hair and my heart is sighing. This is what it's supposed to feel like.

When longing meets knowing.

This is happening. Really happening. Tender turns to heat. That familiar ache in me quickly engulfed by the licking flames of want. He shivers under my touch and grips me closer. Hungry. Eager. His strong arms are enfolding me, and the quiet, dark desire in him sends a shock wave through my system. I coax his mouth open with my tongue and the *sound* that comes out of him. Like every star in the sky, every cell in my body burns with the undeniable rightness of us.

"Wait," Ethan says against my mouth, panting a little.

He draws back to look at me, and his hazel stare is its own deep breath. He watches me carefully. Closely. He leans back and dips his fingers into his pocket.

"I think there's another reason you didn't tell me," he says.

When he pulls out a crumpled yellow paper with blue ink, I almost laugh, though it gets stuck in my throat. Of course he found mine.

"Did you read it?" I ask, stalling. Knowing that he must have.

He nods. "Please, no more secrets, Talia. What did my dad do?"

My voice is a bit strangled at first. "It doesn't matter—"

"Yes, it does." He threads our fingers together and waits.

In the end, I tell him everything.

"He told me to stay away from you. He kind of cornered me when I got to your house on New Year's Eve. We were looking at the painting, but then he started saying all this stuff like I'm a tease and I'm not the right kind of girl for you, basically calling me trash—"

Fury ignites Ethan's features. His hands shake in mine.

"*He's* trash. You're—" He closes his eyes. "Brilliant and gorgeous and—"

I squeeze his hands gently. "And a scholarship student."

He blinks. "What does that—"

"Your parents are the biggest donors to the scholarship program, Ethan. If your dad wanted to, he could mess with my scholarship. Whether I move or not, I could still lose Liberty. I could still lose . . . you."

Saying it out loud makes me realize how deeply I've believed this to be possible. Mr. Forrester has power over me. And way too much of it.

"I would take him down in a hundred different ways if he even *tried* to do that. God, why didn't you tell me?"

"Because he's your dad." Though there's a part of me that feels better for being honest with Ethan, I wanted to spare him the hurt that his dad sucks this much. I didn't ever want to get in the way of their relationship.

His eyes are big and manic with rage. "I don't care, I won't let him do this to you. I won't let him take you from me."

My heart squeezes. I push the curls off his forehead and attempt a joke. "Dang, I get it, you don't want me to go."

He doesn't laugh. He presses his forehead to mine. His breath brushes my lips when he confesses in a rough, tortured voice, "Of course I don't want you to go."

My fingers sink deeper into his hair as I kiss him again. And again.

When we pull apart, I finally voice the fear that's been the hardest for me to identify. "I think I've been the most scared to tell you all this because . . . I'm not the kind of girl who can stay because of a guy."

He squeezes me harder, like he's afraid I'll disappear any second. Then he gently cups a hand around my jaw and whispers, "I know."

His eyes are dancing between the space of terrified and hopeful. A loaded pause that sends my pulse into a frenzy. "But I'm not the kind of guy who can watch you go again without telling you I'm in love with you."

CHAPTER THIRTY-FIVE

Ethan

Senior Sunrise, 10:42 PM

GOD, I'VE NEVER BEEN more scared and sure at the same time. But I had to say it. No more holding back.

I slowly trace my fingertips up to the nape of her neck. That soft skin I haven't stopped thinking about since prom night. In a way, it doesn't matter what happens next; I'll wait for her as long as it takes.

But I start to doubt myself when Natalia doesn't say anything and instead eases out of my arms.

She crawls over to her stuff. She turns her lantern up, and the bright yellow light fills the tent. Hopefully the teachers are fast asleep and don't notice. She rifles through her bag and pulls out her sketchbook. Biting her lip, she flips through it until she finds what she's looking for. She runs her fingers down the page and with a shaky exhale, hands it to me.

It's a sketch. Long fingers, including a warped pinkie wrapped around a pen. My hand. I remember this because she made me hold still forever as she tried to get it right. She kept cussing and erasing, and my hand got a cramp.

She turns the page for me. Another sketch. Me dribbling a basketball; the movement in it makes me want to play right now.

Another page. My profile staring off at the Golden Gate Bridge, my hair blown forward in the wind. She must have drawn this one on our class trip last year. God, that was so much fun. We were so sleep-deprived, we laughed harder on that bus ride than any other time I can remember.

Another page. I'm hunched over my desk in my bedroom studying, my chin in my hand. That was finals last year. She fell asleep and "bombed" her econ final. She got a B, but she was so pissed.

In another, my face is buried in my hands, my fingers knotted in my hair. I'm stressed. Angry about something. I thought I always kept that side of myself from her. But she saw it. Sees it. All of it.

My eyes are starting to burn with every new flip of the page because I get why she's showing me this.

"Natalia, these are so good."

Many are quick pencil or ink sketches; others are vibrant with watercolor or colored pencils. She hasn't shown me her art in years. I've asked, but it's been a long, long time since she agreed. But she's gotten so good. Incredible even.

They're not all of me, either. There are dozens of drawings of her hands and the lines of her beautiful face, her wide eyes, her long legs. Sienna's intricate braids. Rainn surfing on cresting waves. A lot of other people from Liberty from various classes. Her bedroom, her backyard. It's her world. But there's no denying I'm central in it. So many flash images of our friendship.

She turns the page one more time.

My eyes dance across the image, my heart knocking harder against my ribs.

In the sketch, two people are at the beach—*this* beach, clear from the eucalyptus trees framing both sides of the image. They're holding each other like they can finally breathe. Like they're home.

All the other sketches in here are of things that are happening around her on the outside. But this one is different. It's from inside her. I don't know how I know this, but it's clear that she drew it . . . tenderly. With feeling.

I can't take my eyes off it or keep the awe out of my voice when I say, "It's us."

"It's my Lion Letter. My real Lion Letter."

My gaze finally lifts to hers, and she's watching me intently.

"I hope it's obvious why . . ." She trails off.

And it is. But I'm a jerk who's going to make her say it. The longer I stay quiet, the more twisted her hands get.

"I'm so in love with you. It's like . . . I do nothing but love you."

I grin.

I set down the sketchbook, turn off the lantern, and pull her to me, finding her lips in the dark. Natalia is the only one who sees straight through me, to the insecure nerd inside. I'm only me when I'm with her.

Somehow, she *loves* that guy.

When her soft mouth opens to mine, thought ceases. We're frenzied. Gasping. God, I love her. It's unlike any feeling I've ever had. It's golden fucking perfection, and this is really, finally happening. I'm here. She's here. Up and on my lap, straddling my legs. Her fingers clutching my hair, my hands clutching her hips.

She tugs at my sweatshirt, and I yank it and my T-shirt over my head quickly. It's freezing, but I hardly notice because my skin is burning hot. She pulls off her sweater, too, and her long hair tumbles across her bare shoulders, and her eyes are dancing.

The last time we were like this was prom night, and nothing is different about the feeling, but everything has changed. I trace my fingertips down her spine, goose bumps blooming under my touch. I love that I can make her eyes fall closed.

"You're so beautiful. I can't—"

But I can't finish my sentence because her mouth is on mine again. I laugh against her lips, and for the first time in maybe my entire life, I feel like I'm exactly where I'm supposed to be. We kiss like we're running out of time. I guess we are.

I grasp her harder, kiss her deeper. She responds by arching into me, lightly dragging her nails down my back.

Oh my . . . *god*.

I'm not sure how much time passes because I surrender. I'm gone. Sunk. We're in our snow globe filled with her jasmine shampoo and the thick ocean air and the sounds of our breaths, fast and tripping.

After a while, she pulls away gently and we're both panting.

She squeezes her eyes shut like she does when she's thinking. "Okay, I know this is awkward, but—but just because you're not one anymore, doesn't mean I'm about to lose my virginity at a *school function*. I don't care how much I want to, or how hot you look right now."

I have to blink several times because my brain isn't exactly functioning. Blood has definitely traveled . . . elsewhere. I sit up. "It's not awkward. If we aren't able to talk about it, we probably shouldn't do it."

She nods and smooths her hair, which, yeah, is pretty damn mussed because of me. Not gonna lie, I feel awesome about that.

But then I realize what she just said and I ask, "What do you mean I'm not one?"

She bites her lip. "Well, you and Claire . . . right?"

What? I hope the horror is clear on my face. "God, no. Not even close. Definitely still a technical virgin," I say, my neck going warm.

She's quiet a long beat. "Are you serious?"

"I would know."

Her nostrils flare. "Karma better kick the shit out of her, or I will."

I smile and stroke her hair and take a minute to absorb how good it feels to have her body tucked against mine. She notices me grinning.

"What?" she asks.

I shrug. "You think I'm hot."

She rolls her eyes. "No, I don't."

"You drew, like, a thousand pictures of me," I tease.

She buries her face into my neck like she's hiding. "No, I didn't."

"You're blushing," I say.

"You can't even see me," she grumbles.

"I don't have to."

She laughs, this high, girly giggle and she clamps a hand over her mouth because it came out loud against the quiet campsite. She's never sounded so light. So happy. That I have anything to do with it fills me so full I'm overflowing.

"I hate you," she says quietly.

"You love me."

And then in the dim moonlight, our eyes lock and our lips are about to meet again until outside, a nearby tent door unzips. We both freeze.

"Nobody better be out of their tents," Mr. Beckett says, his voice groggy. "Or in tents they're not supposed to be in."

"*Shit,*" she whispers, her warm breath skimming across my chest.

I can hear Mr. Beckett scramble out of his tent, and I think his foot must get caught on the flap because he curses under his breath.

If we move to pull on our shirts, the rustling of the tent would be too obvious, so we lie there, still as prey.

Where is Rainn? He was supposed to be on lookout. But I don't know how long Natalia and I were talking . . . then *not* talking. I guess it's been a while. We were probably supposed to trade out with Sienna and Rainn a long time ago.

Our eyes stay wide on each other as the bob of Mr. Beckett's lantern light and heavy footfalls approach our tent like he's coming straight toward us. Like he *knows*.

My heart is pumping, my arms wrapped around her, my hands clutching the bare, damp skin of her back. There's no space left between us, but I pull her closer anyway.

If we get caught like this, Sacramento would be the least of it. We would be in some Shakespearean shit with what her dad would do.

But not even that would fully ruin this moment for me. I finally have Natalia in my arms and that's worth getting expelled over.

The footsteps stop right beside our tent. Natalia tenses, I hold my breath.

A furious zipper sounds on the other side of the campsite. "Yo, Mr. Beckett!" Rainn's stage-whisper echoes across the dark night.

"Rainn? What is it?" Mr. Beckett asks.

"Um, I, uh, cut my finger."

Mr. Beckett sighs. "On what? Is it bad?" His voice and footsteps fade as he plods across the campsite to Rainn's tent.

Natalia lets out a breath, her muscles relaxing against me. I hope he didn't actually cut himself to save our asses, but we seriously owe him. Our friends really came through for us tonight.

I'm not as alone as I thought.

Natalia and I lie still while we wait for Mr. Beckett to go back to his tent. I trace my fingertips across her lower back, and she hums a happy noise against my collarbone in response. Entwined like this, with her arm slung across my chest, holding me close to her, I feel a deep peace settle inside me. I kiss her lightly, amazed I get to do that. Amazed that her smile goes goofy when I do.

No matter what changes come for us in the morning, at least we'll always have tonight.

CHAPTER THIRTY-SIX

Natalia

Senior Sunrise, 12:23 AM

I GUESS WE FELL asleep.

I open my eyes. It's still dark out, and I hear voices, so it's definitely not sunrise yet. Whatever miracle Rainn and Sienna pulled off, we owe them.

I'm curled around Ethan, his face relaxed and slack with sleep. He hasn't moved at all, his arms still wrapped around me, holding me against his bare chest. I'm all too aware of the way our skin clings to each other, and it makes me feel shy. I've woken up at his house countless times over the years from all-night study sessions and friend sleepovers. But never in his arms. It's perfection I could really get used to.

But that thought darkens as I realize what I've done. What I've set in motion by texting my mom that I want to go with her. I never looked at her responses, and I have no idea what she's thinking or planning. All I know is that I *have* to talk to her and my dad. I need to determine if this is really the best thing for me. Not for them, or Ethan, or anyone. Just me.

I try to extract myself without waking Ethan, but he stirs as soon as I sit up. I pull my shirt and sweater on and watch his eyes flutter open with a nervous clench in my gut. What if he sees me and regrets the way we poured our hearts out to each other? We've both always been so careful with our friendship, and now we can never go back.

He blinks a few times, adjusting to the dark, and when his gaze lands on mine, he smiles so wide, heat and golden heart colors spread through my chest, through my limbs, and I feel like I could fly.

"Hey, you," he says.

It's my favorite Ethan voice. Growly and sleepy. It makes me want to kiss him all over, but I resist. Somehow.

"What time is it?"

I grope for my phone in the dark since I never returned it. "Twelve thirty," I whisper.

I take in the alerts I missed, and my heart rate picks up as I read the message at the top of my texts. "Ethan. Your mom just texted me."

I pass him the phone and press my lips against the back of his bare shoulder while he reads.

Hi Natalia. I know you're on your senior sunrise trip, but in case you see this before Ethan does, will you please have him call me? I don't care what time it is. I need to know he's okay. Thanks hon.

Ethan scrubs a hand over his jaw now fully peppered with stubble.

"I should probably . . ." He trails off.

"Yeah. Do you want me to leave so you can have privacy?" In the distance I hear whispers from other tents. Other people are still up.

He raises a joking eyebrow. "And risk you getting hypothermia? No way."

I tuck closer to him because I hear what he truly means; he needs the moral support.

She picks up on the first ring.

"Ethan?" It's so quiet at the campsite, I can hear her voice clearly through the small phone speaker even as it's pressed to Ethan's ear. She sounds tired, but like she's stayed up too late, not like she was asleep.

"Hey, Mom."

"Did you see?"

He says he did.

Her voice becomes thick with tears. "I'm so sorry. How're you doing?"

Ethan squeezes my hand and I use my other one to rub small circles on his back. "Don't worry about me. I'm sorry you found out this way."

She's silent a long moment, then says, "Honey. I knew."

Ethan meets my gaze over his shoulder, eyes wide. I'm sure mine are just as big.

"What?" he asks.

Her sigh fills the tent. "Your dad isn't that great of an actor, no matter what anyone says."

Ethan pushes a hand in his hair. "Wow . . . I—I knew, too."

He tells his mom everything then, about the texts and the months of secrecy. I can tell with every spoken word the invisible shackles around him loosen. His mom is soothing and reassuring and it reminds me all over again how Ethan has remained so . . . *Ethan*, no matter the celebrity roller coaster.

"What about Adam? Do you think this will make him relapse?" Ethan asks.

"Oh, sweetie, no, no. He knew, too. Your father is far from discreet. We didn't tell you because we wanted to protect you."

"I thought I was protecting *you*," he says in a small voice that elicits fresh tears through the speaker, and a few from me.

"I guess we should've been protecting each other a little less and talking a little more," she says.

Ethan sits in stunned silence while she fills him in on the last remaining details of the day. It feels ... significant being by his side for such an intimate exchange. But Ethan never makes me feel like I'm intruding. The whole time they talk, he makes sure we're touching in some way. Like he's not just my anchor but I'm *his*.

When they hang up, he looks freer.

"Everything I was stressed about ..." He lets out a small laugh. "They knew."

I hug him. I love seeing his burdens lift. I'm grateful I'll get to help him hold them again.

We talk awhile about his brother visiting soon and his mom's publicity plan to ensure the utmost privacy for the family. The betrayal and anger and humiliation Ethan feels about his dad being such a disappointing jerk.

"I'll never forgive him for any of this. But especially for what he did to you," he says, the rage returning to his voice.

We're lying side by side, facing each other, my leg flung over his.

"Never is a long time," I murmur.

"Not long enough. It was fucking wrong." When his hard eyes meet mine, they soften immediately. "I'm so sorry you went through that alone, Talia."

Tears push at the backs of my eyes again. As painful as it is, it's so much better that we're talking about it.

His strong arms fully encase me, and he buries his nose in my hair. "I guess we should figure out how to swap tents back."

I nod against the bare skin of his neck.

"Or ..." He trails off, pulling me into a kiss.

We're tangled there awhile, and it takes a few tries before we successfully break apart.

"I actually need your help with something," I say before we get lost in each other again. "I have an idea."

His eyebrows spring up.

"But full disclosure, we have to break a few more rules."

"You already broke into the letters, stole a phone, and have a guy in your tent when 'fraternizing on a school trip could result in penalties commensurate with the offenses, including but not limited to, expulsion.' Who even *are* you?" he asks, grinning.

I give him a long look. "You did not memorize the Liberty student conduct handbook."

He tries to keep his face passive, but even in the dark of night I can tell when he's flushing. "I may have studied that section in particular before this trip. For . . . reasons."

I smack him, but my heart isn't in it. I love this nerd so much.

"What's the idea?"

I tell him and even though it's going to take some serious sneaking to pull off, and we could truly get in a ton of trouble for leaving, he grins again. I can't remember Ethan ever smiling so much.

I pull on my shoes and slowly, slowly unzip the tent door. Once it's open, we climb out and tiptoe past the tents, hearing dozens of whispered conversations. Almost everyone else is still up except the teachers, whose tents are quiet save Mr. Beckett snoring.

Ethan and I get to the parking lot and slip into his car. The benefit of this ridiculous thing is that it is legit *silent*. He keeps the car at a crawl until we get out of the parking lot of the campground and onto the main road.

I look at him driving, and leaving our little bubble of the beach and the tent and the magic we made there is disorienting.

But flipping through my sketchbook with Ethan, I realized what I could do for the class. After everything we've been through in the past day, it feels worth the risk.

We get to my house and don't have to be quiet anymore. Mom is at her apartment, and Dad isn't due back from his work conference until tomorrow. Neither of us wanted to see Mom loading up the stuff we once shared.

I open the door to the dark house, and Ethan follows me in. We have to be speedy. I know exactly what I need and where it is. We should be in the car and back to the campsite, gone twenty minutes at most.

Ethan follows me to my room. I flip on my fairy lights instead of the overhead one. He plops down on my bed while I pull the huge box of my old sketchbooks from underneath it. I flip through them, pulling out the relevant ones and piling them in a small stack. After several long minutes of rummaging and sorting, I have what I need.

"Okay, ready!" I say.

But Ethan doesn't move. He's studying my artwork I have up all over the walls.

There are several abstract paintings, the style I go back to when I'm in a *mood*. That's often how the paintings in my mind look—streams of color that take on no defined shape but evoke emotion or a sense of place.

He looks at those awhile before moving on to the portraits. I know he's studied those before because he jokingly asked why I never drew him. Well, he knows the answer to that now.

Then he moves on to the few watercolors I've done. I love working with watercolor, but I only ever gravitate toward it when I'm in a softer place. When I feel safe or loved or happy. All of which are rare for me. Especially these past few years.

"You're really talented, Talia." There's a sadness in his tone I don't understand. "If you don't feel comfortable at Liberty anymore because of . . . everything, you should go where you can do this. Because you *need* to do this."

I try to look at my art from his perspective. Try to be less critical of myself and . . . he's right. They *are* good. I shouldn't be so stunned that he gets me; he always has, but it hits through a different lens that he's willing to see it even if it means I might leave.

I wrap my arms around his waist from behind and press my cheek to his shoulder blades. "Thank you. I've been thinking that this might be bigger than Liberty, though."

I think I've been talking myself out of Liberty the way I was talking myself out of Ethan—because I'm afraid to want it only to have it taken from me. It's much easier to reject than to be rejected. But easier doesn't always mean better.

No matter what pathetic men like Mr. Forrester say, I deserve to be at Liberty. I deserve to take studio art from a renowned artist like Ms. Aucoin. I deserve every opportunity my parents have sacrificed for and invested in. I've earned the right to invest in myself.

He steps out of my embrace to turn and look at me. "What do you mean?"

I perch on the edge of my bed, and he settles beside me.

"I don't know," I say, "I guess I've been thinking about what you said—how I eventually will need to decide for myself. Because . . . I want to go to art school!" I exclaim. Out loud.

His expression is far from shocked.

I keep going. "I've wanted that for years. And we're told all the time to trust our gut, right? To trust our intuition. But I've never known how to do that because my anxiety is always feeding me false information, telling me I'm constantly in danger. How do you trust yourself, then?"

I study my art lining the walls again. None of it is perfect. Neither am I.

I go on. "My dad is going to *freak* when I tell him I want to pursue art. And I guess I thought, if I go with my mom to Sacramento, and she sees me do really well in the art program there, then she might help me convince him, and it wouldn't be as much of a problem."

I look down at my hands. "But I think I've been trying to convince myself it'll be better because I don't want to face all the parts about staying that will be hard. Missing her, living with my dad, living with my mistakes.

"But is it really worth missing out on my last year in my hometown, at my school, with everyone I care about, just because I'm scared of having a conversation with my parents that we're probably going to have to have eventually? Like, I have anxiety—if I keep running every time I'm scared, I'll be running forever. I have to try. I have to trust myself."

Ethan's beaming as he envelopes me.

"Did you know that if a wave isn't obstructed by anything, it has the potential to travel an entire ocean basin?" Ethan asks.

And I know what he's telling me, and it makes my heart swell.

"Whatever decision you make, I trust you. We'll be okay," he says.

My eyes fill. "Really?"

His eyebrows come together, all soft and understanding. "Three hours is nothing. You know how many audiobooks I could fit in on a drive like that?"

Three hours is *not* nothing, but I adore him for saying it anyway.

"What if we don't work?" I whisper.

He strokes a soft thumb across my jaw. "What if we do?"

I stare at him, my heart beating out of my chest. The friend who sees me through the worst of myself. Knows that my thoughts spin in a dizzying whirlwind that prevents me from ever trusting how I really feel, what I really think. But he sticks with me. Pushes me. Encourages me to trust myself.

I am my truest, best self with him.

In one day, we fought our way back to each other through the chaos of our hurt feelings and broke through the walls of our secrets. We can do anything.

I reach for him and pull him to me and kiss him. Hard. And then it's all too easy to collapse backward on my bed, the soft blankets a relief after lying on that cold ground. I know we need to get back to the camp-site, but for the first time ever, I don't care if I get in trouble or disap-point someone. This matters more. This is my *life*.

In the glow of fairy lights, as we talk and twine and kiss and laugh, our clothes fall to the floor. I'm so grateful he stopped us on prom night. The pact would've pushed us to a place we weren't ready for, and it would've broken our friendship. It almost did.

And now, I don't have to control or contain my feelings for him, because there's no shame, no question, no fear. Ethan's soft touch trails the swell of my hips, his breath shakes along the underside of my jaw. My hair is splashed across my pillow, and his large fingers thread through mine against the mattress. Our eyes stay locked, and I tell him I'm sure. And I am.

I'm sure that I've never felt safer. I'm sure that I've never been hap-pier. I'm sure that my wild heart is his. It always has been.

Because together, we're watercolor.

CHAPTER THIRTY-SEVEN

Ethan
Senior Sunrise, 5:44 AM

SOMEHOW, WHETHER IT'S GOOD luck or our friends looking out for us or Waluigi's guiding light, Natalia and I managed to sneak back to the campsite undetected an hour ago.

My brain is taking its sweet time catching up to everything that's happened. In space, astronomical objects are on a collision course long before the impact event. The same is true for me and Natalia. We went from hovering on opposite sides of the fucking universe, to crashing into each other exactly when we were meant to. Just like in her picture. Everyone says Senior Sunrise is powerful, but damn.

It's still dark when we climb out of our respective tents like we were there all night. Sienna faces us, her hands on her hips.

"Were my calculations correct?" she asks Natalia, who slides a knowing glance my way and blushes.

"I'm definitely going to Vegas with you when we're old enough to gamble," she says to Sienna.

Sienna grins. It's so smug. I notice Rainn hovering on the edge of the group, his eyes lingering on Natalia a little too long. I walk over to him.

He's been the kind of loyal you read about. The kind of friend every person wishes they could have—selfless and generous and understanding. He hasn't made me feel bad about this once he got it, when just yesterday it was his arm around her.

"You good?" I ask.

Rainn nods decisively. "Yeah. I am."

"You can kick my ass again if you want," I offer.

"Nah. But don't forget that I can."

I put a hand on my ribs and wince dramatically. "Like I could."

He laughs a little.

"Seriously, dude, you're allowed to hate me. I totally deserve it."

His face screws up like he's considering it, then he clicks his tongue dismissively. "I can't get mad at the ocean for making waves, dude. I'm a surfer."

I pull him into the kind of embrace that tells him I get what he's done for me. I hated Rainn yesterday. I couldn't look at him and Natalia and be happy for them. I couldn't do what he's doing. He's so much better than me. And I'm so fucking grateful he's my friend.

There's a massive table set up with breakfast items. Thankfully it was someone else's job on student council to deal with today. Inevitably, Natalia takes an inspecting eye to the spread and, with a subtle look around that only I notice, rearranges the coffee cups. She just can't help herself.

I'm so wired, like I have Natalia injected in my bloodstream, there's no way I need coffee. But I devour two cinnamon rolls pretty much without breathing. After I down a third, a yawn escapes me.

"Long night?" Natalia asks, eyeing me playfully over the rim of her cup.

I grin again. I'm smiling so much this morning my cheeks legit hurt.

I brush my fingertips across her cheekbone as I tuck a strand of hair behind her ear. "Best night," I say.

The memory flashes between us. The glow of the lights, the roar of our hearts. Hands everywhere. Skin forever. God, it was perfect.

The teachers announce we only have twenty minutes until sunrise, and Natalia gets that determined look on her face.

We still have her surprise.

She links her fingers with mine, and we walk with the group to the beach. I can feel Claire's eyes boring into our backs, but there isn't much shock in them. Rainn was right, Natalia and I were inevitable, and everyone knew it. Thankfully, we finally figured it out, too.

We make our way down to the shoreline with everyone gathering one last time. The morning fog is already lifting, promising a clear sky for the sunrise. Right now, it's that misty deep blue that precedes dawn.

The box is still where we put it on the beach just minutes before we snuck back into our tents. We planted it by the firepit when we got back to serve as our official cover story if we had gotten caught being outside. Ms. Mercer looks around and realizes she forgot the jar of Lion Letters. I have to cover my laugh with a cough at the look on Natalia's face.

We all quickly huddle around the fire Ms. Mercer started while we wait for her to come back with the jar.

Natalia stands. "Hey, everyone, I was actually hoping to talk to you all."

She's not met with kind eyes. The class is still visibly angry with her, their gazes staying on the fire or the shoreline behind her. The silence is tense.

She straightens her shoulders and does what Natalia does best: leads. "I just wanted everyone to know that it's been an honor serving as your president the past few years. All I ever wanted was for every experience to be perfect.

"But perfect is impossible. And being a good leader is about more than doughnuts and poster boards. It's about being trustworthy. I've failed in that way. Because of me, several of you had your private letters taken and read aloud."

She catches my eye as she tucks the loose strands from her braid behind her ear again. My heart actually skips.

She looks at everyone individually. "I'm sorry. For being so careless with your letters, your secrets. I *promise* I didn't read them. I accept whatever happens, even if that means I'm no longer the student body president of Liberty. I know this doesn't change anything, but I want to share my real Lion Letter with you all. Because if I were braver, I'd never hide my art anymore."

A few people exchange interested glances. She reaches for her sketchbooks in the box and finds the pages she tore out of them last night. She starts passing individual sheets to specific people. Our hands touch when she gives me the sketch—our sketch—and we share a private smile.

Everyone looks confused until Janelle gasps. "Oh my god, it's me!"

She turns the paper around so everyone can see the drawing Natalia did of Janelle from the school trip to the Golden Gate Bridge last year. The bridge is behind her and she's laughing, her eyes closed. It's quick, but it's undeniably Janelle.

"This is so good. You *drew* this?"

Natalia nods. "I realized I've drawn all of you over the years at one point or another. I know it seems . . . creepy, but I don't mean it like that. It's how I learned to draw. Some are definitely better than others.

I'm still learning. But I wanted you to have them. To know that . . . it's okay to be seen. I see you."

The fire crackles between all of us just as the wind hits the eucalyptus trees, rattling the leaves together until it sounds like sheets of rain. Everyone is silent as they stare at their sketches.

Suddenly, Rainn shoots up and says, "I have something to say, too. Or, read, I mean." He clears his throat, and pulls out a small piece of notebook paper. "'If I were braver, I would go for the big waves.'"

Wait, is he . . . reading his Lion Letter, too?

"'The waves that freak me out. Sometimes I'm scared I'll get tossed and maybe even drown. But I'll never get better if I don't push myself. I guess that's kind of like life. In my last year at Liberty, I want to go for it. I want to get better at surfing, the waves, and life. Mostly, I want to get better at telling my friends I love them.'"

He crumples up the paper and throws it into the fire. Everyone claps. When he finally meets my eyes, I don't know what I look like. But it's probably on the verge of crying because he thumps a fist against his chest twice.

"Me next!" Sienna steps forward, and she winks at me.

That's when it hits me. They planned this. These diabolical wonders planned this. I really might cry right now.

She pulls out a piece of yellow notebook paper. "For the record, we rewrote these because we weren't going to go messing with the jar like *some* people," she says, shooting a teasing look at Natalia.

Natalia's eyes are glassy, and she laughs a little, as do a few other people. My heart swells. The tide might actually turn for both of us because of what Sienna and Rainn are doing.

Sienna clears her throat and begins, "'If I were braver, I would live louder in my truth at Liberty. I want to create a safer and more inclusive space for anyone and everyone who is queer or questioning. So I will finally petition Principal Cooper to start a *real* LGBTQAI+ club—one that is finally funded by the school like all the other clubs, instead of reliant on student-run fundraisers. I will not rest until it has a budget that rivals the since-shuttered Waluigi Appreciation Club.'" She shoots me a grin, and I smile into my hands. "'I will also lead the Variables to a stunning victory over Havenport Prep!'"

I whoop along with the collective cheer. She crumples her paper and tosses it into the fire.

Natalia springs up and throws her arms around her, then does the same to Rainn. "Thank you," she says, her voice thick. It's clear she had no idea they were going to do this for us, either.

Sienna gestures around. "Like we told you all last night, anyone who wants to can go next." She plops back next to me, and I throw a grateful arm around her shoulders and squeeze.

Then we wait. And wait.

And wait.

Other than the rolling waves in the distance and the occasional popping of the wood in the fire, it is *silent*.

"Well, this is more painful than *Dwarf Fortress*," Sienna whispers.

And that pulls a stifled laugh out of me despite it all. I've been so fixated on the drama of the past day with the letters and Natalia and my family, I forgot who I have and will have with me by my side this year even if everything else goes to shit. My *friends*.

"Fine. I'll go."

The group looks. It's Prashant.

He's chewing on his lip, and when he raises his own notebook paper to read from, it's shaking. He pushes his glasses up and there's a visible sheen across his forehead enhanced by the glow of the fire. He's quiet a long beat as he studies the paper, until he finally lowers it again. "Actually, I think it would make more sense if I . . . I . . ." He shoots a nervous glance at Claire before he closes his eyes. "'On the outside, always looking in—'"

And he's *singing*. Prashant Shukla, of the buttoned-up, mathlete variety, is singing in front of the entire class and sounds . . . awesome?

"Oh my god, he sings?" Sienna gasps. "What is this song?"

"It's from the musical *Dear Evan Hansen*," Sara Lui says, eyes misty. Then she and a few others start harmonizing with him.

With that and the whooping of the group, Prashant comes alive. He even starts doing these little hip sways. I look to Natalia, and she is clearly just as astonished as I feel.

When he finishes, the class erupts into explosive applause. Prashant is smiling wider than I've ever seen. He shoots a hopeful kind of glance at Claire, and she looks more stunned than anyone. When the group quiets down, he says, "'If I were braver, I would audition for the spring musical.'"

The theater kids yell out, "You better!"

He ducks his chin and grins harder.

He tosses his letter into the fire, and everyone cheers again.

Prashant's display unleashes something. More and more people stand up, one after the other. Some read from their own papers, and others just talk. Heartfelt apologies, hopes, regrets. Some lighthearted, others heavy enough to cause tears. It's clear that every person, no matter their group or sport or whatever, is going through something. Ms. Mercer, who returned a while ago, is standing off to the side next to Mr. Beckett. She has a wide smile on her face, but I definitely see both of them wipe their eyes.

The sky comes alive above us, the sun rising on our last year together.

Then Mason almost shuts it down when he goes. He stands, the fire casting a long shadow of his hulking frame on the sand behind him. He has a paper in his hands, but he crumples it and straightens his shoulders. He's looking at the fire when he says, "'If I were braver, I would join Sienna's club this year.'"

He lets it hang for one . . . two . . . three long seconds. And everyone looks at him, mouths open. His gaze lingers on Rainn before he quickly looks away.

Oh.

When it's clear Mason's not going to say anything else, Sienna and Leti both spring up and throw their arms around him. He turns about four shades of red. Rainn does, too. But he joins in fiercely when the rest of us cheer for Mason. Well, most of us. There are definitely some uncomfortable looks exchanged among the other football players but screw them.

Before this trip, I thought Mason was a toolbox. Not just a tool, but the whole damn box. But after today, it's obvious that he's actually one of the coolest, most genuine people in our class.

I'm feeling all warm and fuzzy. And then Claire stands.

She waits until all eyes are on her, a practiced move of holding everyone's attention from her years onstage. "Good morning, everyone. Just here to point out that Natalia is obviously trying to manipulate us, and I'm not falling for it. I'm going to watch the sunrise now. C'mon, Janelle."

Janelle stands. But instead of following Claire, she turns toward the group and bites her lip.

"Janelle, let's go," Claire says, annoyed.

Suddenly Janelle blurts, "I'm catfishing Tanner Brown. That's what I wrote in my Lion Letter, okay?"

My eyes go wide. So it was *her* letter that Tanner found. The one that got destroyed during the fight.

"Every time he asks for nudes, I send him pictures of those hairless cats. He's getting so mad," Janelle says. She plops back down in her seat to gaze at Natalia's sketch of her again.

It occurs to me then that this is her version of an apology. I can't even manage to stifle my laugh. It explodes out of me. Natalia, too. Then the rest of the class. Claire stomps off.

Ms. Mercer steps forward and announces, "It's time."

We perform the sunrise ritual of releasing the rest of the letters to the fire. It feels good to watch them burn, especially after so many of us have opened up.

As the horizon yawns awake, everyone scatters to gaze out across the ocean. Natalia presses the backs of her shoulders against my chest. I wrap my arms around her as we stare at the dusty-rose sky.

"Did you know poems written about dawn are called aubades? Serenades are written for someone you love in the evening, and aubades are for that same feeling in the morning," I say.

Janelle overhears and shakes her head. "Okay, Ethanpedia." But it's not hostile, it's kind of . . . chummy.

There's no way we're friends, but it doesn't seem like she's trying to hurt my feelings anymore, either. At least that's something.

Claire marches over to us again, my jacket in her arms. I release Natalia for a second.

"Here," Claire says, handing it to me.

"You . . . okay?" I ask. I'm not ready to forgive her for all the lies and crappy things she did on this trip. But she's not the only one who made mistakes, and I can't help but feel bad for her.

She hugs her arms around herself. "I've been through some shit this year. And . . . I know you won't believe me or whatever, but I'm sorry."

"Thanks," I say.

Her eyes fill. "I want to be with someone who looks at me the way you look at her."

I flick my gaze to Natalia, who is doing a terrible job pretending not to listen to us. "I'm sure you will," I say.

Claire shoots me a curt wave before she finds a place to watch the sunrise on her own.

I walk back to Natalia and slip my jacket around her shoulders. She plunges her arms into the sleeves gratefully.

"You're way nicer than I am," she says, eyeing Claire across the beach.

"I'm aware," I say.

She laughs.

As the sky streaks pink and lavender, it reminds me of Natalia's art. The way she uses color, like every canvas is her sky.

I grip her tighter, unsure how long I'll get to hold her like this. She said she'll talk to her parents, and I believe she'll make the right decision for herself. I know we'll make it through. But I want to soak in every droplet of her jasmine scent and throaty laugh and snarky looks while I can. She squeezes my hands like she's tracking my thoughts.

"I'll paint you an aubade," she says quietly.

"Yeah?" I ask, grinning.

She nods, her hair tickling my neck. "Somehow. I need to do *something* to capture this."

"Which part?"

"All of it. You. Me. This sky." She turns to look at me. "Our beginning."

CHAPTER THIRTY-EIGHT

Natalia

Home, 9:35 AM

ON THE DRIVE HOME, I expect a flurry of texts from my parents. From my mom, telling me all the things she can't wait to do in Sacramento. How she's going to start packing up my room for me. I expect cold, angry texts from my dad.

But instead, Dad texts on the family chain:

Let's talk when you get home. Mom is already here.

Ethan pulls up to our driveway and parks. It's just the two of us, hands twined.

I stare at the weather-beaten house that I love, my pulse picking up pace. She's really leaving. I'm really staying.

"Want me to go in with you?" he asks.

Of course he can tell that I'm nervous.

There are shadows under his eyes. He's got to be as exhausted from our all-nighter as I am. I should let him go home and sleep, but I'd love to have him by my side for this.

"Really?"

He kisses the inside of my wrist. "Really."

We walk into the house, and Mom and Dad are sitting together at the kitchen table waiting for me. They greet us both warmly. Then at the exact same time their gazes drop to where our hands are linked. My cheeks prickle with heat.

Mom smooths over the moment by getting up and pulling Ethan into a hug.

"So good to see you, Ethan," Mom says. "Why don't you both sit down."

We each slide into chairs at the table. It could be weird, Ethan being here for this, but it's not. He's fundamental. Even my parents get it. Their eyes are gentle and concerned. I guess my text got their attention. Finally.

"What's going on, mija?" Mom asks.

I haven't opened up about my life with my parents in forever. We are three separate islands with no inroads to one another. But I guess not talking is exactly how we ended up there.

"When I texted you, Senior Sunrise had gotten . . . intense," I start.

Their eyebrows rise in an eerily similar way, and Dad nods, knowingly.

"It's powerful," he says.

Ethan and I exchange a look. *Yeah, it is.*

"I just— I wanted to go somewhere new. Away from here. Away from myself," I say.

Mom frowns. "You know I want you to come with me. The thought of living apart . . ." She trails off as tears spring to her eyes. "But, moving isn't the escape you think it is. You'll still be you, wherever you go. No matter how much I want you with me, you shouldn't use it as an excuse to hide the magnificent young woman you are."

"I know, but . . ."

Ethan squeezes my hand under the table and gives me an encouraging nod. The rest tumbles out then. Everything I've held in all summer. About the stress and pressure. My panic attacks. That I don't want to have to choose between them as if I'm deciding forever whose side I'm on. Or which side of myself matters more.

"And I want to paint again. I don't want to hide my art anymore."

"I don't understand why you felt that you had to," Dad says, genuinely confused. There's also a hurt that hangs around his eyes. I feel a pang of guilt.

"I mean . . . you switched me out of studio art. You always call my paintings my 'little hobby.'"

Dad leans back in his chair. "Okay, but that's because it *is* a hobby, Natalia. You've never pursued it beyond a few classes. I can't read your mind. I didn't know you had any interest in it professionally."

"Because I didn't even know it was an *option*."

I think of what Ethan said about how I make *myself* miserable trying to live up to standards that don't align with who I am or what I want. But how can my parents know what I want if I've only barely figured it out?

Ethan speaks for the first time. "Have you seen her work lately? She's incredible."

I stare at him, the canvas in my mind turning rose gold. It almost hurts, how much I love him.

"She is," Mom agrees, her eyes misty.

"Talia," Dad says. "This is your life. You're almost an adult." His gaze sweeps over Ethan a little warily. "If you want to pursue your art, I'm never going to stop you. Does that mean I understand it or think it's a wise career move? No. You know how chaotic my childhood was, always waiting for your grandfather to 'make it' with his art. It wasn't until Liberty that I had any sense of real stability. But I love you no matter what. I want you to be happy."

A lump forms in my throat. "Really?"

His eyes go glassy. "Honey, of course. You're my daughter."

It's the first time I've felt as much his as I do Mom's. Maybe the first time I've felt like I'm *mine*.

I take a deep breath. I know it'll hurt to be away from Mom. I know it'll be hard to face the consequences of this day. I also know it'll be worth it. "I want to stay."

Ethan squeezes my hand tighter. Mom nods, like that was exactly what she was expecting. She reaches across the table to hold my other hand. We both cry.

It still feels like a fissure in my heart. Like the final crack inside the split of our family. But even still, our islands feel closer. Yesterday, this choice felt impossible because I was trying to please everyone else. Now, I know that staying is the right choice for me, like leaving is the right choice for Mom.

As she's packing up the car a bit later, Mom smiles and asks how everything happened with Ethan.

I tell her almost everything. She laughs that my dad is going to have his hands full with me this year. That's when we pause and cry. It's not like I imagined it would be, telling her about falling in love. We're not sitting on the corner of my bed. We're not curled up in a house we share. But it's pretty close to perfect anyway. Because love is its own home. One I'm finally building for myself.

Long after Mom drives off, and my tears have dried, Ethan and I sit out on the porch steps in the shadow of the cedar trees.

"You're staying." His voice is quiet, his tone wondrous.

I smile. "I'm staying."

For my art. For myself. For every first with Ethan, and every last at Liberty.

He pulls me into a soul-soothing hug, drawing his thumb back and forth across the skin of my lower back. My fingers curl into his shirt, and I draw him closer. As I press a soft kiss to his throat, he releases a deep sigh.

Time unfurls. We'll sleep eventually and figure everything else out later.

For now, all we do is hold each other and breathe. Because we've waited so long for this.

We've waited so long for us.

CHAPTER THIRTY-NINE

Ethan

Graduation Day

I COULD KILL RAINN.

"Shhh!" I clamp a hand over Rainn's mouth.

Natalia looks at us suspiciously.

I drag him away by the arm, hand still over his mouth, until we're out of earshot. He smacks me the minute I release him.

"Dude, what the hell?"

"It's a secret," I hiss.

"Oh, yeah, I forgot," he says, adjusting his cap. The green-and-gold tassel is dangling in his face, and he grabs it so it stills. "She hates secrets."

I give him a leveling look. "You think I don't know that?"

And I do. I thought this was an amazing idea.

But now, with her adjusting the chairs and flowers on the graduation stage, fidgeting and barking orders at Prashant, who really should be focusing on his valedictorian speech and not on the angles of the podium, I'm reminded all over again that my girlfriend despises anything out of her control when she's stressed. And today, with all eyes on

Liberty, she is *stressed*. I wonder if she'll be stressed about Liberty the rest of her damn life.

I go up to her and squeeze her shoulders. "Hey, it's going to be great."

She narrows those big blue eyes at me, and I have to stop myself from kissing all that red lipstick off her. I go for it anyway, and she leans back, raising an eyebrow.

"You know I hate secrets, Ethan."

I sigh, my head hanging low. "It's not a secret, it's a surprise. And I promise you'll like it."

"But what if it's embarrassing? What if I panic? Is there going to be a spotlight? I will end you if there's a spotlight. You have to tell me."

She looks like her head might spontaneously detach from her body. I squeeze her shoulders again.

"Okay, okay. You sure you want me to tell you?" I ask.

She folds her arms across her chest, one of the few people who actually ironed her green graduation gown, and nods.

"Will you *please* pretend to be surprised?" I plead.

"Yes! I promise. Just tell me before I have a freaking aneurysm."

"They're going to name one of the Liberty Lion Scholarships you're gifting through student council after you. It's going to be given specifically to students pursuing fine arts."

Her red mouth falls open.

"Damn, that's *exactly* the face that I wanted projected on that giant screen right there," I say, gesturing to the wall behind her. I grin because it's pretty priceless to get the close-up version.

"Ethan . . . ," she says, trailing off.

I hold up my hands. "It *was* my idea," I say proudly, "but Prashant and all of student council were the ones to push for it. There was a meeting with the board and everything. You deserve it, Talia. It's your legacy."

And it is. She spent the entire year tirelessly fundraising, wanting to ensure there was a scholarship that was in no way linked to private donors. She raised enough that if student council follows Sienna's projected financial structure, it will be sustainably crowd-sourced for years.

Natalia grins so wide it's our sunrise in my chest.

I trail my fingers on her arms under the belled sleeves, and that's how I end up at graduation with red lipstick stained all over my face. My mom isn't thrilled with the photos, but Adam laughs.

Dad didn't come.

We had a blowout fight when I confronted him about what he did to Natalia. He denied it. Called her paranoid and crazy. Classic gaslighting. Then he accused her of flirting with *him*. That's when I lost it. Adam had to pull me off him.

He crumpled then. His lip was swollen and bloody where I'd hit him.

"I know I'm a broken man," he said through sobs.

"Become a better one." I said. It was a plea. A desperate one.

He went to an intensive therapeutic treatment center not too long after.

"Wish I could be at your graduation, but I don't want to make it worse for you," he told me on our monthly phone call my mom is forcing me to have with him.

I think he's just a coward. Doesn't want to see Mom. Doesn't want to face the stares and whispers that follow him now that his career has fallen apart. Sofía Sanchez revealed in a tell-all that she felt coerced by him on set. Based on everything Natalia told me, too, I believe every single word of it.

I'm glad he didn't come. I didn't want Natalia to have to face him, and I'm nowhere near ready to forgive him. Not sure I ever will be. I want to believe he can come back to us. That he can be the dad I remember. But if he never does, the loss is his. It's on him to mend what he broke.

I have Mom and Adam and Natalia, who lost her mind all over again when the scholarship was officially announced at the ceremony. I don't know if I've ever heard the auditorium so loud. Well, maybe when my basketball team won the Showdown game for the second year in a row, but still.

"Proud of you, E. Still wish you were gonna come to U Dub next year," Adam says.

Adam is now a full year sober and going back to school. I thought about joining him at the University of Washington so I can keep an eye on him, but I realized it's not really my job to do that. I love him, and we still talk every day, but I can't protect him from himself. I have to live for me.

Besides, I fell hard for UC Berkeley's computer science program and haven't looked back. Doesn't hurt that Natalia is also staying in the Bay because she's going to CCA—California College of the Arts in San Francisco. She's going to shut down the entire place with what she can do. A light has switched on in her now that she started painting again. She never struggles with words when she talks about her art.

After the hundreds of pictures and goodbyes with all the families, Natalia and I, with all the seniors, climb on the bus to Grad Night. The final event she's organized as our defunct president. She officially stepped down for the year before student council even voted. She felt it was the right thing to do, both for the trust of the class and for herself.

She's been able to focus on art classes and fundraising and applying for college and scholarships. She has had weekends to visit her mom, and time for therapy. She's only had a few panic attacks since Senior Sunrise. She's taking such better care of herself, and I'm so proud of her.

Besides, Prashant was so busy dominating the mathletes tournaments and starring in the spring musical with Claire, Natalia's been low-key running student council anyway. She shoves the giant poster boards she created under the seat in front of us. The first one is of the freshman year photos she made for Senior Sunrise that on the bottom reads, "How It Started." The second has the Polaroids from every event this year and on the bottom reads, "How It's Going."

"Odds of tonight being better than Senior Sunrise?" I ask Sienna as she and Leti settle in front of Natalia and me.

"Um, zero?" Mason states. He's sitting behind us, next to Rainn. Like Leti, he's an irrevocable member of our crew now. Rainn still seems clueless about Mason's crush on him.

"Nothing can top Senior Sunrise. Dude, you of all people know that," Mason says, assaulting my shoulder with a meaty slap. Some things never change.

"True." I smirk.

Natalia goes my favorite shade of pink.

"How would you define 'better'?" Prashant asks the group. He's wearing the same mathlete varsity jacket Sienna has on, complete with their championship patch.

Sienna points at him. "Exactly. We need specific definitions."

Rainn thinks. "Less drama?"

Sienna pulls her math face. "Odds of that are sixty-eight percent."

Prashant shrugs. "I would've said seventy."

Rainn elbows Mason and rolls his eyes. Mason laughs, and they both flush. Huh. Maybe not so clueless.

"More dancing?" Leti suggests.

"One hundred percent," Sienna says. They share a *look*, and it's so sweet even I have to look away.

"Fewer complaints?" Natalia asks.

Sienna squeezes an eye shut. "You don't want to know those odds."

"Natalia being less stressed?" I ask, and am thanked for that with an elbow in the ribs.

"Zero," Sienna and Prashant say in unison.

Natalia narrows her eyes playfully, and I don't know how it's possible to love her even more than I did that day, but I do. There's no one like her on the planet. Of that, I'm sure.

People like to get real cynical about high school relationships falling apart in college. They like to remind us that we're young and we're naive and that most people don't find forever love at our age. And, okay, that might be true for a lot of people. It might even be true for us. But I doubt it.

Because I know what we've been through. What we've overcome to get here. Any time we hear something like that, Natalia and I grasp our hands tighter and share one of our private smiles. We know that whatever the future holds, we'll face it like we have everything else in our friendship: by turning every risk into a chance. Every kiss into a promise.

Every ending into a beginning.

ACKNOWLEDGMENTS

SO, YOU'RE HOLDING MY lifelong dream in your hands. There are not enough words to convey the oceans of gratitude I feel to everyone who got me here.

First, my eternal thanks to my powerhouse of an agent, the incomparable champion of champions, Chelsea Eberly. Words fail. Thank you in every way for getting me to write my *Rent*.

Thank you to my brilliant editors, Brian Geffen and Carina Licon. From that first call, it felt like talking to myself. You understand this love story down to the marrow. Thank you for your unwavering enthusiasm and for making me a better writer.

All my gratitude to everyone at Henry Holt, including Jean Feiwel, Ann Marie Wong, Mallory Grigg, Lelia Mander, Erica Ferguson, and Claire Maby. A special thank-you for the swoony cover of my dreams to designer Abby Granata, and artist Fevik.

I couldn't have asked for a better publishing team than Macmillan and Henry Holt, and I'm so honored to work with you all.

To Ruth Bennett and the entire Hot Key and Bonnier Books team for bringing this story to UK readers with such devotion and enthusiasm. I am thrilled to work with you all.

A multilingual thank-you to the Rights People team for getting this book into the hands of readers all around the world!

Thank you so much to my film/TV agents Mary Pender and Orly Greenberg at UTA for believing in this book from the get.

I am endlessly blessed with my incisive and enthusiastic trinity: Tierney Anderson, Katryn Bury, and Kara Trella. I cherish your wisdom and insights and friendship so much.

Tierney, my alpha reader, the best of the bests. You've been there for every call, every draft, every tear, from word one. I would absolutely not be here without you. Of that, "I'm as sure as the moon rolls around the sea." Thank you. Love you.

Kate, my fated writing soul mate and war buddy: Thank you (and your Victorian ghost) for getting me here. And for always fixing all my plot problems. Kara, thank you for understanding me and my words in a way that feels like we've known each other decades. I love you all and literally couldn't do any of this without you.

Tamar, thank you for being such a wonderful friend and being the link Kate and I needed!

Ms. Rousseau, my high school English teacher. Thank you for being the first teacher to see something in my words.

When writers are nurtured, so, too, is the writing. Nothing has been more nurturing than being part of the Writing With the Soul community. A special thank-you to my 2022 Scotland crew and Green Group. You know who you are, and I LOVE YOU.

To my personal hero, Adrienne Young, your passion for storytelling is a constant lightning strike igniting my own. What you do for writers, and what you have done for me—there are no words other than you, quite simply, changed my life. Thank you forever. (Now you know why I always cry when I see you.)

Helen Chance, my BE FRI, it was you who first whispered what felt like forbidden words at the time: *I think you want to be a writer.* You saw me, see me, like no one else. Maggie Hofmann, thank you for reading so much early writing, for cheering me on and getting me since Oakenshield. Chelsea Cook, thank you for letting me stand under your umbrella. I love you all forever and ever.

Forever grateful that writing led me to the most lovingly aggressive support system: Alexa Lach: soul twin. Beloved grandma ARMY who never lets me forget my worth, I will never let you forget yours. I HAVE DEAD. Joseline Diaz: Natalia sharing your last name is a sign that we were fated soul friends destined to be Swifties and ARMY together. Your friendship is a tremendous gift and your blurb made me cry. Megan Puhl: my number one hype woman. Leigh Ashford: You make me proud to be a Gemini. You all dropped into my life at the precise moment I needed you, and I'm never letting go.

A very special, crying-while-writing-this-note to Kristin Dwyer. Your mentorship, infectious enthusiasm, story genius, and generosity (mostly about Jin) are unmatched. The day you told me you loved this book is the day I knew it would be the one. I am tremendously uncool about the fact that I'm lucky enough to be your friend.

To Rachel Lynn Solomon, Jenna Evans Welch, Maurene Goo, and Kristin Dwyer, for making my whole and entire life with blurbs I will treasure forever. I'm eternally grateful to you.

To *Write Where It Hurts* listeners: You know what this took. Thank you for being with me on my journey.

Mine is a vibrant and loving family of storytellers, and none of this would have been possible without them. Mama, my loving, trailblazing, brilliant Chicana role model; I'm ambitious and passionate because you were first. Thank you for loving books, and guiding and holding me through every single step of this journey. *We* did it!

Dad, thank you for my lifelong film and music education and for always being a soft place to land. Talking about art (and Paul Simon), or really anything with you is one of my all-time favorite things to do.

Thank you to Jim, for always asking about and supporting me and my writing. Thank you to Mary for your constant support and encouragement.

To all my friends and family (the Fernándezes and Des Laurierses and Doanes) who have been on this journey with me, THANK YOU!!!

Mame, family treasure, I first learned the power of storytelling from you. And to all my grandparents now passed, Pete, Grandma Dolores, and most recently, Grandpa Al, thank you for believing in art and in me. I gratefully and humbly stand on your shoulders.

To the Secret Agent Goddesses, my sisters, Dolores, Carmen, and Nora, you have been there *every single day*. I could (and have) (and probably still will) write novels about what each of you means to me. You are my rocks. Thank you for making me laugh, for always letting me cry, and for being my safe space. Thank God (and Mom and Dad, I guess) for giving us each other. I love you. Paciencia y fe.

To my children, my North Stars, who share their mom with so many worlds, you keep me dreaming and inspired and grounded. I love you with my whole heart.

To the love of my life, my favorite person, Justin. Of course this book—our book—was it. It's for you, the person who has made me feel brave and beautiful and capable since we were teens ourselves. Whose love for me taught me to love myself. Who never, *ever*, let me give up. I no longer hate how much I want to kiss you.

Finally, to you, dear reader. Thank you. I hope this book made you feel a little softer, and a little braver. It sure as hell did for me.